SEASONAL
ROADS

MADE IN MICHIGAN
WRITERS SERIES

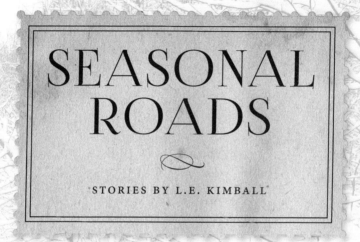

SEASONAL ROADS

STORIES BY L.E. KIMBALL

WAYNE STATE UNIVERSITY PRESS
Detroit

20 19 18 17 16   5 4 3 2 1

Library of Congress Cataloging Number: 2015960095

ISBN 978-0-8143-4145-2 (paperback)
ISBN 978-0-8143-4146-9 (ebook)

∞

Publication of this book was made possible by a generous gift
from The Meijer Foundation. Additional support was provided
by Michigan Council for Arts and Cultural Affairs and
National Endowment for the Arts.

The following stories appeared in different form
in the following journals:

"Deadfall"–*The Way North*

"The Love Charr"–*Gray's Sporting Journal*

"Nothing He Could Put a Finger On"–*Orchid*

"Seasonal Roads"–*Alaska Quarterly Review*

"Spinner Falls"–*Washington Square*

Designed and typeset by Bryce Schimanski
Composed in Minion Pro

FOR HILARY

The distinction between the past, present and future
is only a stubbornly persistent illusion.
—*Albert Einstein*

CONTENTS

ACKNOWLEDGMENTS

A heartfelt thank you to all of the following:

Annie Martin, acquisitions editor at WSUP, who did the initial editing of this project, and who transformed a complicated project into something coherent, reining me in when needed. Many thanks to Emily Nowak, Kristina Stonehill, Kristin Harpster, Bryce Schimanski, and all the staff at WSUP who make the process of writing (and publishing) like a dream, and to Lindsey Alexander for her careful copyediting.

Mike Delp, for his confidence in my work.

Jack Driscoll—as always—for his help and support every step of the way.

Jen Howard and John Smolens, Northern Michigan University, for their support and editorial contributions.

Critical Connection Writers Group: Keith Hood, Amy Sumerton, Jeanne Sirotkin, and Kevin Breen for very early support and feedback. Thanks, Keith, for an early publication of one of these stories that gave me confidence to go on.

Thank you to the literary journals who supported my work ongoing: *Alaska Quarterly Review*; *Washington Square*; *Gray's Sporting Journal*; *The Massachusetts Review*; *Orchid, A Literary Review*.

ACKNOWLEDGMENTS

Ron Riekki, who anthologized one of these stories in *The Way North*, for the great support he gives to U.P. writers.

I would like to acknowledge the use of the website awoman'sfriend.org for part of the wording of the epigraphs in the story "Genitals."

My best friends: Geoff Bowman, Carol Carr, Jo Doran, Charmaine Howell, Karen and Bob Ksionzek, Cindy Lepard. You know how much I love and appreciate you all.

My family: My dad, Dick Kimball; my children, Josh Fay, Hilary Oskey, John Fay; and my husband Dick Fay for putting up with all my craziness and loving me no matter what.

AISSA

SEASONAL ROADS

Aissa watches as Idgy snatches a fly midair, rolls it between her tongue and the mottled-gray roof of her mouth. She drops it, lifeless and saliva soaked, onto Norna's dirty wide-planked flooring. The dog, a beagle-Lab mix, sits between the wood stove and a turn-of-the-century dry sink. Aissa sits on a short stool off in the corner, an elbow propped on a pine work table, trying to keep slivers out of her backside. She examines an index finger the dog has just grazed with her teeth.

Soft mouth, my ass, Aissa thinks.

The dog pants, slopping tiny beads of saliva onto the floor.

You'll run out of that hot wetness, Aissa thinks. We'll all run out eventually, and the cold dusty dryness will spread until there's not enough heat or spit left to wet even the tiniest whistle. It'll be over. Finis.

It's hot here in her mother's kitchen, mid-July. There is a Kelvinator propane-operated refrigerator and a working hand-pump in the cabin, added sometime before Norna moved here, August of 1970—the year Aissa started high school and a year after Norna left Aissa's father because, as Norna said, "they could think clearer each to their own."

The room smells of Norna and of things rotting. Moldy produce—eggs or cheese maybe? On top of the rot is the smell of sex. Sex dripping from the ceilings, seeping up from the floorboards, but when Aissa looks she sees nothing but dried rosemary and thyme hanging from an overhead beam.

It has been two days now and all Aissa has accomplished is to shove a bowl of dry kibbles across the floor to the dog who hasn't touched them. Aissa considers driving off, leaving the dog here alone for all eternity.

"Damn it, Idgy, I don't need this shit . . . come get in the damn car. You won't feel a thing."

Aissa pulls on the shredded yellow clothesline hanging from the dog's neck, but she feels the dog's teeth rake against her knuckles. Not enough to break the skin, but enough to *let her know*. Aissa puts her knuckles to her mouth, and tastes something sweet and slightly salty on her tongue, chews for a minute, then fishes it out on her index finger. A tiny ant.

She hears the door slam on the Volvo, then sees the blonde head appear in the doorway. Jane, her ten-year-old daughter. Only it's Aissa's mother Norna's face looking back at her. Short-cropped sandy colored hair. Eyes, elliptical, opaque, color-blind. They remind Aissa of an Indian word she'd learned as a child—*giwideonanin*: "detour."

Though she hates it, another word comes to mind when she sees the child's face: canine.

"Well?" Jane asks. They'd spent the night in Newberry, at the Zellar's Inn where they'd eaten canned bean dip and tortilla chips for dinner, drank warm Pepsi. Jane had requested sirloin. Sirloin is the word she had used. Why not a filet? Aissa had wondered. Or maybe a huge hunk of prime rib. Strip steak? But no, it was *sirloin*.

After Jane had fallen asleep, Aissa dusted an entire bottle of J. Lohr Cabernet she'd offered the owner of Tom's Mini-Mart and Bait Shop twenty-five bucks for. He'd planned to take it home himself, so she'd offered the big bucks in desperation. He'd agreed, but she'd felt his eyes drop to her breasts and then farther still. She had tilted her head and followed his gaze until he finally looked up at her and at last shoved a pudgy, hairy paw out for her money, ten dollars more than the sticker price. She'd awakened at ten this morning, with the empty bottle pressed between her face and the too-hard pillow. Stomach, head; the effects of the wine alternate now in sick relay waves.

Jane heads for Idgy and before Aissa can move to stop her, the dog rushes to the girl. Jane crouches next to the dog, the girl's head drops over the animal's flanks, their bodies parallel, and it looks for all the world as if they are sniffing each other.

"Jane," Aissa says. "Get away from her."

"What for?" Jane asks. Aissa remembers a time they'd stayed with Norna years ago. Aissa had walked out one morning to find Norna and Jane who was maybe five at the time feeding a mangy-looking stray. Male, small, tawny, it appeared part coyote. Jane was holding a piece of leftover stew in an outstretched hand. Her face held a rapt expression, the same atavistic expression it holds now.

"Because I said so . . . just stay away from her."

Jane parks herself on a stool and Idgy resumes her place by the wood stove, head cocked. One black ear points upward, the other flops forward, an effect that gives Idgy a quizzical expression very like Norna's.

Aissa, what do you think of taxidermy?

Her mother would ask a question of young Aissa, then study Aissa's face, clearly fascinated with the flashes of thought she saw scattered there, the panic she'd see rising. The questions went on and on.

But eventually they'd stop.

Aissa's face would turn blue, her blood would dam up, pressure would build in her ears until she thought her head would explode.

Breathe, for God's sakes, Norna would shout then. *There are no wrong answers.*

Now, despite a few light sprinkles on the tin roof, the sun filters through the window to the west, illuminating Idgy's head like those pictures you see of Christ, and Aissa has her first panic thought for the day: that Norna has taken over Idgy's body for some karmic purpose known only to herself, and that Aissa's purpose in life is soon to be revealed to her in some weird combination of Kantian logic and beagle-ese. Jane turns her fair head sideways to watch Aissa and both sets of eyes bore into her face. Norna's eyes.

Why write, Aissa? Why not be a bricklayer?

Seventeen then, she knew better than to debate with her mother the merits of bricklaying vs. journalism as a career choice. So Aissa had posed a question of her own instead. What do you think of Ted? Ted, who bounced when he walked, and had half-open eyes, as if he found a full view of life more than he could take. He and his buddies did hash and quaaludes down by the trout pond, though Aissa didn't. *What did you think when you first met him?* Norna had replied. The usual: answer a question with a question. Oh, I didn't think, Mother. He made me feel sort of unbalanced, I think. *What do you talk about?* she'd asked. Well, mostly we discuss the size of my nipples. Then Norna's frank humor: *Kind of an inadequate discussion, eh?*

Back then Aissa had had only the remotest feelings for Ted, certainly nothing you could describe as love, but she'd felt grateful to him. Grateful in part, she thinks now, because he was the first and seemed good at sex for someone so egotistical, and in part because they had done it in the dirt at the side of the pond. It was less impulsive than one would suppose, less out of character since Ted was not a risk at all. And the sand had ground into her hair and she could feel the good, solid earth pulsing below her, him pulsing above. Despite her ambiguous feelings for him, it felt solid. She felt connected.

Now, Aissa sees four dusty brown bottles of Guinness sitting on a primitive sideboard. As she grabs one she notices part of a five-cent postage stamp adhered to the battered surface of the pine cupboard. She scrapes at it for a moment with her thumb nail, gives up, and wipes the bottle on the front of her faded I'm-a-Montessori-Parent T-shirt, then uses it to twist off the top. But it doesn't twist. So she bangs it off on the edge of the work table. She sits down in the middle of the kitchen floor, leaning against the Kelvinator, where she can look more carefully into the dog's yellow eyes. Jane kicks off her tennis shoes, leans back in the chair, eyes closed, head resting against the wall.

Well, Mother, Aissa thinks, this particular question, *this* dilemma has an answer. And you and I both know what it is, don't we?

Do it then, she hears Norna's voice in her head. I don't blame you, go ahead and do it. You have good reason . . . only don't be a chickenshit about it. Don't leave it to some insipid veterinarian with the inevitable needle—so neat, isn't it, so sterile? Lose the distance, the voice says, *don't be a chickenshit.*

That's when she sees Norna's .410 shotgun leaning against the corner of the living room, the shells in a silver box sitting on a window ledge above it.

Aissa pulls her eyes from the gun, looks at dog and child. She realizes she's been like this for nearly two days, mostly catatonic, and Jane has been, characteristically, watching her. Aren't you sick of waiting here? Aissa wants to scream at her. You're ten years old . . . aren't you bored as hell?

Two in the afternoon now, Aissa opens the refrigerator, and is surprised to see everything looks fairly fresh—eggs, cheese, milk, broccoli, bacon. She sees a loaf of bread and several tomatoes on top of the fridge. No mold yet. Just a silty gray beauty mark on the top of one of the tomatoes. What, then, is causing that horrible smell? And then she sees it behind the refrigerator. Idgy has killed a chipmunk, no, *pardon moi*, Aissa thinks, not a chipmunk but a baby squirrel. No doubt she's been rolling in it. She grabs a hunk of newspaper and flings the animal through the open door into a tall patch of weeds.

Jane seems not to notice.

"Peanut butter," Aissa says, seeing it behind the loaf of bread. "Make yourself a peanut butter sandwich."

"Daddy wouldn't like that," Jane says, but the words are not a reprimand. No, Aissa thinks. Ben wouldn't like that. He didn't like peanut butter, basements, the outdoors, bookshelves, sweating for any reason, and Aissa's reporter job at the *Lansing State Journal.*

Jane makes and eats the sandwich while Aissa looks around. The cabin consists of two rooms and little in the way of possessions, but Norna is omnipresent in the sparseness, despite—or perhaps because of—the fact that she had always seemed fleeting.

A fleetingness with the terrible power of an idea.

There is a chest of drawers in the living/kitchen area and black-and-white Native American rugs on the floor. A similar rug hangs over an open pantry door where a few brown dishes are partially visible in two neat rows. The kitchen wood stove had been Norna's only source of heat. And in the bedroom, next to the bed, is a pile of books. Aissa knows without looking who the authors will be: John Stuart Mill, Henry James, Freud, Darwin, Plato, Sartre, Heidegger. Heisenberg. Fiction or poetry is a possibility: Goethe, Chekhov. Rilke. No political books per se. Norna was political only when it overlapped with other areas of thought. She believed in capitalism only because it provided opportunity for the most rope. "Upon which people can hang themselves," she'd say. It was all about the questions.

Other people had questions as well.

Why in the world would your father marry your mother after she lived for over a year in a wigwam on the edge of town? With that Indian?

Aissa had no idea why. He was impressed with Norna's ass, she'd overheard her father joke once. Not many women could live for a year in Michigan's Upper Peninsula in a wigwam without freezing it off.

Is it true your grandparents found your mother at the county dump beneath a pile of old newspapers?

Yes. Summer of 1915, John and Rona Ansgar, childless, found Aissa's mother at the Luce County dump beneath the classified section of the *Newberry Gazette*. At dawn. The bears had not even finished foraging. They named the child Norna, Norse for "fate," and took her home. They never reported an abandoned child to authorities and Norna became famous for saying "one might as well be in one dump as another."

Through the years Aissa posed questions of her own. Why ever would you live in this godforsaken cabin when Daddy had money—offered you the inn and a perfectly good house on Drummond Island?

Keep the inn, Norna had told Aissa's father at the time of the divorce.

And Aissa, he'd asked, *Who keeps Aissa?*

A man named Bert had once owned the fifty acres upon which Norna's cabin stands. Norna had lived here since '72 in return for some barn work. She milked cows, cut grass, hauled shit (and some said Bert's ashes) in return for the use of the cabin. One spring when Aissa had made the pilgrimage to check on her mother after the long winter, she'd caught Norna with someone she'd assumed to be Bert, though she had only gotten a glimpse of the man's bare buttocks through the partially opened cabin doorway. She'd left, and, years later when she accused Norna of it, her mother had said matter-of-factly, *Actually, Bert was homosexual.*

Aissa could do nothing more than look at her dumbfounded.

There were so many different guys coming and going up there, Norna had said, *I used to tell him they reminded me of aggregate fruit. He found me very amusing.*

A gay bush pilot? Isn't that what Norna said Bert had done once for a living?

At any rate, Bert died and left the cabin to Norna.

From the bedroom Aissa can see the white Volvo in the clearing. She'd left the driver's door open, and along with the open cabin door, it seems to Aissa a particular omen. She walks through the kitchen, calls Idgy to come. Grabs her by the collar and gets the usual reaction.

"You call her," she says to Jane. But Jane only smiles.

"She's a good dog, Mom," Jane says. "She doesn't look sick to me."

When Aissa picks up the shotgun, she's surprised at how much lighter it feels than she remembers. She pushes the safety, breaks open the chamber to find the gun unloaded but—as all guns are—ready.

It's nine p.m. and Aissa is again sitting in the middle of Norna's kitchen floor, the loaded gun propped between her legs. She drinks her third Guinness, which only makes her feel heavy. Her husband Ben, a dentist, would not approve, because he said carbonated beverages rotted your teeth. Even sparkling water does, he'd say, and especially if you are a sipper. So Aissa has been deliberately sipping, holding the warm yeasty brew in her mouth ten seconds before she swallows. But it's tough to get drunk at this rate, so she has developed a pattern of gulping two huge swallows in rapid succession, sipping every third, swishing the beer around inside her mouth as if she is about to gargle. This accomplishes all her goals, and she feels the beer form a nice head on each tooth like foaming peroxide. She imagines Ben having to pull the rotting things out of her head, dropping them one at a time into the clear rinsing glass he saves for his more distinguished patients.

But Aissa had married Ben for his hands, warmed by the competence she could see in them. An if/then kind of guy, Ben provided the order she'd needed. But lately, Aissa began watching not Ben's hands, but his legs, skinny, with fine silky black hairs that embraced ankles too delicate, narrow feet upon which he wore the inevitable tan medical shoes or if not them, the brown loafers with the tassels. Yes, Aissa thinks, each of her teeth will make clear tinkling sounds like musical notes as they drop into the glass. Like the crystal wind chimes Ben had hung outside their kitchen window despite Aissa's protestation that she hated them.

Aissa knew there had been women. Receptionists, nurses. She's not sure how many.

There's no such thing as a mistake, Norna had said to her a year or so after her wedding.

Aissa can see the Volvo from her spot on the floor and imagines the battery is probably dead, since the door is still standing open, the light dim like a candlelit vigil. Idgy is still watching her, but the dog's head seems to turn every so often to Norna's gun. *Go ahead*, she seems to be saying, *you don't have the nerve.*

Jane, who has been outside sitting by the river, returns now, her short blonde hair curling in crimps around her perspiring face. She sees it in the child's face as well:

You don't have the nerve.

"The blue-winged olives are coming off," Jane says. How does Jane know about insect hatches? Aissa wonders. Norna must have taught her.

Jane moves over next to Idgy in front of the stove. Aissa remembers Norna standing at the stove many years ago, smells the wood smoke and the corn stew like it was yesterday. Remembers Sam Gabow sitting at the kitchen work table in silence. Why are Indians so silent? Aissa wonders. Who the hell was he, Mother? Was he that Indian? The one in the wigwam? And the reply now in her head, *How many Indians do you think I have, dear?* Norna had offered Aissa chilled Popov on the rocks this particular day, with a twist of lime.

Sam, however, had rolled a joint, which made the air in the room sweet and thick and hazy. While the big Indian had moved about the kitchen that day, Aissa imagined Sam's body on top of Norna's frail one. When had it become so frail? Then Aissa remembers black nights, white flesh, Sam's voice floating through the darkness. The morning smell of Norna's coffee boiling in the enamel pot, the eggshells dropped in to settle the grounds, that wonderful smell that makes Aissa ache now. All of it mixed with images of her father's manicured hands, which she somehow can never picture running over Norna's white flesh in the way Sam's must have. *(Your father visited often before he died, stayed here with me,* Norna told her, toward the end. He had? Aissa had never known that . . . was there something familiar about those buttocks she'd seen?)* Sam anointing himself with oil that smelled like cedar. A large sea shell filled with burning sage and herbs, another smell very like pot. Sam blowing tobacco smoke from his enormous lungs all over Norna's body. Sam dancing, banging a tambourine and Aissa expecting him to chant. Why didn't he chant? And then he did. A soft, intermittent sound that vibrates even now inside her head. He had turned Norna's wrists upward, had blown smoke onto them. *You'll need to take tobacco and food from your own portion and make an offering,* he had told her.

Jane leans forward now to hug the dog, and Aissa can see down her shirt, the flatness of her chest, only it isn't Jane's chest but Norna's flatness. It was early days in medicine in 1968, and Aissa remembers the wreckage, the angry ragged streaks of scar tissue, as if someone had tried to scoop a pebble off Norna's rib cage with a machete.

And Aissa remembers again that stray dog Jane and Norna had fed when Jane was small. How Aissa had protested to Norna with the expected concern that the dog might be rabid. She had felt uneasy for reasons more than the menace of the dog, but nothing like how she'd felt two days later when a bigger, black male stray had shown up in the clearing and the dog fight had started in earnest. Norna and Jane had watched from the porch, Aissa from the doorway, as the bigger, blacker dog, obviously part shepherd, ripped at the bowels of the smaller mongrel, whose dying yelps echoed through the ravine. It happened in a surprisingly short time. The blood and saliva mixed in the black dirt and stuck to the sides of the smaller dog so that it appeared coated in chocolate, and the sweet, cloying smell of death assaulted her nostrils. Aissa didn't see much more of the fight, didn't watch or even hear the smaller dog's last raspy breaths because she was watching Jane's face. And Norna's. She watched them watch the battle, the two of them, with nearly no expression on their faces. This had terrified Aissa, but more than that, it had excluded her.

And then she remembers the day Jane was born:

Aissa had watched as her mother had bent her head over the child's naked form in what looked at first to be that lip/belly thing, where adults blow loud air farts in order to make a child laugh. Watched the child's foot move in reaction to the tickling. Aissa, high on morphine had gotten the impression Norna was cleaning the child with her tongue, rough cleansing motions removing afterbirth and bringing pink life to the child's pale skin. An image that has never left her. She might have dismissed the thought as a dream or drug induced memory, but as time went on, she could see how alike they were. She'd watched as Jane slept, feet churning, like a dog running in its sleep.

Aissa looks at the acceptance on her daughter's face now.

"Don't you miss her, Jane?" Aissa asks now. "She was your grandmother."

"Maybe we can live here," Jane says in answer. "You know, when you leave Daddy."

Aissa feels her heart stop. "Whatever makes you say that, Jane? I'm not leaving your father . . ." Jane's face holds the same lack of judgment Aissa saw there during the dog fight, the same maddening acceptance of all things natural, with no need to change life the way Aissa always wants to. Aissa is heartsick with the thought of her failure and not willing—at least not yet—to acknowledge it. Where is Jane's pain? Where is the confusion and pain most children experience? She has a moment of thinking it doesn't exist, then feels even more resentment when the notion strikes her that it's being hidden from her like someone keeping a secret, hoarding a prize.

Like Norna used to do.

It's stopped raining. Steam rises around the Volvo, making it look like it's sitting on a swirling cloud mass. It's nearly dark, and since Aissa can't find a candle anywhere, she digs a large red flashlight out of the back of the Volvo, props it angrily on one of the empty Guinness bottles in the doorway. The beam illuminates Idgy's head sporadically, the dog weaving side to side to avoid it, the effect like bad spotlighting in a child's play.

This dog is holding me hostage. Just like Norna did, Aissa thinks. She has the wild notion that there is only one thing that will free her of them both.

Aissa touches the stock of the gun, knows there will be no time to aim, to sight down the barrel. Idgy is too smart for that. The moment she raises the weapon, the dog will certainly lunge for her. Right now the gun is resting against the side of her leg, her hand running up and down the length of the cold steel, and even that has caused the animal to rise warily to a sitting position. Aissa props the gun for a moment, grabs a length of clothesline, fails to get it through Idgy's make-shift collar since once again she snaps.

"Jane, she likes you."

Jane grabs the clothesline, manages to get it through the collar and ties the end around the leg of the wood stove.

"Where did that clothesline come from, Mom?" Jane asks. "I never saw it on Idgy before."

"It was always there. You weren't here all that much."

But the child is right. Norna would never have put the collar on the dog.

"No," Jane said. "She grew it herself."

"What are you talking about, Jane?" Aissa says. As Aissa backs her way to the door and reaches for the shotgun, Idgy sits more erect than ever, her body taut. Jane moves away from the dog and stands next to Aissa calmly.

Why do you keep Jane away from me, Aissa? Norna had asked her shortly before she died. And then Norna had talked:

I saw my mother once, she said. *Not Rona, my real mother. She'd married and had another daughter a few years younger than I was. When I got there I saw them both hanging laundry in the backyard of a small white house. I watched for a while and then I left. Because I couldn't for the life of me see what clotheslines or dumps had to do with me.*

Inscrutable, inaccessible, indefinable. Even at the end. That's what her mother had always been to her. She had excluded Aissa even from her death.

Death is beside the point, Norna had said at the end.

And Aissa *had* kept Jane away from Norna.

Aissa hears the cell phone ringing in the Volvo, a sound she is sure will break her heart before she can stop it. She's amazed it's ringing since she can only get a fleeting signal out here and usually further up the hill. It can only be Ben. God, she is sick of that sound, of cell phones and sirens and car phones and road noise of any kind. Sick of bells ringing and toes tapping and lips smacking. Mostly she is sick of teeth and everything to do with them. Just when she's about to start screeching, the phone stops ringing.

She turns back to the gun. Opens the breach, checks the shells she knows are there. The chambers smell like oil. One chamber always misfires, something she remembers from the skeet lessons Norna had forced upon her as a child; she can't remember which chamber. She remembers, though, how you have to be deadly accurate with this gun because Norna, who rarely missed, always kept the barrels choked down tightly, the concentration of pellets enabling a quick, humane kill. This meant the gun operated more like a rifle than a shotgun.

Aissa shoves the barrel down and hears the sound of metal joining metal, the safety closing automatically, a sound that for the first time sounds surprisingly familiar to her. The gun's ready, of course. But Aissa is not. Shit! Shit! Not yet, so she props the gun and walks down the pathway to look at the river.

Jane starts to walk with her, then stops halfway. Aissa sees a shovel sticking out of the back of her mother's horrible green Scout and can feel what the splintered handle would feel like against Norna's palm. She is suddenly fascinated with the shape and texture of her own hands so like Norna's, and there is a sudden impulse to dig, but she keeps walking, making her way down until she sees the sign at the edge of the road:

SEASONAL ROAD

Instead of the flatness she expects, the inevitable feeling of inertia, she is aware of covering ground, achieving elevation, then losing it, descending into the subtle depths of terrain.

If Norna's soul had topography, she thinks, this would be it.

It would contain high places where you could see all the way to Lake Superior and unfathomable depths where the trees obscured the sky. It would contain things so beautiful there would be no words to describe them: giant red and white pines, graceful trillium, wild leeks, and gingerroot, and if you listened you would be sure to hear a heartbeat, the wind in the trees, the rhythm of the wild. But, like this logging-ravaged landscape, it would be a scarred beauty, terrible and desolate. Sometimes Aissa knew she'd die of the desolation; a dehydration that seemed to originate from Norna, but came from inside herself, too.

It was the dryness that scared her.

Yes, Aissa thinks, the topography would be remote, private, yet oddly accessible for someone with tracking skills, someone with a sure foot under them.

Someone else.

Aissa sits by the river, throwing pebbles into the brown murkiness.

Anything rising? Her mother's voice comes to her from someplace distant, someplace she hasn't visited for a long time. It seems to come from inside her. Another thought. Was it her mother who had been inaccessible or was it she herself? Suddenly she feels she can describe her mother—in all her indescribableness—in ways she can't begin to describe herself. Shit, she thinks, I've eluded myself for years.

Aissa can feel the impending fall.

And not just fall, but past it. She can see how Norna's cabin will look come winter, snow piled on the tin roof, footprints made by rushing feet on the way to the frigid outhouse, the cedar tree Norna always said was an Indian medicine tree, hanging expectantly over the river. Aissa can see Jane's face at the end of the long two-track. Or is it her mother's face? As if Aissa has followed time down the seasonal road.

It isn't about the bumps in the road, she can hear Norna say.

Aissa has run out of time. She makes her way back. Jane, still halfway between cabin and river. She smiles again as Aissa passes her on the way back to the cabin.

Aissa picks up the shotgun and moves a few feet into the kitchen. Jane is standing behind her now, ten paces off to her left, and makes no move to stop her. *Why the hell not*, Aissa wonders. *Why the hell not?* As she pushes the safety off, she realizes Ben's phone has begun ringing again. And so she whirls to her right, lines up a bead on the cell phone which is sitting on the burgundy car seat. Feels the urge to blast the thing into kingdom come, the car along with it. The cool stock is comforting against her cheek, the trigger cold and silky beneath her index finger. She feels Jane's eyes on her. Idgy has begun to whine at last and she isn't sure anymore whether the ringing is outside or inside her head. But it keeps on. All she has to do, she imagines, is turn and line up that same bead against the side of Idgy's head. When it's done, she thinks, when it's all over, I can simply slide into the Volvo and drive away. I won't even have to bury the damn dog, or so much as clean up the splattered brains and floating hair. *And Jane,* she thinks irritably, *won't even require a fucking explanation.*

The ringing of the cell phone keeps on.

You don't have the nerve.

My God, Aissa thinks. Who in the world was Norna Ansgar?

Aissa turns her body slowly forty-five degrees. Another ten and she knows the dog's head will appear within her sights. She hasn't yet heard the low growl she knows is a surety, but she does hear her mother's words in her head—*you don't have the nerve*—and when the dog's head appears, Aissa's finger pulls back on the trigger—

But it's the barrel that doesn't fire and she hears the dull click inside her head like an accusation.

Just as she had predicted, the dog lunges.

Then the gun goes off, and Aissa feels the explosion inside her own head. The years of being cut off, left out, emotionally excluded, exploding along with it. But it isn't her emotions that are making this mess. Idgy's head has exploded as well. Bits of flesh and blood splash about the room exactly as Aissa had envisioned they would.

She looks up and sees Jane still standing in the open door.

Then it all slows down. Aissa waits for it. Patient. Waits for the sense of freedom she has been expecting, the sense that she's finally taken her life into her own hands, the feeling that she's finally in charge. Has finally done what had to be done. Or at least she expects to feel horror at what's she's done. And she does. But not for the reason she expects. Something is wrong, and Aissa finally realizes what it is: the blood is not coming from Idgy's head; in fact, Idgy is not even lying in the expected heap on the floor. She is whining softly, leaning into the clothesline, straining against the rope and the clothesline, which is still wrapped around her neck. Saliva drips out of her mouth with as much profusion as the blood. And Aissa sees she's failed once again. The bullet has not exploded Idgy's head after all, but instead has entered her shoulder in a downward trajectory, and it appears, has missed even her chest; Norna would never have missed.

Jane is still standing motionless at the door.

"Oh my God," Aissa says.

"Shoot her again, Mom," Jane says, her tone flat like stagnant water in Aissa's head.

Aissa knows she should reload and shoot again, that she really has no choice now but to do that. But all at once Aissa has no intention of shooting the dog again. Jane reaches for the gun, but Aissa pulls it away, throws it across the room. Some madness takes over and she rushes to the dog, drops to her knees and pulls the dog to her chest, knowing full well Idgy, who has never liked her in the best of circumstances, will do nothing less than rip her throat out.

Aissa doesn't care. She's ready. Rip it out, she thinks. Rip it out.

But Idgy does nothing of the sort. She's dazed, possibly from the effect of the lunge, the clothesline cutting off her air and collapsing her windpipe, or maybe it's from the loss of blood. But when Aissa pulls the dog toward her, Idgy drops onto her lap and the blood, like Norna's disapproval, runs across her chest and down her bare legs. She looks up and Jane looks her right in the eyes, tilts her head sideways like Idgy, like Norna. Aissa raises her hands to her neck and checks, half expecting to feel ragged clothesline embedded in the crevices, but no. No clothesline.

There is something there, though. Aissa is sure of it.

Something imperceptible.

NORNA THEN

DEADFALL

She woke, tried to roll over, but her arm was trapped beneath his massive body.

He smelled of sweet grass and sex.

Her arm was long past prickly; a dead weight attached to her shoulder. Was it part of her body or his? She tugged, heaved backward with no luck. Rather than wake him, she left it, wondering how long a limb could remain bloodless before it died.

It was 1957, a prickly time in general. While she would come to terms with the human way of the world, and its inevitable turning—with the dead weight and the deadfall—she had not come to terms to date, and was as stuck with things in the topography of her mind as she was stuck with her arm trapped under the big Anishinaabe man beside her.

Perhaps it was her original failure to bond that had caused her to be temporarily stuck in her mind.

It was her biological mother, not Rona Ansgar, had left her. She was not abandoned on someone's doorstep or left by the side of the road; her mother had taken her across town and relegated her to the local refuse dump.

She was a month old.

She had lain there for over a day, it had been estimated (weather mild in June), under a copy of the *Newberry Gazette*. She escaped notice of the foraging bears, lying in a relatively clean sandy hollow, her head against a fallen cedar tree, with the good piney scent masking the garbage, the incubating warmth of the sun penetrating through the classified section that first day, and the lunar gleam of moonlight rocking her to sleep that starry night, the rhythmic beat, the earth's heartbeat in her ears, along with the gentle rustling of the newspaper. It had sprinkled about dawn, which had wet her lips, rainwater rich with nitrogen, phosphorus, boron, copper, iron, manganese, and zinc, fortifying her like mother's sweet milk.

As that day in the dump gave way to darkness and it in turn gave way to light, her body, predominantly water, slowed its processes, matched the diurnal/nocturnal pull of the earth and then the lunar pull of the moon. And all of it, the rain, the sun, the moon, the easy wind, smiled on her, infused her with a sideways look at the world, and a high good humor that would last all her days.

Time passed, but only so much of it. If more time had gone by she would have joined the other soluble ions that had been broken down by the steady decomposition of (more) time and returned once again to the great body and soul of the earth.

Which would have felt right to her and okay.

Instead she was rescued in the year 1937 by John and Rona Ansgar who named her Norna and took her home. But she had bonded not with the flesh and blood of her own human kind, but with the loamy eternal coolness of mother earth herself. As if she had skipped a step somehow or never left the heavens at all. Had gone instead straight from heaven to the earth. And despite the loving care of her adopted parents—and though

Norna would love them dearly all of her life—the earth, the source of all life, would stand surrogate, always, between them. The bear cubs, the fishes and beavers, the june bugs, and mayflies became her siblings, the rocks and trees, flora and fauna all part of her extended home.

As a toddler, she would wander off and the Ansgars would find her half a mile away, chest deep in some crick or tributary playing with a water snake or a frog. She swam like a river otter, moved with the three-gaited lope of a coyote and her voice had acquired a whip-poor-will quality.

When chastised about leaving "home," she'd look bewildered. The word would mystify her all her days.

"Don't you love us?" the Ansgars would ask her. "Don't you want to live here with us?" they'd ask.

"Of course," she'd answer, not understanding the searching looks on their faces. Not understanding their not understanding.

She left school in her thirteenth year, though she read voraciously, and was possessed of an intellect extraordinary to most people. The women of Newberry, the do-gooders, talked about her now, in this year of 1957. The townspeople would punish her but never disown her; after all she was theirs. They talked about how she had disappeared into a wigwam with "that Indian" this last fall and how she hadn't come out all winter, it now being mid-February. Even though the shack was off the main road and close to the falls, the town people knew all about her, and she was aware that they knew and that they talked. She let their derision run off her back like the spring torrents she was longing for.

It was not true she hadn't left the wigwam since fall. She went out at night often to hear the wind howl through the river valley, feel the snow swirl around her face, see the stars blink at her like long lost cousins. Much later, she would recognize these months for what they were: a young-adult hormonal depression. But at twenty years old, she was not sure if she could or would emerge from that wigwam or if she'd stay there, suspended, forever.

She wasn't aware, for instance, that Britain had just exploded a thermonuclear bomb in the central Pacific, that Dr. Seuss had written *The Cat in the Hat,* or that the world's largest suspension bridge (which was five miles long and had taken three years to build) had recently connected her world of the Upper Peninsula of Michigan with the Lower. But if she had, she would have seen the irony of all three things.

Because these days it was as if there were nothing more in the world than the big Anishinaabe man's hairless chest against her breasts, his thighs between hers, his shoulder-length hair that ended up in her mouth, slick with something her imagination said was bear grease, but was probably Brylcreem.

"Put your hand here," he'd say. "Put your mouth here."

Her mind would become hyper-focused on a patch of his hide or her own until nothing else existed except that patch and that was what she liked most, the disappearing into that infinitesimal piece of flesh.

Given all this, it wasn't surprising she hadn't noticed it at first, so oblivious to things, so turned into herself and their sexuality, was she.

So what exactly was it? What was it that had pushed her to the realization that this *was not the same man coming to her every night?*

It was none of the obvious things: the fact that he wore one set of clothing when he went to work at Newberry Mental Hospital (former Upper Peninsula Asylum for the Insane), came home in other clothing claiming he'd had to change in order to run the trap line; the fact that his appetite for both sex and food seemed to vary wildly from day to day; the fact that his shoes disappeared twice and he claimed he'd had to buy new ones.

How could she be fooled?

You would think that if anyone could know him intimately, it would be she, a keen observer of life; that she of all people would know. Norna was color-blind, but rather than relying on her other senses, she was more focused on the blackness or whiteness.

Perhaps anybody can be fooled.

For instance, what does it mean to know somebody?

Did it mean you recognized their heart and soul? Was their being like a contained body of water in which you lost yourself, diving until you'd immersed yourself in the entire essence of it? Is there a connection between two people that can never be quite the same connection between two others? Did it mean that, in this case, he became predictable to her? That she knew how he would behave, say, in a dangerous situation? How private he was, how selfish, how generous? Did it mean that she recognized the taste of him (garlic and tobacco late at night), his smell (tobacco again, sage, and lye soap mixed with old flannel wool from a shirt several years too old)? Did knowing him mean she had memorized his body? Would she recognize anywhere his wide, square hands, knobby knuckles, hairless smooth fingers with skin the golden color of maple syrup in sunlight?

Norna didn't presume to know him like she knew her own heart.

No, she thought. She would settle for knowing him enough to tell him from someone else.

●◆●

You might wonder and she wondered herself through the years, why she stayed if she was convinced that there were two of them.

Much contributed. This would not be the last time there would be more than one man in her life, and she would be accused of a certain lack, a failure within her character to make commitments. She would never defend or explain this. It was untrue at the time and untrue later. It was, rather, the necessity within her character to overcommit—and not lightly or often, usually due to unusual circumstance—to more than one person at a time. Commitments that would not end when the relationship—as most people defined one—ended. A commitment much as a mother commits to more than one child. Timing, to her, wasn't everything, and ultimately it became about her investment.

She would not be fool enough to fall for their double standard, the one that said that women were immoral at worst, unromantic at best, to care for more than one person, while men, could and would love the masses.

In her lifetime, Norna would love and be committed to twelve people. Six women including her daughter, four lovers, and her parents.

Sex wasn't relevant. That people considered her shallow, frivolous, impulsive, or promiscuous didn't occur to her and if it had, she would have found it laughable.

A personality in such stark contrast to someone who would leave another person in a dump.

●◆●

The wigwam was like this: The stove was in the corner of the shack-like dwelling, and when fully stoked, burned too hot on certain days and forced them to leave the door open for air; conversely, it would die down in the middle of the night turning them to huddled, frozen chunks of flesh on the ground.

They were warmer naked, they found, clasped together in one down sleeping bag, topped with animal furs, lying atop a bright blue air mattress, their bodies forming a frigid "S" pattern, sometimes on their left sides, sometimes on their right, he sometimes behind her, sometimes her body wrapped around his.

They had a table made from the stump of an enormous white pine, several wooden folding chairs, a shelf that held a cast-iron frying pan and miscellaneous cooking utensils, and various Indian rugs. On the wall over their bed, she had hung her only possession, a Scandinavian quilt given to her by her adopted mother, Rona Ansgar.

They bathed, hauling water from the Little Two Hearted River, carrying it in a large tin feed bucket. After warming it on the stove, they would stand in another metal bucket and dump water over themselves in dipperfuls, soaping first and then using the water as rinse.

She would not call herself bored, though the days got long. She'd spend them doing daily chores, reading, or moving the furniture. She'd tilt the log table onto its side and roll it from one end of the shack to the other, settling, finally, with its placement under a particularly wide gap that served as window and offered the most light.

The next day, she'd roll it again.

Originally she had preferred to view the stars through the slits, and though the wind and snow drove through the cracks on bad nights, she was loathe to seal off the wigwam completely.

●◆●

It wasn't every other night she'd notice the switch. It seemed, looking back, that they didn't split their time with her equally; one of them came to her about two-thirds of the time. Some might think (and friends later suggested) that he was just ambidextrous, so the fact that he'd insist on some nights she lie within the embrace of his left arm, which allowed his right hand free to stroke her, sometimes the reverse, didn't necessarily mean anything. Moreover if they were identical twins, some might think it would make more sense that they would both be right-handed or both be left-handed, possessing the same genetic markers and codes and tendencies toward the same physicalities. But Norna believed that hand orientation wasn't pertinent in this case, and she believed she knew the reason for it. And no matter what the people of Newberry (or friends she was to make subsequently) said later to dispel the notion, she was never able to fully lose the thought.

And the thought was this: they'd been joined together in the womb.

She'd seen the slight scars on their opposite thumbs. Instead of floating free in amniotic fluid in probable positions of front to back, or above and below, they were instead mirrors to one another, each with the opposite hand free. Which she knew had joined them mind to mind, and heart to heart. And required that each rely upon the other for use of the opposite hand, dependent on the other for mobility and access to that side of the womb. They likely touched one another's faces in curious adoration, pulling each other close, but they must have, on occasion, shoved each other away just as passionately, in a mad claustrophobic frustration. She imagined the struggle for who would exit the womb first.

Ultimately even this wasn't what convinced her they were two—it was that until she'd spent many nights with them both she'd had an incomplete joining, a partial experience sexually and emotionally. She knew it took both their hands and both their hearts to satisfy her.

So she devoted herself to the study of him or them. Because she so desperately needed a distraction. She was twenty years old and twenty-year-olds fall in love as it serves as distraction from themselves. No one has the stomach to confront themselves at that age, and maybe they never do.

And they both became "Sam" to her. Two sides of one, like moon and sun, part of the same day.

And though she accepted it, she resented it, too. She found herself hoping that he might cut a finger or contract an obvious bruise along the trap line, which, healing slowly, would be conspicuously absent on the other man. She hoped he'd get lice and cut his shoulder length hair, do something that would enable her to trap him like one of his animals, a coyote in a snare or a beaver in one of his wet traps. It became important to catch him up in the lie, to reveal the deceit, and to at last confront him with it, and that is to what she devoted herself this elusive winter of 1957.

Conversation was spare, at least at first. And that was okay with her, since the first things she concentrated on were the physical characteristics. Norna knew ambidextrous people still preferred one hand for certain tasks. They might switch back and forth batting a ball or golfing, but they tended to use one hand while eating. It seemed Sam ate most of the time with his right hand, but not exclusively. So she'd watch and when she saw him eating with his left hand, she assumed he was "the other" and she'd attend closely at those times to the intimacies between them.

But that was harder than it sounds, since it was at those times she most returned to the earth; sex was nearly like dying, or at least not existing, the closest she came to abandoning that false sense of order and purpose to things, the closest she came to just "being." Prayer, in the sense that the Anishinaabek practiced it, was a close second, she thought. Or for them, it could be argued, it was the same.

How soon the trappings of the world (in sharp contrast to the earth) intruded after sex! And she suspected that this momentary erasing of self was something that appealed even more to the male psyche. An end in itself, a dying over and over like a mayfly mating.

As Norna's suspicions grew, and she found physical identification inconclusive, she began promoting more of a dialogue between herself and the big Anishinaabe man. His name was Sam Gabow (though he would confide a spirit name later that winter, a name she would never divulge, and later she'd ask herself if it was his spirit or the ghost side that visited).

"How crazy are they?" she'd asked him once of the inmates of the Newberry asylum where he performed custodial duties nightly.

"Windigo," he answered, the Anishinaabe word. "My people are afraid of those who are touched, but they don't fail to recognize their gifts, the special knowledge the rest of us lack. They are usually either great healers, or see things others can't."

"Women, too?" she asked, of the inmates.

"Oh, yes, at least as many in there."

"Tell me about them," she said.

And he'd gone on to tell her about a woman named Rose who claimed her husband had had her committed so he could marry a third cousin who'd arrived a few years back from Ontario. "It's pretty much his word against yours, and all they have to do if they choose, is drop you off in the bin," she'd told Sam. Norna asked him if she'd seemed crazy, and he said he'd watched her one day, an enormous red-haired woman with chalky-white skin, pick up a black carpenter ant and put it down the front of her shirt as she lay on her bunk, crossing her arms over her chest protectively, as Sam put it, "like she had an infant or maybe a million dollars shoved down there." Another time she had hung her head out the window and howled like a mad wolf, shouting "God save the queen." Though, who knows how crazy you'd be, Norna pointed out, if your husband had you incarcerated like Anne Boleyn in order to marry someone new.

• ◆ •

"White people always ask questions," Sam said. "Anishinaabek wait until the answers are revealed."

"I want to know about the trap line," she'd said.

He didn't answer.

It was early March now and the Day, as he called it, was always changeable this time of year, was driving snow, more nearly hail, at the door of the shack. She had him backed up against the wall of the wigwam. She was naked; most women feel at a disadvantage, but not her.

"What is it about this trap line?" she asked. "Why do you do it?"

She'd been living with him for months and this was the first time she'd asked.

"I only work part-time at the asylum, but I'd probably do it even if I didn't need the extra money."

Verbalizing reasons for running a trap line always proved tenuous for the Anishinaabek, she found. So many factors. They retained hunting and trapping rights, which somehow made it more acceptable for the Native American; the intrinsic right to do it seemed to distract from the why. The wigwam a "temporary" structure (built out of scrap lumber and pieces of slanted corrugated metal to serve as roofing and constructed on state land), in accordance with the hunting and fishing rights bestowed upon the Anishinaabek under the Treaty of Washington written in 1836.

• ◆ •

Norna helped in the shed; she was good with the fleshing tools. Sam would come in with his catch—maybe a coyote, a red fox, a raccoon—she'd insist on working with him in the shed. The lean-to was attached to his wigwam, the proximity of which decreased the likelihood of the catch being destroyed by investigating bears; though there were nights they'd have to come screaming out of the shack, pots and pans banging like steely thunder in order to protect their catch.

The animals would have to be tended to immediately. As soon as an animal's fur was dry, the big Indian made the cuts from one back foot to the anus around to the other back foot and removed the skin like you would a bulky sweater. (Coyotes were reluctant to lose their hide and had to have more cuts made on the forelegs before it could be peeled off their reluctant forms.) But it would be Norna who would stand at the fleshing beam, holding the skin in place with her belly, clasping the two-foot-wide metal tool in each hand, pushing the flesh away from her in a scraping motion, the fat mounding in front of the tool like pinkish-gray rice pudding. This would free him to adjust the stretching boards, and when Norna was finished with a pelt, he would then tack or nail the skin to the board.

Sometimes they'd skin a rabbit; he'd clean it, hand her the meat—rabbits so cat-like in size and shape—and they'd make stew, using wild sage, and bits of bacon and vegetables, wild mushrooms. But whether he was selling pelts, hunting for food, or fishing the streams, she saw the prayer in his eyes, thankfulness that this time the creatures of the world had sacrificed for them, conscious of how easily it could be reversed and how eventually it would be. Recognizing their part in nature as temporary and not proprietary, without a sense of entitlement. And when he made love to her, she saw in his face the same soulfulness, the same thankfulness, the same conscious attachment to the act, not a moment taken for granted.

Once, in the middle of their love-making, they were lifted off the floor, tossed in the wind, and they'd heard the thunder threaten (thunder and lightning in a snow storm, the odd juxtaposition of electrical disturbance on top of blizzard, the driving snow illuminated by flashes of light that looked like the blinding glare of a knife through a white cloud of confetti). It was the act of joining with each other that was the strange thing, and as her body orbited his, it was this strangeness that kept them both safe; they were not part of the earth, nor part of a thunder cloud, or the storm, or the electrical field, not one thing and not another thing, and therefore not vulnerable.

But it was the animals—specifically their deaths—that connected them. His attitude toward sex, she thought, unproprietary or not, was not that different from the animals he caught and skinned, the sacrificial nature of sex, disparate from all things.

* ◆ *

"What kind of traps do you use for what kind of animal?" Not an idle question.

He pulled one of the large furs—a blanket made of pieced and carefully stitched muskrat—around her bare shoulders, covering her breasts as if he suspected they would become part of his downfall. She left the blanket where he'd put it, accepted the handicap.

"Wouldn't you rather play poker?" he asked.

The Anishinaabek loved mystery of all kinds.

"What kind of traps?" she asked again.

She listened as he listed: snares, leg-hold traps, Conibear kill traps, trou-de-loup traps (the bear pit type with spears in the bottom of the hole, a trap he didn't use anymore), the old-fashioned boulder dead-fall trap—each of them in a variety of locations—dirt holes, culverts, open water rivers, under ice-rivers, cubbies, hollowed out logs.

"What do you use most?" she asked.

"Snares and leg-hold dirt-hole sets, since I mostly trap fox, coyote, and raccoons," he answered.

• ◆ •

Stir crazy.

What happened next might be blamed on her self-imposed cabin fever, her intense desire to know the truth, or the fact that her body had betrayed her and she had been running a temperature. What happened was significant in that it would be the last time she would believe that her "desire to know the truth" could be satisfied by any set of circumstances or reasoning to explain that circumstance. That is, that answers existed in the sense that we think of them. But back then she still believed in answers, and this answer seemed to represent to her, in her fevered state, the answer to everything. This answer:

Who was Sam?

• ◆ •

His Day had become her Day.

The Day had had the feel of acupuncture, needles descending from the sky in driving sheets, piercing her skull as she hauled wood from the pile and stacked it next to the fully stoked stove, unable to keep up with the relentless wind through the cracks.

They were camped too far north, close to the trap line, but only four miles from Lake Superior in the snow belt, and this would be the start of yet another four-day blizzard that would require digging out every few hours. It had been raging only a couple, and she'd been out shoveling twice, huddling beneath the hood of the beaver coat she'd made from Sam's pelts. She'd returned to sit next to the wood stove, chilled through, wondering if Sam would make it in time or be forced to stay in town leaving her alone to battle the storm, when he arrived in a rare state of inebriation, out with the Potter boys in town it seemed, and when he reached for her she reached back, thinking this was the fastest means to her end. He had extraordinary endurance despite the whiskey, and her offer to move up top was declined as it always was.

She waited until he fell asleep on his back. She listened to his snoring, how much it sounded like the whistling of the wind through the slats, and she pulled her arm and body out from under him (the deadfall weight of him), which she accomplished without waking him from his drugged state. She crawled cross the wigwam on her knees and added short pieces of beech and a few pieces of coal to the wood stove.

Then she went to work. She wasn't sure what style to use, but had settled on a form of foothold trap, made with strips of wet rawhide (some kind of metal handcuff would have been a closer imitation, but she didn't know how she would get her hands on a set). She wrapped and wrapped the leather firmly around one ankle, knotted it several times and then using longer pieces of rawhide, she tied several strips securely through the hole in their enormous log table, then back through the foothold trap, which would serve quite effectively as a "drag." He might be able to move the table, but would not be able to pull it through the doorframe of the shack. She decided one leg was enough, but since he was an animal of the human variety and she needed to harness his brain as well, she rolled him gently to his side and managed to bind his hands together firmly behind his back. The strips would tighten and harden like molded concrete to remediate any looseness in the bonds or inferiority in her knots. Then she covered him so that he would not become cold, and poured herself a cup of coffee from the enamelware pot, thought about who would check the trap line, and what time Sam was due at work and she listened to the rhythm of the earth and Sam's breathing, watched the contours of his body in the sepia shadows in which she saw all things then looked out at the night and saw the black humped bodies of fallen trees, another kind of deadfall, imagined small creatures, the vast wildlife huddled under them and under the cedar sweepers, thought about the pressing darkness that intensified the storm, and waited for him to wake up.

Which he did about daybreak.

He took one big heave in an effort to sit up, bound leg preventing it, and flopped back to his side.

"What the hell's the deal, Norna?" he said.

She hadn't considered what she'd say, an explanation for her actions, yet the look on his face (though he'd asked the question) told her he knew what this was about. There was no betrayal in his eyes, no accusation. Was it her imagination or did he understand the nature of the game between them—that since he acted in accordance with his nature, she could only act in accordance with hers? She said nothing, and he watched her without speaking. She'd begun to sweat now, her fever rising with the Day and the continuing storm. The room swam and she felt she might fall off the stump on which she sat and she leaned her head and body against the wall; she wasn't sure she hadn't dozed off. When she opened her eyes, Sam was still watching her, but his eyes had become small and fox-like (yet his countenance more bear-like), and she saw him clearly for the first time. And how easily things could have been reversed, and maybe still were.

The big animal shifted in the trap.

He pulled himself up on one knee. Norna loosened his trousers, and held the bucket while he relieved himself.

"Do you think this matters?" he asked her.

"I don't know," she answered.

She wasn't sure if she expected the other Sam to show up when this Sam didn't. If she expected to hear he'd been at work when she knew he couldn't have. Or if she expected him to confess in order to get her to release him. She didn't know. She didn't even know what she intended to say or do next.

It was hard to tell predator from prey, she knew that. When she'd tied his bonds the night before, she'd realized it was not merely a measure in self-defense; she recognized every role inside her: victim/oppressor, lover/hater, exploiter/exploited.

"It's not a trap, you know," Sam said. "When you trap creatures, there is a volitional aspect to it . . . animals decide to walk into the trap."

"Oh, you set yourself right up for it."

He was quiet for a minute.

"True," he conceded. "But suppose I choose not to recognize myself as being trapped. Suppose I choose to accept it as a sort of vacation." And when she offered him rabbit stew, he refused, stating that he had decided to fast. "A vision quest," he announced. "You may be happier I've chosen this path since you've made it hard for me to relieve myself." And he smiled at her, making her wonder again who was trapped and who was free, and how it was hard to tell.

"You might give thanks," he suggested. "If one creature benefits, another sacrifices."

"No trust, eh? No such thing as a symbiotic relationship?"

"Happens," he said.

He closed his eyes and she imagined him in his mental wilderness, the place where you see the face of God. Sam referred to Him as the Day, consisting of light and dark, day and night, consisting of all sides of a thing, all aspects of the all-knowing and all being. And as Norna watched him, she felt the Day envelop her, too, her head leaning against the shaking wall of the wigwam, a fevered weariness overcoming her, pulling her along. But no, maybe it wasn't the Day pulling her so much, it was Sam, wolf-like now, hand held out, inviting her on his quest. Yet, despite his invitation, she was acutely aware that this was a vision quest of her own, that they might start off together, but that was the best case.

Together but forever apart.

It began to seem more like a journey to her than a "place" of discovery or contemplation, which seemed right. And she followed along behind Sam for a while, through clouds, or maybe fog, but then it turned to a raging blizzard, wind whistling through the trees, snow driving in horizontal sheets. They trudged on in the dark, he occasionally looking back to see if she was still there, but taking no responsibility for her welfare. After a while, she seemed to be the ground breaker, with Sam on her heels, but when she looked back she saw what looked like a pair of bear cubs leaping through drifts; the two of them looked helpless, motherless, and she had the feeling they were trying to keep up with her. Then she couldn't see them anymore, heard what sounded like a wolf or coyote howling—songs of prayer in the night.

She wondered if Sam (the Sams) were still back there and if he had seen the face of God yet, because so far she had perhaps only the vaguest feeling of the Day. And then she was at the falls, which had frozen into ice cycles the size of swords and in which she was able to see her own reflection. She suddenly had the feeling that she could see the Day in the reflection of her own eyes.

"Norna." She heard her name, several times, and woke to see Sam had dragged the table over to her. She had slipped off her stump and was lying on the dirt floor, her head propped on the wood pile. He was nudging her with his head. "Norna," he was saying. "Are you all right?"

She opened her eyes.

"How long have I been gone?" she asked.

"Twelve hours, maybe a bit less." It was dusk, she thought, or maybe dawn.

She stood, weaved, and grabbed the wall. She located the hunting knife from the shelf and cut the rawhide binds from his hands. He grabbed the knife and cut the binds on his foot, then helped her to the door, supported her as she squatted in the snow, then lifted her into bed. He stoked the wood stove, climbed in with her, pulled the furs around them, and together they listened to the storm rage on.

She didn't apologize for her behavior and it was clear he didn't expect her to.

It was impossible to apply principles like good and bad to a trap, to any circumstance; your vision was simply not broad enough to do that, your evolutionary vantage point not clear enough. There were no answers in that sense, no order, no black and white attached to the finite. You could only wait and see and live in each moment that had been provided.

They survived the storm, or rather, she survived it, and they resumed life in that winter of 1957, she watching him, he providing for her, she helping in that shed of slaughter that somehow became as much her responsibility as his. They made love and played games of chance at night, or she'd read to him aloud from Rilke, her favorite poet.

She never asked him directly.

She didn't know if Sam had deceived her; didn't know how much she'd deceived herself, and it no longer mattered. Her experiences increased her compassion, caused her to demand less of others.

And that was good.

•◆•

She had been in Sam's shack since November and as she knew she would do eventually, she walked out in late March. Sam told her about the origin of the medicine lodge, the story of the North Star, and finally he told her the creation story. It could only be passed, this history, orally, the magic a testament to their intimacy, the extent to which they had surrendered to the trap. This was something that would be lost if told indiscriminately or written down for the eyes of a casual reader.

There would be no record of him or her having been here this long winter of 1957, except that which had been written on each of their souls.

In late March, the first thunderstorm swept through the region marking the end of the Anishinaabek story telling season, dragging off part of their roof, and creating a distance between Norna and Sam they would never eliminate, but would, paradoxically, never widen.

He helped her pack up the burlap bag which held her books and the few clothing items she had come with, and her quilt. They swept the floor without speaking, sometimes rubbing up shoulders, and when they were finished, they left the wigwam together, he walking south toward his trap line and she, without a backward look, making her way toward Lake Superior, and finally west to the town of Grand Marais.

JANE SOON

THE THINGS
THEY ATE

They sit opposite one another, two men approximate in age. The air within the log structure has the dreamy, silty look of windblown chaff in an August wheat field. But it is October. And this is not a wheat field.

The men lean toward one another across a primitive kitchen work table, search one another's eyes in what looks like an effort for clarity, then lean away. First one pushes back, followed by the other, middle-aged men trying to gain focus in a darkened room. They shove shoulders against the strong spindle backs of eighteenth century Windsor chairs, but neither seems to achieve the proper distance and they again move toward one another; there is ground to be negotiated.

"I read a novel once," the first man says. "About how war does nothing to encourage virtue, how it provides no framework for human behavior, and moreover, how it never ever restrains men from the things they have a natural inclination toward. I'm paraphrasing. The guy was right, maybe, but I think the author was playing with our heads."

"Did you go?" the second man asks.

"Vietnam, you mean? No. John went." He looks the other man in the eye now. "It's all my fault. This whole thing is my fault."

"And how does the war thing tie in?"

"War is more honest. People don't try to pass it off as a dinner party."

The man seems to gush words now. An arterial sort of flow. First he talks about his wife's clothing, then something about her "whiteness," then something about not knowing what to do with her books. The other man, a detective, seems used to the full spectrum of human emotion and makes no attempt to staunch the flow; better, he thinks, to let this kind of thing run its course. He mumbles the usual about it all being difficult and routine and part of his job.

"I'll make this painless as possible," he says predictably. "And anyway, I have just a few more questions. We've been over most of this at the hospital."

The detective stands. Loosens his belt a notch, scratches. Maybe he has eaten a large meal recently? Or perhaps he's been suffering from an outbreak of eczema? Or hives? Or even poison oak, some skin affliction which might cause him to scratch repeatedly around the belt line. Which he does now, the white shirt rumpled from the lateness of the day and the extent of the scratching. But is it only a rash causing him discomfort? His hand moves to his jaw as if checking whether he needs a shave. Or perhaps there's an upper-left wisdom tooth giving him trouble? In which case home will begin to sound better and better, it being four o'clock on a flagging Friday afternoon. He seems the type possessed of a wife willing to slather him with a variety of things soothing and greasy, maybe calamine lotion or some form of cortisone cream, though certainly nothing much will help a festering wisdom tooth.

"It was just the four of you, I have that right?"

"Oh yes, just the four," the man answers. "My wife, Jane, John, who has been a friend since childhood, and a somewhat annoying woman we know from Marquette I invited on the spur of the moment, just to round things out. Hannah, her name is."

"Long way out here, huh?"

"My wife's notion."

"You look like a city boy to me," the policeman says.

"Oh, I am a city boy." The man has a wistful expression. "Jane always appeared fragile," he says. "She had a porcelain doll-like quality about her, but she was the tough one. I am most certainly out of my element here."

"Hmm," says the detective. "Where would you feel in your element, would you say?"

The man doesn't answer. He has fine, sandy hair, parted neatly on the left but with enough of a wave to appear unruly. There is a compelling, untouched quality about the face, perhaps a certain lack of bone structure, the hint of an underlying softness or fleshiness that stops short of weakness. But there is a pervading sense of boyishness about him, too. And a resiliency despite the softness that seems to go beyond, or maybe even to invade, appearance. No solid physical character about him, only characteristics.

"Just how far are we off the main road?" asks the detective.

"A good twelve miles on the two-tracks. But the roads are passable and dry in October."

"Yes, I suppose that's true. But it took me half an hour to get back here. Sure wouldn't want to do it all the time, live way the hell out here like you do." The detective looks through the north window, sees several vehicles parked under a clump of fir trees. "See you got the vehicles for it. Humvees always look awkward to me, too wide for their intended purpose—at least in Michigan. Not to mention one hell of a price tag."

"Well," the man answers. "We've been here four years now. We have a generator since there's no electricity, and all the necessary supplies. Jane and I have . . . had . . ." he stumbles over the word, "staples and canned goods enough to last several months if necessary. Of course, they would have been used only in an emergency. Certainly not something we'd eat ordinarily."

"Who plows the road for you?"

"Jane does it. We have a loader with a cab. Still it's half a mile to a plowed road."

"Why here? Why the U.P.?"

"My wife has family attachments. Her grandmother Norna lived near here for many years until she died and now her mother Aissa lives in the cabin—maybe twenty miles from here."

The man looks out the window and the detective's eyes are drawn out as well, toward what's left of a fresh herb garden and beyond that to an expansive vegetable garden, ravaged now by several killing frosts. Perhaps he is thinking of the way they normally eat, or used to eat, the two of them? The detective stares intently at the first man as if something about his face is vaguely familiar.

"I met you several years ago," the man reminds the detective. "A friend of ours died of an asthma attack on one of the small lakes. Must have been three, four years ago maybe. You were assisting another officer at the time, I believe."

How could he have forgotten? "Yes, I remember now. Sad thing, wasn't it? She was a young woman in her midtwenties, I believe. Attractive."

"Yes, very."

"I was there, but I didn't come to the house. Must be why I didn't place you right off."

"Sounds right," the first man says, and he appears as if he's about to comment more, but apparently changes his mind.

"And it *was* asthma that killed her, I remember that too," the detective says. "No chance the girl had drowned." A statement yet it had the quality of a question.

"No chance."

Silence. Nothing to say in the face of this more recent tragedy.

"So tell me about this 'battle,'" the policeman says to the man. "What happened at this dinner party?"

The detective's face is not your usual cop face. Instead it hints of masters' programs, socio-psychological schooling. Complexity.

"I told you already I was culpable."

The policeman has seated himself in the Windsor chair again, while the first man stands and paces the kitchen, wiping down counters. Counters that have been previously inspected, the technical, forensic part of the process now complete, food containers confiscated, details accounted for. Despite the agility of his words, the first man appears violated, nearly wasted, though in no way indignant.

"Yes, you did say you were culpable. I remember you said the whole thing was your fault—that's a common reaction, you know. To believe everything is your fault."

The detective watches as the man moves about the kitchen. He moves past a gleaming stainless steel refrigerator, Sub-Zero kind of arrangement, over to a large commercial gas range with the word Viking just below the oven door in block metal lettering. Beyond the appliances, a close examination of the cupboard has revealed international spices such as tahini paste, nam pla fish sauce, Sriracha, basmati rice. Shortcuts, much of it, for anyone who really knows cooking, but delicacies indeed to someone like the detective. The first man hands the other a cup of Darjeeling tea who then holds it next to his left cheek (soothing to that wisdom tooth?) and the "gush" continues without further official prompting.

"She was off-kilter about things, there's no denying that. Jane was normally calm, had a dry, intrepid sense of humor. Relentless. But this week she was driven in some calm sort of frenzy—strange way to describe her, but that's how she was. Spent the week stripping down the pine stairway leading to the loft. The treads had become worn, she said. Though I couldn't see a thing. 'Of course, *you* don't see it,' she'd said to me, 'you would never see it.' And she was right, I didn't. Things I should have seen much earlier. At any rate, she spent the week with those harsh chemicals, sandpaper, and steel wool. Scrubbing until her fingers were raw."

"Those stairs near the front entryway there." The detective makes his way to the front of the house, the blonde man following.

"Yes."

The detective walks over and inspects what appears to be a wedding picture of the man and his wife, Jane. He shakes his head. "I don't think I've ever in my life seen a woman's face look more hopeful," he says. "Affirming, but as you say, tough somehow, too, despite the fragile look." Then he looks up. "This is really quite a house. Feels like a church somehow despite the logs and the fact that it isn't that large. I wonder why? I've seen lots of log homes with vaulted ceilings and they remind me of lodges, not churches. Perhaps it's the sparseness of the furnishings."

They sit, still across from one another, in a set of brown leather chairs.

"Possibly. Anyway, there was the hunting. She'd been hunting all week since we needed the rabbits for dinner. Refused to buy them. She raises game herself, axis deer, black buck and nilgai antelope, all imported from India. Among others. But no rabbits, and she refused to buy them. She trained horses and hunted only for fun—it was the game that paid the freight. Oh, and she was a truly accomplished chef, mostly self-taught, though she'd made a few trips to New York. That's where we met, when she was studying at the Culinary Institute. At any rate, she insisted on hunting, not butchering anything, and she got three rabbits several days before the dinner party, field dressed them, and hung them in the potting shed. You have to bleed them, you know, the longer the better, a couple weeks if you've got the time."

The man talks on, a hypnotic but not quite rehearsed quality to the speech, more grief-stricken?

"They dripped most of the first day, congealed blood on the potting surface. She left it there for the next three days. The blood gathered chunks of lint and dirt like black honey would collect flies. I asked her to clean it up but she would only smile. Did you know, by the way, that unless you examine the organs carefully a skinned rabbit is indistinguishable from a skinned cat?"

"And how does the cat compare to a rabbit if you were to eat one?" asked the detective.

The man smiles. "We hope we don't know the answer to that, huh?"

The policeman stands. He can see the potting shed, visible out the window. It has whitewashed wood planking, and has been reroofed with green, multi-ridged galvanized metal. The building is old, perhaps used as a sugar shack once, too big for an outhouse.

"It's temperature controlled to forty-five degrees," the man informs the detective. Certainly "potting shed" is a misnomer. "But anyway, Jane was troubled . . . somehow she always seemed to be around when somebody died. Should have given people the creeps, but later they started asking for her when it came their time . . . so it was more than the scrubbing and hunting bothering her," the man goes on. "It was something about a recent death that weighed on her. An old woman, not a child or anything, yet she kept saying something about Shirley's life, that's the old woman, being 'too linear,' something wrong about that. Kept saying her husband didn't understand time. Or realities. She wasn't sleeping—Jane, I mean. She said she wasn't sure if she'd dreamed Shirley and George or if they were part of some other 'migration.'" I'd turn over and see her sitting up in bed at four a.m. Naked. Moon shining off the whiteness of her shoulders, shoulders so white I felt sometimes like shading my eyes from the sight of them." He pauses.

There is a whiteness about the man as well, though it's a different kind. He is dressed in a taupe-colored pullover shirt and matching denim pants. There would be no dirt under the fingernails of this man's soft white hands, and the lack of color in his hair and clothes seem to add to the picture of someone untouched, unsullied by life's harsher realities. The man's face reveals grief, and something else. Something remote. Regret, maybe? Resentment?

The detective shifts a bit in his chair, but otherwise makes no comment.

"She was staring out the window at the morning star. Venus, she said it was. The skies had been unnaturally clear for more than a week. 'It won't leave,' she kept saying to me. 'It won't leave. . .' It looked like any old star to me, but she said no, it wasn't symmetrical, it simply 'didn't look right.' She was interested in physics, though she never pursued it as a vocation, Einstein, Born, Bohr. She referred to something called 'glimpses,' and 'migrations,' whatever they were, and she said time was illusory, that our conception of it was off. Something about 'forty-nine days.' This not sleeping went on and on, night after night for weeks, though much worse the last week. I'd speak to her sometimes, but she didn't seem to hear me, though she insisted once she'd seen other 'possibilities for my outcomes. It got stranger and stranger. And wolves—'where are all the wolves?' she kept asking."

The blonde man shudders. Is he shivering at the primitiveness he has come to realize had been inherent in his wife's personality? He seems to shrink, become smaller as he stands at the sink. Diminished? Reduced somehow, even after her death by all the scrubbing and daily scouring?

"It's not something a food critic can allow to become general knowledge, but I could easily become a vegetarian," the man admits. "Food has become nothing but a business to me." The detective nods, empathetically, though he himself appears to be the hunter type and not squeamish. He is, after all, a detective.

"I see dog dishes there by the back door, but no dogs running around?"

"No, Jane's mother gathered him up and took him to her camp. To be sure he was cared for while I was at the hospital. He's a mongrel, mostly chocolate lab. His name's Max."

"Good hunter?"

"Amazingly good."

"I see, well, I interrupted you. I'm sorry."

"John got here at ten minutes to seven, early as usual. As I said, we go back to childhood, he and I. Grade school. I think you have all that, am I right?"

"Somewhere in Minnesota, I think?"

"About a hundred miles northwest of Duluth."

"We were able to talk to John before the end," the detective said. "He said there were things between him and you, or maybe it was the three of you? Kept talking about his mother or maybe it was your mother. Some confusion about that. Something about her being the whole problem."

"Yes, things always seem to be the mother's fault, don't they? Have you ever noticed that? I'm sure they, whoever they are, have studied rhesus monkeys. Or maybe adolescent mice and decided that any behavior that indicates the tendency toward 'personality disorders' or anti-social/violent/psychotic/sociopathic characteristics can be linked conclusively to the mother's not washing them immediately after birth, or her arbitrary habit of giving all the cheese to a younger sibling."

"Yes."

"And did this seem to you be an accusation of some sort?" the man asks.

"Exactly what I asked him," the detective says, "but he said no, it was not precisely that."

"John was a bit incoherent at any rate. Toward the end. But he was right. There were things 'between' the three of us. Hard to believe they're both gone . . .

"Anyway, Jane was cooking that night . . . We both cook, but again, she was the talented one."

"I understand you've made quite a name for yourself as a critic. Pays well I hear?"

"Oh, yes, good money in it once you've established a name for yourself. If you have the nature to withstand the capriciousness of the publishing business."

"I suppose such things are possible. To make money at it, I mean. Always surprises me. I understand you now own this food magazine, Faire La Cuisine, is that what it's called?"

"Yes, that's correct."

"But you had your success apart from your wife's business, I understand."

"Yes."

The details continue. The haze has not disappeared from the room, but the camera angle has somehow altered. And the change in angle along with the approaching evening has turned the haze to a warm glow, which in turn seems to form nebulous halos around wall sconces and floor lamps.

"After dinner we played lawnmower, a form of blackjack in which there can be any number of players all playing against one rotating dealer. It was during lawnmower that much of the battle was waged, since lawnmower reveals a lot about the people playing. But it began earlier than that in the kitchen where we watched Jane cook. That's the usual thing to do with a chef as skilled as Jane, part of the evening's performance. The guests get a chance to watch a master at work. They expect it and Jane doesn't mind obliging them for the most part. But Hannah was sipping sherry and hovering, which drives Jane up the wall. She refers to an invitation extended to Hannah as the 'Harrowing of Hannah,' though she admitted the woman was too stupid to be truly evil. She said Hannah was simply boring and affected and too old for John. But none of that mattered to me. I had invited her on purpose, as a tactical diversion. But it didn't work like that."

"How so?"

"Well, there was still plenty alluded to. About trusts broken, time wasted, things missing, things that were either gone now or were never there to start with, but should have been. The degree of directness might have been different, but the subject matter was the same. Nothing was said, though, about babies . . . she'd lost a child once. She was only in her teens. Very traumatic. She wanted children. I wasn't making her happy, that's what it boiled down to. I'm certain her mother, Aissa, would confirm that."

The detective seems to be considering that, making a note—*confirm with Aissa*—then interjects suddenly: "She was naked, that young woman. The one who died of asthma out here several years ago, she was naked. I just remembered that," he says, though the expression on his face seems to reveal a man who never forgets anything.

"She'd been skinny-dipping." There is an open, honest quality about the man talking.

"Someone else was there along with you, wasn't there?"

"John was there, we were both there."

"Go on, tell me about the dinner, then. You served wine?"

"Naturally. I picked it out myself, a 1990 Chateau Lafite Rothschild, a Bordeaux from the Pauillac region of France." Seeing the detective's questioning look, he adds, "About five hundred dollars a bottle."

"I have a recipe for rabbit casserole. Has broccoli, cheese, and cream of mushroom soup in it. My wife always enjoys it."

"Yes, I'm sure." The first man smiles, and there is a pause. The man resumes his seat at the table. "You want to know why we didn't all get sick, though I'm sure I've explained this before. It was the method of preparation and individual eating preferences in this case." And he went on: "Jane was preparing a sautéed rabbit chasseur, but she prepared the chasseur sauce separately, a sauce that consists of quantities of butter, shallots, garlic, white wine, tomatoes or sometimes tomato sauce, tarragon, chervil, and parsley, reduced, to which she added, as you know, the wild mushrooms. The rabbit was jointed, larded with bacon fat to retain moisture, sautéed, and then braised separately, approximately an hour in a mixture of butter, oil, and spices. Normally, Jane would have served the sauce over the rabbit, sprinkled with chopped parsley, but in this case Hannah announced at the last minute that she detested mushrooms, which forced Jane to serve it as an accompaniment.

"And there you have it." The man's smooth face reveals emotions that run the gamut from anger, fear, and finally resignation.

"There is no formal recipe, I take it," says the detective.

"Oh, no. Cooking is complete improvisation once someone becomes as skilled as Jane. There would be no need for that. None whatsoever."

"And yourself?"

"Myself. I had been having a slight stomach disturbance and decided the rich sauce wouldn't be prudent under the circumstances."

There is no sound in the room except the slightest motion of air caused by a circular fan located high over an indoor grill. The man looks up with distaste, walks to a wall switch located next to the grill, and turns it off.

"And the 'fault' you are referring to?"

"Jane knew mushrooms as well as any expert. Only if she were under great strain could she have made a mistake like that."

"Most of the mushrooms we tested were fine, that's true. But it doesn't take much of a certain type, does it? And you were with her when she picked them, I understand."

"Yes, but I don't know food and cooking like Jane does. There's much more to it than people realize. Did you know, for instance, that kidney beans are poisonous dry? Or that quail will gorge themselves on great quantities of hemlock, and though hemlock is quite harmless to the quail, consumption of the bird by humans can be deadly? And some mushrooms, while tasting delicious, are poisonous. Even if tiny amounts of certain species like *amanita verna*, which are sometimes found in the autumn, become mixed with good healthy mushrooms, they too can become deadly poisonous simply by association."

"Yes, so we see." The detective reads from a clipboard containing notes. "They are hemispherical to flat, cuticle white, silken, normally without velar remains. Gills white and crowded, stipe narrow at top, white with ring and membranous saclike volva, base sometimes slightly enlarged. Flesh white. No odor in young specimens. Incubation period of eight to forty-eight hours, death occurring four to seven days after initial symptoms. Common name: destroying angels."

"Yes, well Jane always picks the mushrooms herself and, at any rate, has the means to make chemical and microscopic examinations, something she normally does as a matter of routine. She told me, after she became ill, that she had checked them carefully."

The detective nods. "She told us that as well. There will be a formal hearing, of course." He rises to his feet, walks through the kitchen on his way to the front door. Hesitates.

"What did you mean when you said that author was playing with your head?" he asks, as he pulls a jacket over his white shirt. "The war thing?"

"Well, he calls the book a novel, says it's fiction, but he uses his real name and the names of other real people. You know part of it must be true, but not all of it. He weaves his fantasies into the truth until you wonder if anything at all happened to him in Vietnam. Until you wonder whether or not he invented every bit of it to justify a personal war experience in which he was his own worst enemy. You suspect it consisted primarily of chasing his own neurotic fears along a continuum of insanity. And he wants us to feel the insanity as well. And that was his entire point, which is allowed, of course. Self-indulgent. But it's not that hard to do, jerk people around like that."

"Hmm," says the detective. He grabs a piece of lint that blows crazily around his head as he opens the front door. Hail has started pounding the metal roof, making a sound like horse's hooves on pavement.

•◆•

The detective, Lieutenant Lindstrom, reminded me of my father. In the way he held his head, and in the way he used it. That same deceptive plodding quality, that laid-back passivity you might mistake for dullness if you weren't careful. I admire these qualities.

I haven't seen my father in fifteen years.

Just his name signed in a square, definite hand on the bottom of the checks that got me through Boston College.

Mother married him in 1952, but she'd waited three years to have me in order that he might finish law school. Something both my mother and his parents, who owned a small deli northwest of Duluth, had pushed hard for. After graduating top of his class, he plodded at corporate law for a firm called Benson, Benson and Lieberman, and for the next ten years we lived in the slightly upscale community of Bemidji. All in apparent tranquility until my father's own father died in 1965 and he informed us that he was using his small inheritance to buy a farm near Rockford, Illinois, where he intended to raise Holsteins. And possibly some pigs. Or chickens, he wasn't sure yet. When my mother refused to go with him my father left anyway, refusing to engage in the requisite emotional tug of war that would more naturally precede such a strange and sudden leaving.

I look like him, she tells me. Without the calluses. And certainly without the wafting aroma of cow shit. But I don't know that for sure since I refused to see him and pictures can only tell so much. I'd refused to see him despite the fact he'd done well as a farmer and had always been financially responsible for me. Not, as my mother assumed, because I was hurt by his desertion, but because he posed other difficulties for me.

"You were right not to go with him," I told her. "Totally right."

And she had had to agree with me.

I knew she was tired, that there was a side of her that needed someone, that there were times she thought about looking for someone to replace my father. That she needed to feel the touch of a man. But I knew that would never do. Evenings I'd sit on the floor and stroke her feet, despite the fact I've always hated the feel of other people's skin, while she watched *The Price is Right*, or *Gunsmoke*, and ate boxes of Screaming Yellow Zonkers and PayDay bars. I don't remember her ever cooking.

"Don't stop, honey," she'd moan.

They never want you to stop.

• ◆ •

"We can skip it if you want to," Jane had said the morning of the party. "Just call it off." But I knew she didn't mean we really could. There was too much she had planned.

There had been some hint of forgiveness at one time. Not really any talk of it, just what I would call a barely perceived attitude towards it. But I have found that when people "forgive" you, it simply means the punishment will be exacted indefinitely, subtly, so that you nearly believe it's not happening at all.

And if I hadn't known already, I knew that week that something had changed. I watched this deliberate nightly ritual between her and Venus. It had been performed naked for my benefit. Or at least partly with the malicious intent of insinuating moist, unwelcome body parts into my mind. But she was right about one thing. It felt as if things had shifted, that the alignment of the stars had sent all nature cockeyed. The nightly news had been full of a rash of shark attacks on the east coast, dogs attacking their owners in New Mexico, alligators in Florida eating poodles and small children. Women murdering their husbands and putting them in chest freezers . . .

Jane was crouched over the stairway leading to the loft as we talked, scrubbing away, her blonde hair tied back, her white face and hands smudged with oily stain remover and dried finish. When I asked why she was scrubbing, she replied to me that she believed in ideas. But an idea, she went on to say (and this is the gist of her sentiment), should never take on a life of its own. People should not become the embodiment of a thought, should never separate themselves intellectually or emotionally from the good earth, because then, she said, the idea becomes sterile, and the people devoted to it, dangerous.

It was important in her case particularly, she said, that she should feel the "good" wood grain beneath her fingers.

"As well as those 'good' slivers under your nails," I pointed out.

"Absolutely essential."

"Whatever, we may as well go ahead with the dinner," I said.

"I don't know why you invited Hannah, it won't make any difference to anything."

"Perhaps not."

Jane had been at her mother's for nearly two months, claiming the forest fire that had nearly engulfed her mother's cabin kept her longer. When she returned, I had the feeling it wouldn't be for long, but she'd tarried into the fall. What was keeping her from going? I stooped and reached my fingers toward Jane's cheek, moved even then by her beauty, the contrasts in coloring (blonde hair, pale skin, colorless eyes) and in personality (fragile but savage, that flat-out relentless up-yours quality I'd never been able to deal with). She reached her hand toward me, the one with the steel wool in it. I could see the poisonous residue coated on the outstretched palm. Her eyes got wide.

"Touch me," she said.

"Oh, for heaven's sake, you're the one not grounded."

She shook her head. "Not about grounding," she said. I could see the flesh of the wood within the steel, shreds of it mixed with the harsh chemicals, and I had an impulse to take it from her hand.

"Touch me," she said again, and for a moment I remembered what it had once been like to be this close to her, the buoyant, supportive essence we'd provided each other. Then I felt regret that she had become what she had.

Was there any chance of a new beginning? At that moment I wanted that more than anything and I searched her face for any reciprocal sign of regret. She didn't pull her hand away, but I could not make myself reach for it. Her eyes searched over my face, and for a moment I could see the softness under the wildness of her. But then she seemed to see something that brought her up hard against the wall we'd built between us. Her hand closed around the steel wool, and dropped to her side.

"She won't eat half of what I cook, you know what kind of eater she is," Jane said.

Hannah was a hair dresser in a salon I patronized. She'd been here for the holiday wild-game dinner last year and only picked at bowls of nuts and chocolate balls. Jane was right. She wouldn't appreciate the rabbit, and did I recall rightly—she did not like mushrooms as well? Yes, I was sure she didn't. Well, I knew it wouldn't matter, either way. There had been a time I had needed her. We had enjoyed a fleeting rapport even though she was inordinately stupid and self-interested and entirely too sexual.

I studied Jane a moment longer.

"What is it you think you know?" I asked her.

"I wouldn't claim to 'know' anything," she said back. "Did you know they said Hitler had no sex life? Sacrificed everything to some bloodless ideal."

"You could hardly call Hitler bloodless," I said.

"He was a vegetarian."

"Hmm," I said.

"He was removed from the blood, distant from the act. Don't you get that? I doubt if he could relate to his body at all. Probably found it a nuisance even."

"Hmm," I said.

"I believe in sex," she said. "And sweat."

"Yes," I said. "I know you do."

"I'll bet a nickel," Hannah said, pushing her own nickel toward the pot in the middle of the table, though she couldn't bring herself to let go, and one bright orange nail rested on top of it. The game was a form of blackjack in which the dealer starts with a pot of two bucks or more, plays each person consecutively around the table, until he gets back to himself. He can only take the pot and go home if he has made it all the way around and he must at least triple his initial gamble. If he doesn't, he has to go around again. Jane's game.

John dealt the second card face up to Hannah which proved to be the ace of hearts.

"Oh, I better have another one," she said, telegraphing (as she did everything else about herself) that she had a lousy first card down. John dealt her another ace to which she said she had better have one more and then he dealt her a four of clubs that decided her to stay. John flipped over the king of spades, dealt himself an eight of diamonds, and announced he'd pay nineteen. Hannah flipped over a two and reluctantly shoved her nickel into John's growing pot; tie goes to the dealer.

The evening had developed about as I had expected. John arrived early. Hannah straggled in half an hour later, wearing tight jeans and heels, an effect she imagined showed off her long legs and bony ass. She had tried to waylay me near the doorway, brushing up against my arm with her barely restrained breasts, leaning toward me in order to whisper some amorous triviality that at one time I'd have at least appeared to be receptive to, but I steered her into the kitchen.

"Killians," John said when I asked him.

There's more to him than the beverage might suggest. Though he could never be called truly discerning, John has an educated palate. He's the type of person who would eat chipped beef on toast and foie gras with the same relish, and while I might do that as well, John would have less appreciation for the difference in finesse. There is one thing about John I admire and that is he'd likely call the stuff goose liver. Hannah would never eat goose liver, however, she'd insist on calling it foie gras; she ordered the usual sherry. Jane, who needed to let the Rothschild breathe anyway, sipped a bit of that, swirling it in the wide claret glass that red wine necessitates, a contemplative look on her face. Normally, circumstances such as these might require a clear head on my part, but I'd tossed these balls airborne long ago and a gin martini or two at this point would make no difference in the least to how they fell.

And so having eaten dinner, and having cleared away most of the mess, we were now huddled around the old pine gaming table in the main room, a fire raging in the stone fireplace and Willie Nelson playing, "Milk Cow Blues" on the CD player; Jane's choice. But one I had to admit was not too bad, if slightly monotonous. During dinner she'd played Miles Davis and Keb' Mo', I think. I prefer classical music, or, better yet, silence. It can never get quiet enough for me.

"Great dinner," said John. He had hardly spoken all evening. He'd merely been watching me as if he not only had suspicions, but as if he knew it all somehow. I gazed right back at him.

"Thank you," said Jane.

"So you really, like, killed those rabbits yourself?" asked Hannah, staring sadly into the money pile.

"Yes," Jane answered.

"I don't think I could do that," Hannah said. "It's just too . . . too barbaric. I know we have to eat, but . . ." Hannah kept crossing and uncrossing her legs every couple minutes, to get me thinking: triangle and fuzz.

"That's the point," Jane replied, and I could see the amusement under the words. "Do you know," she asked Hannah, "what is involved in field dressing an animal?" Jane had no intention of waiting for her to say she had no desire to hear or know and talked on, the description of what felt remarkably like the act of field dressing Hannah.

"You have to be careful making that first cut," Jane said. First remove the sex organs. "Then be careful as you cut from the vent to the sternum that you use force enough to cut only through the skin and just the muscle. You don't want to puncture an intestine and contaminate the whole carcass. If you do it just right, the entrails will roll out intact. Then you can open the body cavity and remove the heart and lungs and finally the trachea and esophagus."

"Yuck," said Hannah. "How can you do that?"

I felt clammy myself, and I knew without looking at her that Jane was watching my face.

Jane still looked amused, but then deadly serious. "It's an important process," said Jane. I knew what she was getting at, of course. The same old rhetoric about the distance between ourselves and an act of brutality being directly proportional to the guilt, or lack thereof, blah, blah, blah. Jane kept talking.

"People who hunt are not more barbaric than anyone else," she said, "they may be more compassionate. When I reach into the open body cavity of a steaming animal and pull out its heart and lungs, it's tough to pretend I'm not doing that." Rehearsed, I thought. In anticipation of Hannah's sensibilities.

"Why are bloody hands ever necessary?" asked Hannah.

Here it comes, I thought. I'd heard it so many times before. "Because emotional pain works just like physical pain," she would say any minute. "It has a purpose, like removing your hand from a hot griddle . . . prices to be paid for resorting to palliatives rather than feeling emotional pain . . . we're still getting burned, we just don't know it." But remarkably, she didn't say it.

"What is it about people that make them unwilling to accept blood and sex?" Jane said instead.

She looked at me then, and I thought then how Jane and I had both accused each other, and rightly, of absolute purity as if it were a dirty word; we both possessed the uncompromising single-mindedness of the fanatic. "Is it a question of acceptance, Jane?" I asked. "Or is it simply that some of us don't choose to wallow in it as you do? We all have to take a shit, too. I notice you don't bother wallowing in that . . . but I guess in a way you do like wallowing in shit, don't you?" I laughed to try to lighten the atmosphere in the room, since Hannah had moved to the edge of her chair, and Jane's dog, Max, had positioned himself between us.

John laughed and spoke finally. "Yes, there are always peons to do the wallowing, isn't that the way it works?" A reference, I presumed, to his having gone to Vietnam?

"People like you think things all add up in the end," I said. "But of course they don't." My comment was directed more to John, since nothing about Jane added up, or ever had, and that was part of what attracted me to her and what repelled me now.

"You know my first boyfriend, Rob his name was, had a rabbit's foot," Jane said, a bit irrelevantly, I thought, a dreamy sound to her voice. The amusement was back as well. "He said it was what was holding us together. He'd rub it along my cheek and down my arms, and then we'd both kiss it for luck, and then kiss each other."

"Ah," I said. "Why have I never heard anything about Rob before, and what happened to him might we ask?"

"I heard he died," she said. "I must have got all the luck." She peered into each one of our faces, and when she came to Hannah's I saw a look of guilt cross her face.

"Look," she said to Hannah. "Don't mind me. Hunting's not for everyone." Hannah met her eyes gratefully, and she softened, as most people did around Jane.

"No," I said. "It certainly isn't."

Willie's flutey voice floated around the room: "I could tell my milk cow, Could tell by the way she lows." The ceiling fan continued to hover like some great winged predator, air brushing oppressively over my skin, and I wondered then. How abrasive we'd been to one another, Jane, John, and me. How abrasive, and yet how necessary.

"Well, obviously, you know what you are doing in the kitchen," Hannah said to Jane. "I give you five stars."

"Funny," Jane said. "That's what my husband gave me once upon a time. But I doubt he'd rate me that high any longer." Her voice was light now, soufflé-like in its consistency. Like I remembered it had been once. She'd been one of several young apprentice chefs working temporarily at Lutece at the time I wrote the review.

"I said she was one of the few chefs around who understood basic simplicity in cooking, who remained honest to the particular fare she presented. Thank God she hadn't served me skinless, boneless chicken breasts smothered in raspberry sauce. That way I didn't have to lie in order to write it."

John glanced in my direction. I found him harder to read tonight for some reason. There was a time I considered myself intellectually superior to him. Believed he was possessed of no complexity or subtlety. But I've realized I was wrong. What he lacks in raw intelligence he makes up for in intuition.

John designs fly rods, primarily out of bamboo. Before that he'd taught college English for many years in St. Paul, something he said he'd enjoyed. He'd inherited money (not a lot but enough—both his parents being dead and he an only child). He had vacillated between a very early retirement in Bozeman, Montana or here, finally deciding on Michigan's Upper Peninsula several years back.

I watched as he shuffled the cards, and that's when I saw it on the back of his right hand. Raised, like someone had abraded his skin, it ran the full distance between the base of his thumb to the knuckle of his index finger. I felt startled for a moment, almost as though I'd forgotten about the scar, and then I thought how silly that was because of course I would never forget it. It had been my eleventh birthday, the summer before my father left, and since I was having a party and had asked for a Ping-Pong table, my father decided we should construct one ourselves.

"Nothing to it," he'd said, as he rounded up plywood, saw horses, green and white paint. He planned to make the net out of cheesecloth he would then attach to the table with glue, using carpenter's clamps.

"We can afford to buy the kid a nice table," my mother had said.

"This will be better," my father said. I knew what he was getting at. It was an expensive present to just give a kid for his birthday. My father intended to impart to me the importance of doing the work myself, wanted us to experience it together.

But I refused to help much, holding the edges of the plywood only when he directed me to, in stony silence.

But John, whose own father worked endless hours of overtime at a plastics factory, wanted to help. John had nailed the first piece of plywood to the sawhorses and, as I held one end of the board, he took the hand-saw from my father and began ripping down the second piece. Somehow the blade slipped, or he'd gotten his hand in the way, I don't remember, but he sliced a three-inch gash in his left hand, severed the tendon between his thumb and index finger, and it was while my father wrapped the cheesecloth around it to staunch the blood flow that I realized it was their table, John's and my father's. More than that, I realized that far from being resentful of this, I was relieved.

John and I played Ping-Pong over the years, the ball flying between our two paddles, like the tension between us, dividing the wins pretty evenly. I always claimed to not hear the slight ping of John's ball should it glance off the rough plywood edge to which he always replied, "Fuck you."

And then I'd see his face in the shadows. I'd see his impatience, his quick temper, but also the open generosity and loyalty of him. Certainly I saw the violence. But there was something else more terrifying. The closest I can come to describing it is faith. An expression that told me he knew I was redeemable at the end of the day . . . something that told me he needed to believe it, and he would believe it. Because the alternative was incomprehensible to him. And through the years, he held his faith out to me like a lifeline, the scar a testament to his loyalty.

Years later, he covered for me if I found it necessary to be out of the house all night. And finally, after it was all said and done, I'd given him Janet Earlbach (a girl who seemed vaguely interested in us both) in exchange for his friendship, his sacrifices, and his faith.

John dealt me one card down now, and I peeked under it while he took another of Hannah's nickels. My card: the two of diamonds. I looked up, smiled brightly, but not too brightly, tapped my knuckles on the pine table for a card, and said, "I'll take the pot." About forty bucks. John then dealt me, face up, the queen of diamonds. I smiled and said, "I'm good."

John smiled back, but didn't turn over his own card. In fact, he stood up, walked over to an antique beverage cart, and said he just had to fix himself another drink. Would I like one? No, I was nursing my Calvados, a fine Sire de Gouberville. Anyone else? No, they were fine.

"I think they're all fine," I said to him. "We're all just fine."

He poured himself an amaretto and more coffee from a black carafe, walked over to the front window, and peered out at the night. I remembered a dove he'd killed once when we were kids, the way he'd inserted the stick through the neck cavity, down through the small body and out between what was left of the legs. How it smelled oddly sweet as the flame seared the pink skin. I remembered, how sometimes when he cleaned something, he'd say to me, "Here, just touch them. Hold them in your hands." At the time, I thought he wanted me to become less squeamish, but now I know differently. I thought about what Jane had said about pain and how little she understood it. How something so subjective could ever, even remotely, be objective.

"It's starting to blow," John said. "I talked to my Aunt Jan yesterday. She told me she saw your mother not long ago." This was addressed to me.

"Hm."

"She's having fewer coherent days, I understand."

"Well, they are having to use stronger drugs to keep her comfortable," I said.

The home had written to me a couple weeks back. The letter had come from a Dr. Joyce Anderson, the director of The Reflections of St. Paul, informing me, essentially, that mother was driving them crazy. She was insisting on her nightly ritual of two Wheat Thins and one saltine cracker, along with two Maalox Plus tablets. They didn't carry those brands of snacks, they said, and the Maalox gave her the runs. But none of that was the big problem. The big problem was that she was regaling everyone, visitors primarily, with tales of the staff abusing her. Dr. Anderson was requesting I deal with the situation or move her immediately. But neither request was possible.

"Homes," Jane said, "are wonderful places, aren't they? They take over your burdens for you, only what people don't realize is that they save them for you, like in a bank reserve vault, and though they keep them away from you, out of sight, they sit there accumulating interest. Either you pick them all up someday, or worse, you don't."

And then I saw in John's face that he got it finally. Or accepted it. We don't really fool people; after all, they fool themselves. He returned to the table, and as he did, he placed a hand on the back of Jane's neck in a gentle squeeze. Not too familiar, nothing inappropriate, something I'd seen my own father do to him once, and then I noticed he no longer seemed to be watching me at all. Instead he looked at Jane. Then he picked up the deck, turned up the card which had been sitting in front of him which turned out to be the eight of spades. John dealt another card—the eight of hearts.

"Ahh," he said then. He still hadn't looked up at me.

We both knew that a Vegas dealer would be required to hit sixteen, but in lawnmower the betting is different since the players play their own hand without ever seeing the dealer's card. No splitting pairs or doubling down, either. What this boils down to is that in lawnmower there are no rules. Which makes it much more interesting.

"Are you going to play?"

"Maybe," said John. I turned from him to watch the others. Hannah was babbling away to Jane about how she'd spent the day looking for a blow-dryer that had been missing several weeks now. Did other people lose things like she did? Should she be worried her brain had atrophied? What brain, I thought. Jane, dressed comfortably in blue jeans and moccasins, had folded her legs under her, semi-lotus position, and appeared to be doing deep breathing. Trying to see out of her third eye, no doubt.

"At any rate," John said then. And he smiled when he said it. Because we both knew, had known for a long time that John was the only one who had ever understood me. Probably had, really, all along.

"I think you're bluffing. I'll pay seventeen."

• ◆ •

You'd tell yourself everything was so perfect. And it would be at first. Some of them served as buffers, human shields, stepping stones. In all cases, they were camouflage. And there was never any trouble attracting them:

You, Jane. Unexpectedly, there had been no accusations. You went so far as to pretend nothing was any different between the two of us, that you'd never intended any of what I knew you had planned, professed love for me in fact. You made me wonder for a moment if it could be true, but in the end I knew better. I felt your hands close around my heart. You had been merely massaging gently, but I could picture the blood on your fingertips, knew it would be only a matter of time before I heard the word divorce.

But then there had to be you, John, carrying not only your faith but a fly rod, happening upon us at the pond that night. Jenna (another woman I'd needed for various reasons), had her cold, wet, arms around me. Tentacle-like and grasping, she attempted the inevitable advances. She had lowered her head into the water, sure her warm mouth would arouse my obvious disinterest, a circumstance brought on by a combination of frigid temperatures and a deeply fundamental indifference. Before she'd grasped the futileness of her gesture, the cold water caused bronchial spasms, aggravating a brittle asthmatic condition I had known nothing about.

I underestimated you, John, all along. And that was a mistake.

But then you underestimated me. You would have called me a coward, but that couldn't be further from the truth.

Put yourself in my place. When you think about it, couldn't this happen to anyone? To you even? This is how it starts. Phantom odors. Ammonia, vinegar, wet wool, gym socks. That dry, dusty odor of decomposition. Or maybe not, maybe it's not those things at all and it's you yourself you've smelled. Simmering away in your own juices, some crazy hodgepodge of technique—poaching, braising, browning, clarifying, sautéing, stewing. Deglazing. You have become a dilution. A reduction. In danger of being plated soon with limited prep time and much fanfare. With plenty of attribution for the chef . . .

But whatever has caused it, you know it's the bloat that has become more than you can handle, an insidious, creeping loss of appetite that has invaded everything. It isn't just that you've lost your taste for sweetbreads and headcheese and blood sausage. No, you've lost your taste even for wild oysters with fresh morels, the "Holy Trinity" of cassoulet, spider crab timbale, roasted guinea hens, legs of lamb en croute. Even passion fruit with crème anglaise, though the last seems bloodless in comparison. But with each passing day it increases . . . this anorexia of the soul.

And then, there are the mushrooms. Mushrooms are fungi, lacking the pigment chlorophyll. They reproduce both sexually and asexually. Without getting too scientific, let us say that the relationship between green plants and fungi is a symbiotic one; the fungus extracts excess reserve sugars from the roots of the plant but rather than harming the plant it enables it to increase its root apparatus, which then increases its ability to absorb mineral salts and water. There is even a point where the plant cells that are under attack begin digesting the fungus cells. And it all works out beautifully. The fungus has its sugars; the plant gains in nitrogenous substances and mineral salts.

Like lovers.

Though you try not to think of it, you know this: fungi occasionally become parasitic. If they do, they attack specific hosts. Plants, insects, even other fungi.

And that is when they must be stopped. . . .

You can see that detective now, hesitating as he did at the front door, standing in the half shadow, in that lingering silt of a shifting perspective. Just like your old man would have, the certain knowledge revealed in his face, yet with that disarming quality about him that makes you wonder if things might, just maybe, have been different.

You look out the window and see Jane's rotting cooking garden in the half-light of a diminishing day, yet suddenly you can see it burgeoning with life, abundant with heirloom tomatoes, zucchini, exotic peppers, rosemary, mint, tarragon, chives, all of which you could have sworn were dead, and you rub your eyes like a small child would do. You can see the potting shed partly revealed in the late afternoon shadow, and the carnage, the eviscerated carcasses dripping there through the years.

AISSA ONCE

SPINNER FALLS

I'm not sure who came first, but it must have been either Chevy Chase or Steve Martin. It was too early for Tim Allen, though he comes often. Not Steve Martin, though. The last time he arrived in my dreams, he never went on at all. Just hid under my desk because he said if he came out, I'd force him to have sex with me.

I assured him I only wanted him to fix the oven.

You sleep naked now. Before he had insisted upon it. Now it's your personal revenge.

Next to your bed stands an oak nightstand that once belonged to his mother, too massive to please you, dark, heavy grained, upon which rests a delicate lace doily, a pair of dime store reading glasses, a few books written by your women, the ones he refers to as "your harpies," and a book called Trout Stream Insects, *an Orvis Streamside Guide. Oh, and that collection by Kafka you stumbled upon at the library reading selection of the month.*

Next to the books there is a square jewelry box your own mother gave you—made of glass the color of purple oxidized blood. It has a matching lid that is attached on two sides with antique brass hinges. It's lined on the bottom with plushy white satin—stark against the red glass—and on top of the colorless satin the daily ritual: the results of today's foraging.

Not too extensive; certainly not a collection as diverse as what is featured in the Orvis Streamside Guide *(in fact, your collection doesn't appear in the Orvis book at all). A couple mosquitoes (one you slapped after it had sucked a bit of blood from your knee cap), a medium-sized house fly, a papery, mud-colored moth, and two tiny gray spiders . . . not the real fuzzy kind because, after all, that could be a bit much. All small, because that is what is needed.*

All dead.

Oh, and tweezers. You always need tweezers.

It's that cutting brilliance I admire about the comedians, I suppose. Lines delivered with surgical precision and equally little compassion. Massive gray cells on legs. Limber. Loose.

Always lethal.

But then there's that underbelly, that barely camouflaged, suffering angst that appeals to me, too. I don't blame them for the angst. I'd rather die than do stand-up.

So I don't.

I lie down.

And most of my comedians do that as well . . .

Which I think is cheating.

You sleep naked, but he has a vengeance of his own: he's a big man and he has slid his feet out to escape the confines of the mint-green sheet (doing this inevitably causes the sheet to wrap around the solid stumps of his legs) so that, as happens often and is the case tonight, only half your body is covered, the softness of the fabric covering one foot and dimpled thigh, cutting you straight down the torso, shielding one oddly pointy breast and dividing your crotch and the entirety of your body into two equal halves, leaving one fleshy side absurdly exposed. A snowshoe, one of a dilapidated pair of antique bear paws given to you by your grandmother, protrudes from the bookshelf between you and the floor lamp, forming a waffled, prison-wired shadow over your half-exposed chest. You are hypnotized by the incongruous effect your naked body has on your own sensibilities, the firmness even yet of those high, pointed breasts, the one you can see anyway, pointing away, the deceptive swelling of your traitorous abdomen, deceiving in that it has never issued a child. And the persistent, dry ache you feel between your legs where the sheet divides and will continue to divide—in every way that could possibly matter. You spread your leg a bit wider to see if the act of doing so will split you physically as well as figuratively. Surely you have become dry enough. Like an abandoned wish bone left too long on someone's window sill in the sun, brittle and decomposing and fleshless.

(This is mostly bullshit, and you know it. But you think like this sometimes.)

You do have a child, a child you wanted desperately, and evidence of her "issue" spreads across your abdomen in a crooked smile, low pointy boobs and off-center navel forming a ludicrous upside-down happy face as you look down. The child has mass, volume, and casts an imposing shadow. You raise your leg one across the other in a half-Indian position so you can reach the bottom of your foot. You start peeling the skin off in strips.

Anyway, Chevy, Steve, Tim, who else. Oh, Tom Hanks . . . Robin Williams of course. Sean Connery and Harrison Ford (I consider them very funny), Kevin Kline, Bill Murray, Jerry

Houser (the gas station attendant in *Seems Like Old Times* who handed over the Zagnuts when Chevy Chase knocked over the candy machines at gun point—and after he'd been shoved out of a car doing fifty, rolled down a hill doing seventy-five, and left for dead by the bad guys—B. G. and somebody; I probably have that all wrong). Anyway, Martin Short comes sometimes, and much to my dismay, Woody Allen. No black comedians so far. No women.

Profile. You always think of him in profile even when he sleeps. His yellow skin has begun to pucker and dimple slightly, like a two-day-old pear abandoned at the back of someone's kitchen counter—just the hint of a brown mushy spot so far, to the left of his nose, but you can see the impending decay. His mouth hangs ludicrously open. Slack. Gaping. Trout-like? (He'd prefer that comparison; he'd never want to be compared to a fruit.) The slow tedious process of degeneration . . . no, transformation? Metamorphosis? To steal Kafka's metaphor.

Now a few seconds of sepulchral silence and you know precisely how he will look stuffed and mounted (bagged and tagged?) but then the next shuddering gasp rakes down your nerve endings and forces you to grab the edge of the mattress to keep from being sucked in and down—over the lips, over the gums, look out stomach, here she comes. . . .

The rasping, sawing noise continues next to you for a few uninterrupted measures, then teeters on the brink of an endless rest but is only about twenty seconds long according to the clock, then resumes in a blasting, snorting, howling crescendo. You glance down, smile, the bed sheet rising in the vicinity of his crotch, forming a tent—a teeny tiny pup tent, a bivy maybe?—over the lower part of his frame. You are tempted to lift the edge of the sheet and take a peek, curious about the extent of the damage, but don't want to take a chance on waking him.

Never wake them, your mother said once.

Kevin Kline was nice, I thought. He didn't talk French to me or sing "La Mer" to me like he did to Meg Ryan in French Kiss *or talk about his ass twitching. But he did take me all around a fancy Hollywood-type cocktail party introducing me to everyone there as if I were the love of his life. That's one thing that's pretty consistent with my comedians; they all seem to adore me (except on the odd night when Steve wouldn't emerge from under the desk). Anyway, things were going well with Kevin at this cocktail party, everything had this fuzzy gilt-edged look to it when he suddenly turned into Bill Murray, whom I kind of liked in* Groundhog Day, *but has always made me feel ever so off balance because of his sarcasm. I spent most of the night trying to morph him back into Kevin since I was pretty sure he wasn't gay in this particular dream, and with whom all things seemed to glow.*

The days foraging.

Some days are good, of course. The days when the catch all seems to parade right past you like lambs to the slaughter, without your having to move a muscle or lift a finger; they seem to nearly dive into the crimson box. Ripe, plump, sleek bodied, the beetle types—lots of legs. Or sometimes fuzzy and squat, caterpillars and spiders, still with plenty of legs. And fliers too, moths and mosquitoes. Always willing to make the sacrifice and you wonder why they are. But then there are the can't-get-your-fill-days when the box lays barren and empty . . . soft, padded, expectant. Who's sorriest on these days?

You see him from the side. You like his profile but he always seems to be laying it on you; never looking you in the eye. There had been things you liked: he was a big man, intelligent. He had this habit of walking through a room hiding his thumbs inside his fists. Vulnerable. You figured there was a safe, benign quality about a man with no thumbs. . . . Best of all, he laughed. With you. At you. Over you. It didn't matter.

As long as he laughed.

I say I was dismayed when Woody Allen arrived because I knew someone who resembled him once. Sickly, anemic looking. Shreds of hair clinging to an inflated-but-still-insipid looking head. Severe acne, purple, clammy skin, and worst of all, what I imagined was an imposing body odor. (Well, that's what this guy had.) Anyway, in my dream I didn't see any signs of abominable hair dryers that would blow the last remaining shred of hair off his head like in *Play It Again Sam*, or any signs of looming liberated lobsters moving toward my ankles like there were in *Annie Hall*, and he didn't seem sexually deprived and pathetically needy as he did in nearly all of his films, and not particularly funny, which was a relief, because funny was tied to all of the above. Instead he sat calmly and earnestly next to me on a piano bench and explained to me how Aristotle had claimed there was only the slightest difference between tragedy and comedy; and he talked about Death of course, how Borges had said that to prolong the years of a man's life was to prolong the agony of his Dying and multiply the number of his Deaths. Then he played me the new song he had composed. Just for me.

Your father laughed a lot. The key, he would tell you (and you presumed from this, he meant the key to a man's heart) is to keep them laughing. Do nothing but that, not another single solitary thing, he said, and they'll tolerate anything. Turns out you don't know much about comedians or comedy routines.

You know too much about audiences.

And then he said this: The ultimate failure, the unforgivable sin, the quintessential kiss of death (quite seriously, he'd say this) is to bore them.

Never . . . ever . . . bore them.

The whistling. That's what I like most about Chevy. *Fletch Lives.* White suit. Dancing me down streets of graceful live oaks, animated creatures cavorting at our side, Chevy's and mine. Singing:

Zippity doo dah, zippity ae,

My oh my, what a wonderful day.

Plenty of sunshine . . .

You're dressed in white, or rather it's an ecru lace, something high necked and Victorian and not your cup of tea. Matching shoes, but your friends have told you they will never do. Black is the only thing these days with a white dress, an absolute must; only it's a dream and the black shoes elude you like things do in dreams. At last you find them. You're wearing a veil which means his face is covered with scrolly disjointed patches; parts of his nose and most of one eye have disappeared beneath a lacy flower. The ceremony hasn't quite begun yet, but you can feel the wedding ring on your hand, seared there. Your loved ones are gathered in front of you, behind the minister for some reason, and the air feels heavy though the sun is shining brightly. Everyone takes a step back as the minister walks toward you, Bible in hand, when they all disappear into inky blackness.

Or you do.

Nothing under your feet but air. You are not holding hands, but you know you are falling together, know you are going to die together, and there is no way out for either of you.

They always say if you land, you'll die.

But amazingly you do land, and lightly, on the balls of your feet, you walk away together, toward the reception. It's time for you to change, but before you can get the wedding dress off and your traveling suit on, you see him off in the distance, fondling several of your maids of honor.

You reach over the bedside table and pick up a book, Life Before Man *by Margaret Atwood, one of your "harpies." He doesn't say this disdainfully; that would be too confrontational. He's never read them, but he knows enough to assume they are man-eating Medusa-like spider women and they make him fidget. Only thing she reads, he tells people. The women. Which isn't true. You read mostly men actually. Jim Harrison, Tom McGuane, Richard Ford. There are others. Hemingway, Faulkner. But you do like your "harpies." Margaret Atwood, Joyce Carol Oates, Lorrie Moore, Annie Proulx. You find out a lot of fascinating things by reading them. For instance, that's how you found out that a male octopus sometimes loses an arm when mating, that dinosaurs probably had no penises and that a snake sometimes has two. But you know an odd thing or two yourself. Do your harpies know it's possible for a woman to have an orgasm if she simply stands on her head long enough? It is; but eventually you found easier ways.*

A mosquito buzzes next to your head, lands a moment on Life Before Man, *then conveniently on your left arm. You slap him with your right hand, pick him up by the wings and plop him into the jewelry box along with the others.*

I always have trouble with Steve, it seems. And that's unfortunate because I always have such hopes for us. There was this one night he showed up (he was our next door neighbor and we all had sloping front lawns in the dream neighborhood) and he was exasperated because the trees and bushes—anything and everything he tried to plant—slid down out of his yard into a big pile in the road, accordion-like. We were used to this in our own yards. But Steve thought this was my fault; I thought so, too.

He doesn't do confrontation. Did you say this before?

You left the orange peels in the sink again, you say. No reaction. No sign of life in his face. You're tracking mud all over the house. Not a flicker. I don't like it when you drink every night, especially in front of the kids. Nope. Not even an up-yours, kiss-my-ass kind of look. Nothing. What was it Margaret said? It was a riddle. What is more powerful than God, more evil than the devil, the poor have it, the rich lack it, and if you eat it you die?

Nothing.

The answer was nothing . . .

The laughter has changed. (When did it change?) He uses it now like some people use smiles, a means of self-defense, camouflage, a diversion. And when you have sex, he ignores your body from the waist up, stays just out of reach, as if he's afraid of the snapping jaws.

He does make business arrangements. Or rather he starts to. Real estate investments, property management; though he's a dentist by trade. You're the control freak, he says. You do the books, line up the little numbers. He can't be bothered with details. He's relegated you to chief peon and head secretary. You know how you tell the head secretary, don't you? She's the one with the dirt on her knees.

The jokes have changed along with the rest. But that's okay with you. Playing secretary is okay, too.

Apparently, he never studied Russia under Stalin.

Your friends tell you straight out. About wine bottles and glasses on innocent shopping sprees, back rubs in chance moments they've spent alone with him. Vague suggestions that you better keep him satisfied. He whines to each of them in turn; has developed a unique relationship with each. You generously provide the framework for their closeness. He dissects your life (you won't say your relationship because a relationship would require participation on his part), pores over every nuance of it with each of them. Once, you protected them from him. Now, you no longer bother.

Let them fend for themselves.

He insisted you go fly fishing once, a few years back, on one of his business things, along with another contractor and his wife, a compact boyish woman with highlighted blonde hair that separated into strands—like snakes.

You stand in the middle of the spinner fall, the trout right in the center of the river, "the feeding lane," the contractor calls it, but when you all move into the river they mostly look like shooting, darting glints moving from the sun into the shadows and back again. You like feeling the current pushing against your legs, like the pull of it even through the borrowed waders . . . you fall in a sink hole and the waders fill full of water, threatening to haul you under or at the least drag your ass downstream with the force of its energy. The struggle appeals to you. The circadian rhythm, the pantheistic images. River of God . . .

"You'll get used to it," the guy in the fish store tells you later. He wears khaki Gore-tex shorts—short shorts, matching shirt. Strawberry-blonde hair like Robert Redford in Out of Africa. *Would someone dress like that really? Still you watch him, standing over a big wooden compartmentalized display case with a pair of oversized tweezers, while he picks a dozen or so varieties of flies: tiny blue-winged olives, medium-sized Adamses, a couple wet flies, some gaudy streamers, and even a nymph or two.*

He gets you "straightened away" with the basic stuff; leaders, tippets, rod (rod—never pole. And nymphs, too—you know who invented this sport), fly vest, clippers. He'll give you lessons, he says, just give him a call here at the shop. You are unsure if this is a come-on, but it doesn't matter. You look down at his legs bulging beneath the khaki shorts and imagine the water rushing between them—no waders for him—flattening the reddish hair around his calves and thighs, the river shoving him a step this way. That way. Maybe your way?

Later you dream you are tangling filament around huge protruding rocks while attempting to shoot line during a forward cast; next you fail to let go of the line in your line hand and only cast out about six feet; or you fail to end the cast soon enough, slapping the rod tip onto the surface water ahead of you, scaring away any dream fish that might have been. Mostly, it seems you have yards of slack line lying in unmanageable heaps on the water. Until all at once you seem to get it: you drop back and let out a great, soaring cast.

And snag yourself an airplane.

Which goes to show you what can happen when you wave an empty hook around long enough. This is some pretty amazing line and leader material, too, you have time to think, and some extraordinarily well tied knots (a source of great pride for you) because he takes a run upstream on you, actually over stream, and lifts you a full six feet out of the water. You spend a few seconds trying to break the line before you go ahead and let him have the rod. You see it disappearing over the treetops as you wake up.

Windows.

Or doors.

Why is it always funnier to watch someone doing something asinine if they run by a window or a door, far away? Like Chevy in *Funny Farm*. Watching him wrasslin' that snake down on the lawn looked so much funnier through the window with his wife unaware of his predicament than it would have looked up close. I wonder who the first person was to figure this out and just exactly why it is.

Maybe it's easier to laugh at people from a distance.

You dissected one of them in college and you can still smell the sweet sickly smell of the formaldehyde in your nostrils; in fact, these days you can smell it nightly. They have blood that resembles a man's, but they breathe not only with lungs but through their skins as well. Their ears sit directly behind their large bulging eyes; they can change color. Hibernate like bears. They may or may not like water. They have only three chambers to their hearts instead of four. In some species, the eggs are wound around the legs of the male. In other species, the male carries the eggs and tadpoles lovingly in his mouth. In your case, his very body seems to form a bridge providing the connection between you and the child.

You brushed up against one another a while back. One winter, when you both used to get out of this bed, when there was life outside of it, and this life had a continuum, well really a spectrum left to it. Ranges of color and opportunity. Perhaps it was an accident, but somehow you collided with one another. Something the shrink said maybe, or his growing realization that you might actually leave; there was a moment where you could feel him engage. A spark. A fraction of a second when you felt a connection. His skin was slimy against your body, cold, lumpy, unfamiliar. His lips wouldn't stay together, his tongue had become sticky, incredibly long. But none of that mattered because you had actually collided; it felt strange and your heart caught in your throat for a moment. You felt something, then, you're sure of it. But eventually you realized you were still numb from the waist up. And he had begun to show a real affinity for the water. Even then.

Synchronicity. Jung invented the word which means (according to him), meaningful coincidence or a causal orderedness. Like when a person suddenly starts thinking of an old friend, keeps expecting to see him everywhere she turns, and then she does. Or like when there is some issue troubling a person, and everywhere she turns, she hears people discussing that very subject, television or radio announcers discussing it, drunks boring each other with it, all of them providing extraordinary and unexpected enlightenment. It's when things become "ordered" beyond the realm of accident or chance. Jung seemed to think synchronicity actually made a case for indeterminism and free will. Not to mention ESP. But I had problems following his premise through to that same conclusion. When people experience synchronicity, the whole point it seems to me, is that we believe the coincidences are more than accidents, have some cause, usually we think a divine one. But that, after all, is still a cause, not an accident.

The reason I mention this is that Tim showed up one night and we spent the night looking for hood ornaments. Like in his book, *I'm Not Really Here.* Everywhere he turned there were hood ornaments. He looked at me seriously at one point. Comedians, he told me, are the only people who know that the *Divine Comedy* is a journey from Heaven through Purgatory ending in Hell, not the other way around. I wasn't sure what Heaven and Hell had to do with hood ornaments.

But I was thinking how my comedian phenomenon itself is synchronistic in nature. Well, maybe it isn't, I guess they'd have to really show up in my bed to qualify, but it seems synchronistic just the same.

There are worse things than eating you, you know that now.

It has glands that emit poison. Only it doesn't have stingers or fangs or a tail that deliver this poison. It oozes through the skin. It sits back waiting. Bloated. Maddeningly passive. Pathetically inert. Blowing in and out of your air space, croaking inanely, until you can no longer take the detachment, the limpness, the sameness, the BOREDOM, and you reach over at last and bite its fucking head off, despite the fact you knew all along that as soon as you took the first bite, it would kill you.

And it does.

It kills you, surprisingly, even though the damn thing no longer has any balls. You've seen to that, you're horrified to say—

Two of the four posters of your bed loom in front of you. Like goal posts. How long has it been since you got out of this bed? Oozing bedsores fester on the backs of your legs. Your child wanders in and out, exempt. She doesn't notice the moss collecting on the edges of the sheets. She doesn't notice your nakedness or his hibernation. She leans over for kisses and seems unaware of the horror. She doesn't know that tonight is like every other night for you, specious, spurious, spectral. She doesn't know you can't trust anything, not even yourself. Night, Mommy. Night, baby. As she leaves, you notice there's a slit at the bottom of the window shade, and light from the street lamp intrudes amongst the shadows, forming a happy kind of party hat across the bare wooden floor of the room. Party hats. Did you ever wear one? Yes, you remember now, you wet your pants, your mother said. The anticipation, she said.

You remember the day but not the anticipation.

Instead you remember the insects—how they hatch over rivers in the early evening.

Mate and die.

You close your eyes for a moment and see bulging legs from under khaki pants, river rushing against them and against you. But it's too late to push back. Isn't it? You open your eyes and see there are tiny moths flitting about, making ticking sounds against the shade of the floor lamp. Tick, tick, tick. You squash one against the paper shade, add it to the box.

These days comfort comes only in your ritual.

And you do it not just for you, but because you know he needs it, has come to depend upon it more than you do. He heaves, mouth hanging open like usual. Pink sticky tongue oozing out of the gash that is his mouth, all of it vibrating with the shuddering gasps of his next breath. The light from the floor lamp isn't much and the red fly box, your mother's jewelry box, looks nearly as black as his eyes have become these days. You're tired and you think tonight that maybe you'll skip the whole thing and just go to sleep. But it's the only thing left for either of you and it must be done.

You lift the tweezers from the bedside table, open the glass lid of the box and poke through the assortment. Nothing unique there tonight, but enough to keep him going. One of the snowshoes falls against the book case with a loud thud, disturbing his cadence slightly, so you make your selection while you're waiting for him to settle back into a regular pattern of breathing. You look over and see if there is any further change. His teeth seem shorter, mouth bigger. Thumbs—does he have thumbs? It's something you'd like to know, but his hands are tucked along his sides, under his buttocks.

What will it be? You decide on the mosquito, the one you slapped this morning while reading Margaret, and using the tweezers you pick him up gently by one papery wing. Is he quite dead? Maybe a wiggle or two. You drop it then—carefully onto his tongue. As far back as you can manage it.

Then it's gone. With hardly a falter in the cadence of his breathing. Now what will it be? Maybe the spider next. You're careful not to get them too hairy or too large. Might be more than he could handle yet.

You lift the spider, a semi-fuzzy, grayish brown one, by one of its back legs, hold it suspended over his waiting, eager mouth. You wait . . . you wait . . . keep waiting. There's plenty where this came from, you assure him. Yep, plenty. The party hat looms toward you across the expanse, no longer seeming to touch the floor.

You drop one more insect . . . the moth—into his eager, greedy mouth.

And you think: Never . . . ever . . . bore them . . .

Zippity doo dah . . .

JANE

THREE FIRES

Thou art Earth, Thou art Water, Thou art Fire, Thou
art Air, Thou art the Void, Thou art consciousness
itself, Thou art life in this world; Thou art the knowledge of self, and Thou art the Supreme Divinity.

Fire is one of the four ancient elements; male Fire and
Air at odds, always, with female Earth and Water.
—*Mahanirvanatantra*

ONE

Fire cleanses, they say.

That's what she'd told herself as she sat outside in her lawn chair and despite the fact the fire department had told her to evacuate twenty minutes ago. "Take what's on your back and in your hands and go," they'd said. Jane had looked down at the periwinkle coffee cup in one hand and the *Newberry News* in the other. "Fuck you," she answered because she knew nothing less would get their attention.

They told her they had other people to get out and she said, "Then you better get movin."

"We can't guarantee your safety," they said, and she said, "Can you guarantee it if I leave? Will you put that in writing?"

That's something she'd like to take to the bank.

They left her looking at the sky to the southwest. They yelled out the window to her that she was a fool while their tires spun in the loamy sand.

It's her mother's camp, and Aissa is downstate visiting a friend. Jane considers packing up some of her mother's belongings, family pictures, or even her grandmother Norna's bamboo fishing rod, but decides to hose down the house instead. The hose isn't long enough to reach all the way around it, but she starts squirting the wood siding, the water spraying anemically two-thirds of the way up. The pump is a one-half horsepower, 110 V, 60 Hz well jet pump. The well is a two-inch sand-point-driven casing down to sixty-five feet below ground level.

Aissa could use a new well.

Since it's been cloudy the last few days, no solar, she's not sure how long the batteries will hold out. *A generator would have come in handy, that's for damn sure,* Jane thinks, *but it's not hooked to the propane: solar is enough for one person in the summer.*

Jane has been here for weeks. She'd needed to get away from Alex to gain some kind of perspective between them. He'd objected, but she'd gone anyway. She thinks about her own ranch, knows it's not in the path of the impending inferno, and keeps hosing down her mother's place, a place that had once belonged to her grandmother Norna years ago. She wonders for a moment what Norna might be doing at this moment in an alternate migration, but lets it go. After all, Norna might be dead in another world, too; in some migrations she never existed at all and neither did Jane—the possibilities always endless.

Time is like that.

Now, in this migration, John's Bronco rolls into the driveway.

"Where's Alex?" Jane asks, referring to her husband. John is his best friend.

"I'm not certain," he responds tactfully. She knows he doesn't want to tell her that Alex has no desire to be there.

There is nothing between John and Jane.

Nothing except love.

TWO

Jane picks up the swatter and looks at her mother, Aissa. She hands her a cotton jacket.

"No synthetics," Jane tells her.

"Tell me again why we'd do something like this?" Aissa asks.

"The DNR does prescribed burns all the time, Mom. Fires are natural and help certain habitats. Sandhill cranes need it. Sharp-tailed grouse, bluebirds, deer. Blueberries and morel mushrooms all benefit."

Aissa nods but shakes her head while Jane points out the firebreaks. The property backs up to Dawson Creek on the south side and they've bulldozed wide breaks to the east and west. It's before green-up, early April, and the frost is still in the ground—the safest time to burn. The wind is out of the north and forecasted to be five to ten mph. The fire plan called for them to burn the area in strips for a total of one hundred acres.

"Besides, I need to clear some of this area for pasture for my livestock," Jane says. "I have too much mature woodland and mature forest."

Jane's grandfather had left her money enough to start her five-hundred-acre ranch when he died in 1994 which enabled her to commercially raise axis deer, black buck, and nilgai antelope, all imported from India. All grass-fed. Non-GMO feed. She planned to expand into elk and buffalo soon, in anticipation of the expanding interests in organic farm practices. And she needed area to grow crops as well.

"*Controlled* burn," Aissa says and looks across the ten acres to where Alex is waiting to light the first headfire. They can barely see him through the trees, but he's standing on a rise and now appears to be digging at something in the ground with a shovel. "Seems scary," Aissa says again. "Controlling fire."

"You got to," Jane replies.

Aissa throws an arm around the girl.

"You are such a fine chef," Aissa says. "Odd business plan, training horses and raising commercial livestock, but it seems to be working. You are multitalented. Horses scare the crap out of me."

"Horses. A horse always reminds you, no matter the rapport, that there is a fine line between trust and crazy. They are never quite domesticated and they'll let you know it."

"I can see how you belong up here and not downstate. Me? I am never sure where I belong."

"And yet you're here now, too."

"Yep." Aissa had never sold her mother Norna's camp after she died and now spends most of her time "being" what she calls that "brook trout out of water." Jane smiles at her until Aissa turns away. Aissa zips her jacket, pulls the collar up against her short brown hair, and all the while she keeps watching Alex who has moved closer to the barn.

"Why don't you like him, Mom?" Jane asks.

Aissa faces Jane once again.

"I don't know that I dislike him, Jane," Aissa says. "Your grandmother always told me there was no such thing as a mistake."

Jane smiles. She lights the backfire on the downwind side of the perimeter of the burn site with a highway flare, holding her sprayer and rake in either hand. She doesn't answer, but watches the fire burn for twenty minutes.

"It's burning just right but we'll mop up behind it, too." She demonstrates with a combination of spray and rake which turns the burned spots to a smoldering black, steam rising around the women like swamp gas.

"He was kind to me, Mom," Jane says.

Aissa nods, but the nod seems again to turn into more of a headshake. "Kind or charming?" she asks.

"Both, I suppose. And sad somehow, there in New York. I was sure if I could get him out of there part of the time, he'd start a new migration. He needed me."

"You and your migrations," Aissa says, smiling.

Jane thinks about fire and how it cleanses. She wonders if it has the potential of rejuvenation and forgiveness or whether it might perhaps veer them off onto a new path.

Or whether they'd just be engulfed in the flames and lost to one another forever.

The women continue on, the two of them working on the back and flank fires, mopping steadily behind the flames for another hour. At last Jane waves over to Alex, on his feet now, who ignites the head fire with a drip torch. They watch as the wind blows up the flames like a big bellows and they race toward mother and daughter. The women back up behind the fire breaks and Jane thinks for a moment that Alex has ignited, too, no longer visible across the expanse of clearing.

THREE

Last night, the night before the fire, Jane had been awakened at three thirty a.m. by a pulsing light coming through the trees to the north, and there was simply nothing to account for it. Heat lightning was simply not that rhythmical, and she'd jumped in her Jeep and driven the eight miles (four miles as the crow flies) to Lake Superior in an attempt to account for it. The roads were all gravel and so dry that the cloud of dust she was creating looked orange behind her as the sky kept lighting over the treetops.

When she arrived at the mouth of the Two Hearted (parts of which will burn to the ground over the next few days), she saw the pulsing light at the horizon, exactly where the water meets the sky, only it wasn't white any longer, it was lavender. The campground was surprisingly quiet, though Jane thought she heard a reverent whisper or two, and she watched as the purple pulse spread across the heavens and turned shimmering green. She was certain at first she was seeing the aurora, yet, just as quickly as the flashes came, they retreated, and once more she saw only the pulsing rhythmic purple light at the horizon and wondered as she always did if it was a portal, or maybe even a wormhole, or a reflection from a black hole, in which energy would suddenly shift downwards infinitesimally and cause them all to disappear. She sat there until the morning light all but obliterated the flashes, then she returned to Aissa's house and watched the looming white pines from her window without ever falling into a deep sleep.

Big Bangs. The sun's gases. All manner of fire comes to mind now as she squirts the building. The eastern and northern skies have not a cloud to mar the blue, but the gusts of wind well over fifty mph blow a cloud of smoke from the southeast that has now covered the sun, and she can smell it encroaching like a giant campfire set by God.

ONE AGAIN

John steps out of his Bronco, takes the hose from her. He continues squirting and she sits for a moment on the picnic table and watches. They don't speak, and after a half hour the original fire department members arrive once again in their pickup trucks and hound them to leave. But Jane knows if she leaves, they will control the roads, and she will not be allowed to reenter. They cannot, however, arrest her and force her to leave her property. They appeal to John who promises to reason with her, and once again they depart in a cloud of black flies.

"How'd you make it in?" Jane asks.

"Logging roads, of course. Came through Pine Stump."

Jane begins moving the log pile from under the lean-to on the side of the house using a wheel barrow, trip after trip, moving it fifty feet away from the house, and John pulls tall weeds away from the foundation. They work for hours until the day disappears on them and Jane notices that the smoke cloud has moved west and is no longer covering the sun. She isn't fool enough to believe she is out of danger, only that there is a momentary reprieve.

They sit for a bit when the wind dies down and each eat a piece of Stilton, closing the windows to reduce the heavy smoke that fills the air. It's stifling with the windows closed, but they listen to the local Newberry station, the Eagle, and learn that the fire is three miles wide and twelve miles long presently, that the wind that had been blowing it at them had switched and shoved the fire two miles west. The wind had set down for the night as it often does, and the local firefighters had gone home, intending to resume their battle at daylight.

The evacuated area, they say, is County Road 414 between County Road 500 and the 410, and north on 500 to Crisp Point. The public is urged to comply.

Jane knows they are safe for the night.

She has a chicken thawed and she picks cucumbers and wild asparagus. She lights the charcoal grill since it's clearly too dry to cook over an open fire and too hot to use the propane stove Aissa has installed this last winter.

Jane dispenses with seasoning other than salt and pepper and as the chicken roasts, she and John sit at the picnic table sipping a couple porters she's iced down. She throws the asparagus on the grill and slices the cucumbers and it feels as if they are sharing the last supper. They clear up the dishes and Jane watches the slow stream of the water, wondering about the water table in this drought. Afterward, as the sun and black flies recede, they move outside, their chairs around the empty fire pit, *the nonfire*, and sit under a smoky sky.

Jane thinks of the food that should have been cooked there, but wasn't.

The wind kicks up again on Friday.

The radio keeps them informed that the wildfire is out of control now; it's four miles wide and eighteen miles long and it's a conflagration, running north to Lake Superior, taking everything in its path. It's already burned numerous homes and structures south of them. Miraculously it shifted west, and now is burning camps and stores and campgrounds to the north and west of them. It will burn all day until it reaches the great shoreline where it will rest; but she knows it will then begin creeping east—and once again—south.

Jane spends the day loading family pictures into the Jeep, and John continues to move anything flammable farther from the log structure. Luckily, it has a metal roof, as the news is reporting that everything that doesn't is probably doomed. They are 30 percent contained, they say, which is a joke since the containment line at that point is nothing more than Lake Superior and County Road 500. The firefighters quit yet again at six p.m. leaving those that remain to their own devices, and in time to make the Newberry fish fry.

And yet nobody has been killed, you can say that for them.

They'd finally gotten air support from Grayling and from the nearby Seney Refuge fire. The DNR arrives and Jane, once again, tells them to leave. On the third day, Jane and John are as organized as they can be. If they do have to leave, they will close the windows and go. There is no rain, but the sun, at least, is charging the solar panels and the batteries, and every few hours, they hose down the house and grounds. The bulldozers arrive at noon and announce that the new eastern "containment line" will run through Aissa's property.

Jane doesn't try to stop them.

While they are at it, they doze down several stands of jack pines that are still too close to the structure for which Jane is grateful since they had run out of gas for the chain saw. The huge machines run over Norna's thirty-five acres for hours, like huge dinosaurs ripping at the land, and when they are gone it looks like a war zone, nothing left but thousands of black flies disturbed by the scarified earth, swirling like living tornados over their heads.

"The fire is now moving east and south toward you," the dozer operators tell her. "Maybe not as hot as that fire that raced to Superior, but it's heading your way nevertheless. You should get out."

Jane nods.

Jane makes dinner instead. She wishes she could use a wood fire, but knows it is out of the question. She had studied culinary arts at the Culinary Institute in New York after she graduated from high school, yet simple cooking over a wood fire is still her favorite.

The fare, though, is often far from simple: Lobster tails in cilantro butter; cioppino with mussels, shrimp, crab, and chorizo sausage all seasoned with Pernod and fresh tarragon, basil, fennel; decadent racks of lamb or venison; porterhouse or bone-in rib-eye steaks; ruffed grouse breasts; rare tuna sliced with pickled ginger and wasabi; grilled pears topped with brandy butter. Yet sometimes it is simple: a few brook trout pulled out of a stream with a bit of olive oil, salt and pepper; a few raw shrimp tossed on the grate; a boneless chicken breast coated in olive oil; a hamburger, rare, which she'd later top with mushrooms and blue cheese; potatoes roasted in the coals, both red skins and russet, all seasoned with a handful of fresh herbs such as mint, rosemary, tarragon, sage, thyme, basil, cilantro from out of her herb garden.

She has shrimp thawed tonight.

She throws it on the grill in a fish basket and then atop some lettuce since it's too hot for anything else. Jane pulls out the cribbage board and they play at a small gaming table on the eastern side of the camp. The windows and furniture have a fine layer of silt, but Jane doesn't bother cleaning much. John wins two games to Jane's one.

"How were things at the ranch?" Jane asks belatedly, knowing John must have discussed coming here with Alex.

Jane wonders if John belongs to her in this universe or some alternate one—or even if he belongs to her at all. They move, once again, to the non-fire under the smoky sky.

John shifts in his camp chair, and she can't help noticing his fingers slide up and down the porter. Jane's mother always talked about knowing a man's character from watching his hands. John's fingers are not slender, but strong and shapely, just slightly knobby, the palms wide. She pictures these hands making those bamboo fishing rods now that he no longer teaches English, and knows that even though John can be pigheaded, there isn't a gesture he makes that isn't generous spirited. John becomes aware of Jane's attention to his hands because she sees him look at the sixth finger on her left hand.

John doesn't answer the question. "I noticed you picked your fourth finger to wear your wedding ring on, not your third," he says, though it's clear John is remarking on the ring's absence.

"You know, reality is a funny thing."

"Yes, it's a perception thing—nothing to do with the 'real,' as I used to teach in post-structuralist theory—the one part of it that ever made any sense to me. The 'real' is the unknowable, unconscious part of ourselves."

"Maybe the place where the destructive side of humanity resides."

"Yes, and maybe the place love and art and creativity reside as well—scary eh?"

"Yet hopeful, somehow," Jane says.

"Yes, hopeful."

"The place where things might be otherwise than they appear," Jane says.

"I hope they are."

Quiet again.

"How long have you been here?" John asks.

"When I leave in a few days, it will have been forty-nine days."

"Ah, and on the fiftieth day . . . enlightenment?"

"Not many Jews observe the Counting of the Omer, a forty-nine-day period of self-reflection and spiritual renewal, but Tibetan Buddhists still have burial rituals that last forty-nine days." Jane picks up the shovel and pokes around in the dead ashes.

"Something like that," he says.

Several charred logs remain in the cold fire pit around which they gather. They are both aware of how strange it is that the fire, instead of being contained within the rock perimeter at their feet, is instead hovering over their shoulder, menacing, and yet intoxicatingly provocative.

"The Anishinaabek tell tales called Sky Legends of the Three Fires," Jane says. "The first tale is about how the Creator gathers flowers to fill the night sky with pictures. He falls asleep and Coyote, the trickster, steals the bag and runs away, though the bag rips open and the flowers are strewn across the sky at random. Coyote howls at the disorder, but Creator leaves the task of making star pictures to the Anishinaabek."

John looks at the sky. "The Creator left more than sky pictures to man, I'd say."

For a minute, Jane thought she was going to get a glimpse of John's life as she has seen so many lives before, but her vision goes dark. She wonders if it's because John's hands will have no place in her life. Or because they will.

"I wouldn't have pictured the two of you together," John says.

"Perhaps I saw what might have been," she responds. She knows John is aware of all the other women in Alex's life, women who have been part of this reality for many years now. "Not sure I get your own friendship with him."

John nods. "We were children and his father was part of the relationship, I guess you could say. I loved Alex's father, though his mother was another story and his parents didn't stay together long. Then I felt sorry for him, I guess."

Jane knows that Alex has never deserved anyone's loyalty, let alone John's, yet she can see the loyalty on John's part has to do with John's character and nothing to do with the relationship. Jane felt an ineffable and limitless emptiness fill her. The coyotes howl their wild yippy barks, and John moves his chair closer to Jane.

"I'm the one scared," he jokes.

Jane entwines her hand in his and his gentle fingers play with the extra pinky on her left hand.

"I was pregnant once," she says. "I lost the baby late to a genetic disorder. Thought it might have been for the best, but I never look at that extra finger, I don't think of her."

Jane fancies she can hear the fire in the treetops, but she knows she merely smells it. She imagines her life's pictures in the stars, the way the Anishinaabe described them. The very moment she feels now, her hand in John's, resides in the past and the future, like the stars above.

"How do you stand it?" Jane asks him of his wife, who had disappeared years ago without a trace.

"I don't," he answers, and he pulls her hand up under his chin, closes his eyes, like it's made of cherished mink.

"I'm not going back to him," Jane tells John. Or rather she will go back, but long enough to settle things, to sort things out, to come to terms with him. She's shocked at how little she'd known about Alex to begin with for someone with gifts like she possesses, and reminds herself that could be true of anyone.

"He's got a dinner party planned, you know," John says. "He's invited Hannah. Told everyone you were cooking."

"Alex sees things differently sometimes."

Alex, as things will turn out, doesn't think much of Einstein. He doesn't believe in alternate migrations, sliding doors, black holes, or concurrent realities; he believes the past stays in the past and he can move on without it. Alex will not believe in a world where Jane has instead picked some nerd-like poet rod-maker or a horse-trainer somewhere, or a starving chef maybe, to be her lover and husband, and not given Alex a single thought.

Jane doesn't waste her breath telling John to leave her there and get out. Because she knows he won't go. Instead she tucks John away again in one of the beds upstairs and sleeps herself in the side loft. They open the windows on the east hoping for a bit of fresh air, but keep those to the north and south closed to minimize the soot. There's not a sound, not a coyote, not a cricket, nothing.

The next few days the fire creeps closer. They can see it in the treetops across Norna's tributary and to the north they see just the smoke. It is now over twenty thousand acres and though they claim they are 80 percent contained, there are hotspots that compromise the containment line and keep the crews busy. The evacuation orders have been in place now over a week. The helicopters drop water at the perimeter of their property and they stay inside so as not to go from inferno to monsoon.

They think about leaving, but don't.

They know the DNR is escorting people in for short periods of time to survey their property or get valuables, but still Jane and John don't leave. They aren't sure what set of events will prompt them to drive off, but they know that so far, it has not occurred. To Jane it seems as if the edge of her world has been cauterized.

Finally, the wildfire slumbers, leaving the remnants hanging in the air so she can't tell them from horse flies or even black flies. Jane and John remain, cook racks of venison and then grouse breasts, all over the small grill, and they watch one another.

A few days later, though, even John returns home.

Jane makes her own fire at last, small and well-tended, because eventually you *have to*, but she doesn't cook on it.

She imagines Norna around alternate fires, Norna free or trapped in her own questions, either one possible, and she thinks of herself having chosen more wisely in some other migration. She thinks of the proliferation of blueberries and morels that will soon arrive. What will she serve John and the other guests Alex has summoned for dinner back at her ranch

Rabbit perhaps.

She drives the Duck Lake fire area on her way home and is shocked to see the bright green ferns emerging under the black trees, like poppies do in a war zone.

NORNA AND AISSA
AND JANE ONCE
UPON A TIME

TO GIVE THANKS

Aissa was twelve. She stood with Norna in the state land where the DNR had planted the jack pines; they reached, now, to Aissa's knees. She could see a very long way, all the way to Lake Superior and she thought how nice it would be to go to Crisp Point and look for agate or just sit on the beach and watch Canada.

You could only see it on the clearest of days.

There was a row of stumps out about fifty yards left from the original clear-cut and Norna had placed six jelly jars on each of them. She was carrying her twelve gauge, but she'd bought Aissa a double-barreled .410 and Aissa, who hadn't wanted to upset her mother, had said nothing.

A gun was the last thing she wanted.

A caravan of ATV enthusiasts passed by and raised a hand to Norna, whooping and hollering as they tossed a beer can into the tall weeds.

"Idiots," Norna had said as she walked over to retrieve it.

"Okay, try it again," Norna instructed. Aissa loaded two new shells into the chambers, closed the breech, moved the safety to the side. She raised the gun to her right shoulder. Without taking time to aim, she closed her eyes, squeezed the trigger, and managed to hit the stump below one of the jelly jars. The discharge rattled inside her head.

"Okay," Norna said. "Now do it again and don't close your eyes."

Aissa had already explained to Norna that she had no interest in this kind of thing. She missed Drummond Island. She missed the call of the loons, the Maxton Plains, the birch trees, the close proximity to the water and the humidity.

She missed her father.

She hated the abundance of jack pines at Norna's which when grown looked like bony arms reaching out to grab her like the witch's trees in *The Wizard of Oz.* They poked her in the eye once and another time ripped her favorite blouse.

They kept at the target practice.

Kept at it for days and when they weren't shooting jelly jars or shooting clay pigeons with the hand-held target thrower, they hauled water from the cistern, chopped wood, and cooked over a wood fire, while Aissa perspired under the hot August sun and found her mother as inscrutable as she'd always been. She longed for school to start and she missed Ginny, her best friend with whom she canoed around Potaginnising Bay. She missed helping her father with the guest's luggage at the inn, and even cleaning the rooms, of which there were exactly thirteen, a number she considered lucky. Norna was always interested in how she spent her time and when Aissa told her they played jacks or hopscotch or with a Ouija board or sometimes threw stones at robins, Norna had said, "hmm."

Somehow she survived the month with her mother.

School started at last, but that seemed not to be the end of the ordeal. Mid-September, Norna had insisted Aissa come for a weekend visit, and she'd met her mother at the ferry in DeTour arriving in her '58 Chevy pickup, driving the forty miles back to her camp, a trip that seemed interminable to Aissa and was a harbinger of the weekend to come.

"Why don't you come home?" Aissa asked Norna over their whitefish stew.

"I am home," she'd answered. Norna said she was planning on getting a dog soon.

"Did Daddy do something?"

"Do you like living with your father?" Norna asked. "You may live here with me instead if you choose."

"No."

The stew, Aissa had to admit, was excellent. Better than her father's cooking. Whenever she could, she talked him into eating at Hilka's Diner where she had a turkey roll or a big hamburger and cottage fries to avoid the tasteless goulash and the pot roasts or Swiss steaks which were always rubbery and hard.

After Aissa did the dishes, she talked Norna into a game of cribbage because the only alternative was reading, and Aissa was simply not in the mood. She had just fallen asleep, it seemed, when Norna woke her. It was barely light and Norna had prepared toast and cocoa with some slices of melon.

"Why are we up so early?" Aissa asked her.

"Hunting, we're going hunting."

"For what?"

"Grouse," she answered. "Season started yesterday.

"I brought hot dogs," Aissa responded, but Norna handed her a hunting jacket that was too large as well as an orange vest and hat while she dressed herself in a similar fashion.

"I don't want to go," Aissa said, and when Norna handed her the .410 and a handful of shells for the jacket pocket she felt mild disbelief at the notion that Norna intended to force her to accompany her.

Nevertheless, she did as she was told and they piled into the pick-up heading down Betsy River Road. "Lots of poplar and beech this way," Norna announced. They drove about twenty minutes, veering off on a two-track road so high with vegetation that the tire marks were barely visible, becoming less so as the tree branches scraped the windshield and down the sides of the truck. Norna crossed a small feeder creek and then stopped the truck. The path continued as far as Aissa could see, skirting the edge of a small lake or pond. They got out and Norna instructed Aissa to walk with the gun unloaded and over her right arm, breech open, like you'd drape a scarf, but to have her shells where she could reach them easily or keep them in her left hand.

Aissa had no intention of needing them.

Norna did the same, but there was an expression on her face Aissa didn't recognize.

"If they fly up, shoot them like we did the clay pigeons. But they might not fly up, either. Sometimes you'll see them just sitting by the edge of the road and if so, just shoot it there—this isn't about fairness today," she said.

Aissa's stomach felt slightly off and she wondered if the butter had been rancid on her toast. The morning chill was still in the air, the dewy grass wetting her jeans, but she could feel the heat underneath that threatened to pull the day into Indian summer. She heard the chirp of crickets and the belch of bullfrogs; grasshoppers hopped quickly out of their path as they walked. There were blackberries out still and even a few blueberries remaining, and Aissa knew the likelihood of meeting a bear in this area was greater as well. They stepped over a pile of scat and Norna said, "Coyote."

But it wasn't bears or coyotes that had put Aissa on edge.

"Do you know how they make hot dogs?" Norna asked her.
"No."

"Look it up sometime."

It started sprinkling just then, a drop or two, and Aissa was surprised since it must have come from the only cloud in the sky. She'd heard stories of people being hit by lightning on a sunny day. It stopped as quickly as it started and they kept walking up a slight rise. "Bird Hill," Norna announced. They'd been walking for nearly an hour and Aissa complained that she was tired and wanted to rest. Norna had a small flask of water with her and gave Aissa a sip, but insisted they walk on. Norna had dropped back, so that Aissa was a step or two ahead of her and that made her heart skip. She wanted to tell Norna she had no intention of shooting anything. Aissa adored her father, but Norna terrified her. Terrified or not, she'd do anything to please her, to get her to finally love her, to get her to come home. It was she the girl worked so hard to please. So she said nothing and kept walking even though the hiking boots Norna had bought her for her birthday were wearing a slight blister on the big toe on her left foot, and a slight one on the top of her right foot.

It was another twenty minutes of tough hiking after they'd gone up yet another rise that Norna stopped walking. "Listen," she said. Aissa heard a slight drumming sound like someone playing a quick riff on a pair of bongos, and as they walked slowly forward Aissa could see a bird at the edge of the gravel, perched on a fallen log.

"Put in your shells," Norna instructed to which Aissa replied, "No, you."

"Put in your shells," she said again, and Aissa did as she was told.

"Normally, I'd flush this bird and shoot it on the wing, but I want you to shoot it just like it was that jelly jar sitting on the stump."

"It's not a jelly jar," Aissa said.

"Good," Norna replied. "Glad you realize that. Now shoot it like I taught you—do it now."

It seemed like it took forever for Aissa to get the shells in the gun. Her hands shook and the gun wavered, and she even shuffled her feet a few times, which all seemed to take hours, but the bird sat there, apparently enjoying the warm sun on its back. Norna didn't say anything more, but she'd moved behind Aissa next to her right arm and she nudged her. Aissa waited and Norna nudged her again, while Aissa felt waves rise in her chest, hard and unrelenting.

Norna nudged yet again.

Aissa closed the breech, released the safety and raised the gun. She couldn't seem to see the bird as she looked down the barrel, only the dead log. She closed her eyes and when Norna nudged her for the fourth time, she pulled the trigger. The bird flapped and flapped in the gravel as if it were trying to take off and instead flew in wild circles in the dirt. The flapping went on interminably.

"Got it mostly in the wing," Norna said. Aissa felt her stomach heave and watched as Norna picked up the bird and handed it to her. "Wring its neck," she said.

"No," Aissa answered. And when it seemed that Aissa would disappear forever, and that something unforgiveable was about to transpire between she and her mother, the bird suddenly died on its own. Norna nodded as if this was as it should be, an unfathomable moment averted.

"You carry it," she said.

"No," Aissa replied. Her face felt flushed and hot, and though she was certain she was going to heave, she didn't.

Aissa sat down on the log, and Norna sat down, too.

"Let me know when you're ready to go back," she said.

Years later, Aissa would read a story Ernest Hemingway wrote about the horror a young boy felt at the killing of elephants in Africa for nothing more than their tusks, the horror at how many elephants were killed for no good reason, and how disgusted he'd been at his father. Aissa had to admit that Norna was nothing like the headhunters in Hemingway's story.

But that didn't lessen her disgust.

Aissa sat there for a half hour, while Norna pulled out a small paperback book from her back pocket and read what looked like a field guide to mushrooms. Aissa became more furious as the minutes passed. She thought she could find her way back to the truck if she had to, but all of a sudden she picked up the bird from the ground where she'd dropped it, holding it by the legs. It was still warm and Aissa couldn't believe how limp, like so much rubber. They headed back toward the truck, and every step she took, she could feel the bird's body sway and knock gently against her thigh. She carried it in her left hand, the gun draped over her right. Norna flushed two more birds and shot them on the wing, and they walked the rest of the way back to the truck in silence, the sound of their boots over gravel mixed with the notes of the songbirds.

When they reached the truck, Norna insisted she clean and skin her bird. She stuck her knife below the breastbone and Norna instructed her how to "pull" the innards in the field before heading back, so the cavity would cool and prevent spoilage.

And after Norna helped her do this, Aissa bent over a log and threw up until she had the dry heaves. Norna put her arm around her for a moment.

At camp, Norna helped her finish skinning the grouse, which now looked to Aissa about half its original size.

Norna got out her big butcher knife and cut off the legs and thighs which she wrapped in plastic, then in aluminum foil.

She would put them in her small freezer.

"I'll wait until I have a quantity of them, then braise them one night for myself," she said. "They are too tough to do over the wood fire."

"Normally, I'd hang these birds a couple days," Norna went on, "but we'll have these tonight." Aissa watched as Norna cleaned and skinned the other two birds, saying not a word, and doing her best not to breathe. Norna went into the camp and brought out olive oil, some cut herbs, salt and pepper. She had slit the breasts in a baking pan and she rubbed them with olive oil and all the spices. They waited for the fire to burn down.

"What was wrong with hot dogs?" Aissa asked her.

"It's hard to bring one of those down on the wing," Norna answered. "And you have to sit in the woods for days just waiting for one to come along, and when you're cleanin' 'em, you have to put skin on 'em, instead of takin' it off. It's a tough way to go."

Aissa didn't smile.

Norna roasted the breasts slowly over the wood fire, a piece of bacon lying across each one. It was getting dark early, storm clouds gathering to the west, and the temperature had dropped considerably. "Set the table," Norna said, motioning to the huge stump between them, and Aissa went for dishes and silverware while Norna sliced tomatoes and finished the bacon on the side. When Aissa threatened to not eat, Norna said simply, "Be a shame to throw that bird away now, wouldn't it." And Aissa took a bite.

It tasted something like chicken, Aissa thought, with maybe some hint of a nut or berry flavor.

"You can taste what they've been eating." Norna read her thoughts. "Quail sometimes eat hemlock seeds, which aren't poisonous to them, but can kill us. But they don't grow near here."

Aissa finished the bite, then fed the rest to the new puppy Norna had acquired from heaven knew where. "Idgy," her name was. Aissa vowed to herself that Norna would never again force her to do anything, but it would turn out that her vow was a wasted one. Norna would, indeed, never again pressure her to do anything.

There would come a day when Aissa would have come back and relived this day over and over again, even if a hundred grouse had to die.

•◆•

"Like this," Norna said to Jane. "It's like taking off a tight sweater—we could throw him in boiling water and pluck him, but this is easier for your first time."

Jane had done as her grandmother Norna told her: gutted the grouse first, slitting it from the breast bone to the anus, slitting the skin under the rib cage from thigh to thigh being careful to not go so deep as to puncture the digestive organs, then pulling the breast away from the legs with her free hand, pulling the entrails out through the anus ring which smelled sweet and noxious. A cross between someone

NORNA AND AISSA AND JANE

farting and the sulfury way the water smelled sometimes at home. Jane thought it smelled "warm" somehow, too, though she knew that wasn't possible—it was just the steam she felt on her hands as she saw it lift from the bird's cavity that influenced the perception. The way you associate chlorine with warm when you're in a steam room. As instructed, she'd used Norna's Swiss Army knife to cut around the bird's feet and wings in order to loosen the "sweater," and then started pulling it over the bird's neck cavity until the bird was naked, its skin coming right along with the it.

Jane remarked how ashamed the bird must be without even its skin, and Norna only nodded.

"Your mother threw up for an hour after I made her do this and refused to eat meat for an entire summer."

Today, it is just Norna and Jane.

Jane's bird had been taken on the wing. Not because Norna had flushed it, but because it had flown at the very last second. They walked slowly back.

Jane would have a future with death, and perhaps she knew it even then. She had "glimpses" of lives in other times, past and future, and sometimes even other migrations, other realities. She knew animals shared her "glimpses" more readily than people did, she could see it in their eyes. Though this ability didn't give her as much comfort as it might seem it would, it did give her an acceptance of things that her mother, Aissa, lacked.

There were some other differences.

Jane had that sixth finger on her right hand which helped her steady the gun—she was a better shot. It had rained lightly all day and the air was heavy with the smell of decaying leaves. Idgy wasn't much of a hunting dog, but she loved bounding ahead of them through the woods. Norna was thinner and tired, and somehow taller. Jane will remember her grandmother as someone who left a light imprint on the world in some ways. She was like a thought, possessed of an airy, ethereal quality, yet she, at times, came down with all the force and weight of a sledgehammer. Norna's weight didn't come in the form of conclusions which often translated into a maddeningly and perpetually judgmental quality; it was nevertheless Norna's questions that would wear on one.

"The Semites believed that the 'Goddess' (who they replaced, by the way, with a 'God'), was transformed into the 'Angel of Death' whose approach can be seen only by dogs—which is why dogs howl at the moon. And the Romans believed 'the Great Goddess' was herself a wolf, the 'She-Wolf Lupa' who suckled Rome's founders, Romulus and Remus."

"Do you believe in Gods and Goddesses?" Jane asks.

"I'm not sure," Norna had answered. "I do believe in canines."

Norna had put her hand on Idgy's head.

"Norna, why doesn't Mom visit here with us ever?" Jane asks.

"I left and went to Marquette for a couple days last week and when I came back there were coyote tracks all over this place—must have been at least six of 'em."

Norna had told her the Indians believed fire had been hidden from man and it was Coyote, the Trickster, who had recovered it for them. Good/bad always; two sides. Like belief.

"And you think that's why Mom doesn't come here? The coyotes?"

"No, I imagine she doesn't come here because I didn't answer questions like your first one," Norna says.

"Why didn't you answer?"

"Because my answers wouldn't satisfy her. You cold?"

"Not too cold most of the time," Jane answers, but she moves the green camp chair closer to the fire, shoves her hands deeper into the pockets.

"I'm short on hardwood for the stove inside and didn't want to fire up the cooking stove in there when the soft pine will work fine out here in the open. "

Jane nods.

"And I like the fresh air."

There are only a few inches of snow and the seasonal road into Norna's house is still passable, but it won't be for long.

Norna stirs the stew, adds a can of green beans, stokes up the coals and replaces the lid, leaving it slightly ajar. When she bends over, Jane thinks of her chest. She'd seen it once, one side nothing but ribs and pink, like a side of pork might look hanging in a meat market.

"She used to come more," Norna says. "Before she got writing about environmental issues. She doesn't like my thoughts on that."

"Why not?"

"It's good she does it. But since it's probably better for the environment for us to all live in cities, and since living in a city would kill me, I feel hypocritical chastising others."

Jane looks at her questioningly.

"Criticize, you know, I don't want to criticize. Plus, scientists change their minds every year on butter. I conserve because it's the right thing to do—not because I've been sucked into their political hoopla."

Jane will remember thinking that the reason her mother didn't come had more to do with Norna's ideas about doctors than about her ideas on the environment. Or maybe she'll remember Aissa's version of it later which supported the doctor version.

"Why do you like it here, Norna?"

"I loved Drummond, it nearly had me, but I was born near here, or dumped near here." She grins, referring to her birth mother having abandoned her at the Newberry dump. "I've lived in towns, downstate for a while with your grandfather for instance, fancy houses on Drummond, but I can think better here. And I can visit towns any time I want to. Which isn't often anymore. I've got friends here, too, you know. Listen! That was a coyote howling just there, it's early for it, so they must be on to a kill. Sometimes they sound like a pack of miniature poodles, all that yipping."

Jane listens to Norna's "friends" and the hair stands up on her arms inside her wool sweater. The yipping is high, maybe poodle-ish, but there is a wildness to it you can't mistake. Idgy moves toward the camp uneasily, but Norna calls her to her side and the dog sits down warily. Jane isn't really worried, though. She thinks of Norna's friend Sam, the big Indian she'd met once. She remembered her mother yelling about how Norna had given up medicine for Sam's voodoo, and how it would shorten her life by five years, maybe ten. Yet that was at least five years ago, Jane thought. She was only six when Norna had been diagnosed. Jane will hear numerous arguments over the years: Aissa accusing her mother of choosing "silly superstition" over science.

"Don't be a fool, Aissa," Norna would reply. "Faith and science can't be separated, they are all part of a whole. 'Faith' in chemotherapy takes a lack of intelligence more profound than any silly 'faith' in God."

"So you'd rather put your life in God's hands."

"Not a God personified. Whatever healing is possible originates inside us."

"You could do both," Aissa would say.

"And I would if the doctors in this particular case made any sense whatsoever. But they are idiots."

Now, Norna leans over the fire and that is when Jane had gotten her first "glimpse." Her first glimpse ever. Her first idea that she, Jane, had lived not only in the present but in the past and in the future simultaneously. She'd later find out that Einstein's physics theorized that linear time was illusory.

Through the years, Jane's glimpses would be more often about other people's lives than her own, but this time she sees herself sitting in front of an infinity of fires, a few more visible than others. If she turns her head one way, she sees herself warming her hands at the future age of fifteen; a bit farther out, she sees herself aged twenty-eight, sitting in front of a cold, dead fire with a man she doesn't recognize. And when she tilts her head the other way, she sees herself warming her hands as a very old woman, leaning over a large hearth, with the distinct feeling that not only did the past, present, and future exist at the same time, but that there could be any number of migration realties with infinite possibilities. Which migration is she glimpsing? This doesn't give her comfort that day; rather, it startles her into remembering what she'd forgotten. It makes a certain amount of sense to her, but explaining it to someone else would be something else altogether.

Even Norna. She can't tell even Norna.

"Let's eat," Norna says. She carries the huge pot by the handle with an oven mitt, and Jane follows behind her. As soon as they step inside, the stew emits a delectable aroma, and Jane's stomach growls again so loud it makes Norna smile. Once inside, Norna cuts them huge slices of French bread, with cold cakes of sweet butter, and pours Jane a glass of milk, herself a glass of red wine. She spoons stew into brown bowls, sprinkles dried chives over the top and they sit down at the seven-foot pine harvest table.

Jane was nine years old that day, and it was a year from the day Norna would pass on.

Jane knew Norna saw the pain hovering over her, but she saw all the way around it, time like a giant piece of cloth and the pain only a shred, a tiny flaw in a vast enormous quilt. It stretched around everything, Jane knew, and she saw how that comforted Norna and how it comforted the animals who saw, too.

It didn't comfort Jane, at least not yet.

•◆•

No one hunts here. Not people anyway.

Isle Royale is forty-five miles long and it is nine miles wide at its widest point; the bedrock is basalt and sandstone.

Norna visited in 1972. Alone.

She met a team of researchers on the island who had just initiated a new phase in the study of the wolf population: the continuation of a fourteen-year-long project begun in 1958. The wolves in the study had never been handled by people nor were they pressured by them competitively as in most ecosystems, and the study of this population fascinated Norna. It seemed ironic to Norna that though the study was about wolves, Rolf and Candy studied mostly moose bones.

And they studied fox and deer mice.

In 1958 there were two packs of wolves, a group of fifteen and a group of three, and one lone wolf.

In 1970, there were eighteen wolves in three packs plus two lone wolves.

Since the alpha male and alpha female are usually the only ones who breed, a healthy lone female will sometimes separate from the pack and attract a lone male and a new pack will originate.

Wolves eat mostly calves or old moose since a healthy full-grown moose cannot be taken down by wolves. Norna finds out the kill rate is about one moose every six days for a wolf pack, calculated by observing how frequently wolves kill moose. More specifically, according to Rolf, the kill rate is the number of moose killed, divided by the number of wolves in the population making those kills, divided by the time spent observing those kill events.

Norna stays two weeks on the island in 1972 and will return every year for two weeks until 1980.

In 1980, Candy and Rolf have an enormous collection of moose bones—gigantic jaws and metatarsus bones—and all joints arthritic.

They have become at home with bones and death.

In 1980, a year before Norna passes, there are five packs and fifty wolves on Isle Royale, nine hundred and ten moose; she will not know that, due to accumulated problems with the gene pool, inadvertent introduction by humans of the parvo virus, and reduction of ice bridges to Canada from winters too warm, by 2013 there will be only eight unhealthy wolves left.

In 1980, Norna base camps at Moskey Basin, visits Lake Richie and Three Mile Campground, and at night she slaps mosquitoes, shivers during the forty degree nights spent in a tent in July. She nurses her sore hips, tired from scrambling over rock and slogging through mud. She comes face to face with a moose cow and two calves and quickly moves out of their path, the musky smell of the cow's warning huff so close she can nearly taste it. She watches a loon kill a merganser duck while its mother looks on; and she watches an eagle kill a loon baby.

Hunting goes on here without us, she thinks. No apologies.

She thinks about her Indian friend, Sam, and wonders if each predator appreciates the sacrifice in the way Sam would.

She listens, silently, to the wolves howl at night. Wolves that don't, as people think, howl at the moon, but for reasons of communication: a rally cry for wolves to gather; a signal to let the pack know of a wolf's location; a warning to keep outside wolves out of a pack's territory.

When they lose a loved pack member.

Sometimes Norna stifles her own howls with her fists.

JANE THEN

TUESDAY

She reaches her right hand toward him, but he doesn't make a move to shake it. Her six fingers would tend to put some people off, but not him. He wonders if somehow this added appendage causes her pain. There would be people who wouldn't hesitate at all, would grab her hand immediately, as if to show her it made no difference to them; they were the ones most filled with revulsion. He wonders if she could sense it, if she'd perversely hang on to their clammy hands a bit long the way he might.

Someday he'll decide hands are not indispensable, even optional. But not yet.

Minutes go by and he makes no move toward her at all.

"Your mother said you do horse trainin," he says. "But I'll bet you don't really."

She points toward the barn, and when she does, his head turns slightly left. She looks toward his right hand which has been held close to his body and purposely out of her view. It dangles from a buckskin suede barn jacket and is made of flesh-tone plastic.

"Mostly train quarter horses around here, but my specialty is dressage."

He's eighteen years old and he thinks she appears to be two or three years younger than him. She is boyish, tomboyish, but graceful. Not unfeminine. He will soon conclude the girl possesses a delicateness-over-toughness, a trait he couldn't know is inherited from her grandmother. And he'll get a taste of her stubborn arbitrariness; even a whiff of her fear before the day is gone. But at this moment, he sees just that her hair is a colorless ashy blonde and that her eyes seem to reflect the green of the grass or the blue of the sky, alternatively.

"You're Jane," he says.

"Yes."

"I'm Seed."

They walk toward the large barn; it's stained a dark charcoal color. The sun glints off the corrugated metal roof, the galvanized horse tank, and the exercise pole. A row of yellow and white daylilies line the fenced riding arena—everything around the barn looks neatly tended, a rarity for farms in the Upper Peninsula of Michigan. There is an extended pasture, and Seed finds, upon entering the enormous barn, a small indoor exercise area and six box stalls, a tack room, a feed area, and an open area between the stalls and arena in which there are cross ties and stacked galvanized buckets. He hears the murmur and gentle snorts of the horses, hears them shift, stamp feet, tails patiently swishing away insects. A liver bay raises its head and Seed can see it grinding grain between enormous equine teeth.

"Weird to have this big barn way out in the woods," Seed says.

"My mother built it for me, but someday I'll have my own place." Aissa would someday turn the huge barn and pasture into a greenhouse and garden.

"Seed is a different sort of name," Jane says.

"Seed-faith, I guess. My mother is a Jesus freak."

"Ah, mine brushed up against it for a short time. Do you like horses?" Jane asks him.

"I've been saving my money, considering buying one, but I suspect my parents had something else in mind bringing me here."

Jane nods.

"Do you have any for sale?"

"Possibly," she answers. "I'm training a quarter horse for some people and they are considering selling once he's trained." She points toward the liver bay, Seed's favorite color. Monochromatic body, mane, and tail. Liver bays are rare, a bit more common in Thoroughbred race horses and Morgans than other breeds. You see it in the occasional quarter horse. Seed loves the way the sun glints off their coats, the same as a black, only slightly warmer in color, like a dark, dark polished pottery clay or obsidian rock.

She puts the bay on cross ties, runs a brush and curry comb over him, cleans his hooves with a pick, and starts to saddle him. She grabs a western saddle, cinches it up but leaves the knot loose at the top while she bridles him with a gentle snaffle bit.

"His name's Basalt, but I call him Stony."

She tightens the cinch strap again, makes a loop, draws the strap through the loop like a tie, knots it. "Gotta wait for them to let out their breath before you finish tightening it, or the saddle—and you—will be hangin' underneath in short order." It seemed a comment on life.

His attention is riveted on her process.

She looks at him. "You could have them adapt this saddle to an arrangement closer to an English saddle, with holes like several belts you fasten—it would be easier for you."

From someone else, Seed would have taken offense, but he'd watched to see if that extra finger seemed superfluous or whether she used it. She read his mind. "I use it for everything but typing," she laughs. "For that, the extra pinky just sticks up there like a little flag wavin'."

She saddles her own horse, packs a saddle bag with water, tins of smoked oysters, a box of crackers, a few sticks of kindling, some matches, a treated fire-starter, and a flask of something, adds several sheets of paper towels, and they are off. Her own horse is dappled-gray and is what she refers to as an "Anglo-Arab." Both horses are at least sixteen hands tall, Seed figures, the minimum height he would consider in his own horse.

"You've ridden some," Jane says.

"About a year, I guess." He holds the reins in the plastic hand. Most people would have thought he could feel the horse's mouth better with his normal hand, but it was exactly the opposite. It would have been customary, though, to hold both reins in the left hand when riding western, right hand resting on the right thigh. Seed does the opposite.

"You've lost just your hand," she says.

"Lost. Such a funny word, isn't it? As if I've been careless and misplaced it somehow."

Jane is unapologetic and not put off by his remark.

"Yes," she says. "Let's see. You are 'without' just your hand, you are handicapped just to the extent of losing your hand . . . hey, you didn't misplace the rest of your arm, that was extremely conscientious of you!" Jane grins. "Good job, there."

He smiles. "Whatever you do, don't ask me to lend you a hand, or worse, give you a hand. Have you ever heard the sound of one hand clapping? Oh, and yes, if a boy is alone in the woods and gets his hand cut off and no one sees or hears his screams, is it still the father's fault?" He clunks the prosthesis on the pommel, and Stony's ears perk up in surprise; he increases his gait. But Seed gently pulls on his mouth, and rests his left hand on the hollow of his neck. "Sorry, old fellow," he says.

"He's only two and a half," Jane says.

They break into a trot, and Seed says, "I'm sold."

Seed knows you judge a western pleasure horse by this gait, the trot, and Stony jostles Seed back and forth in the saddle like he's sitting in a rocking chair, Seed's backside never rising off the saddle. "I've never sat such a trot," Seed says. Jane nods. "That's why they are asking a pretty penny for him . . . and because he's out of Satin Doll by Earthquake."

"Would you show him?" Jane asks.

"I don't know. I might like to train horses someday like you do, though I'm sure I'll have to have a day job, eh?"

"Yep."

"Do you believe in defining moments?" Seed asks her now. "Moments that shape a life forever that can never be taken back or atoned for?"

"Yes . . . and no."

She stops near Duck Lake—one of the Swamp Lakes— after they've traveled ten miles down the North Country Trail. She dismounts and ties the reins around a bush, then makes a small campfire. There's a slight chill in the air, fall impending. She breaks open the crackers, the tins of oysters, and hands Seed a bottle of water. It's early evening and the sun is setting orange over the lake.

"Why didn't your parents just cut it off?" Seed asks her.

She shrugs. "They just figured that would be up to me, I guess."

"And you want it."

"I know it's an option . . . I doubt I'll ever take it, but it's my option."

"It seems unnecessary," he says.

"But it's not not necessary," she says, smiling. "How did you 'misplace' it?"

"I flew off an ATV riding behind my dad when I was a kid. The ATV landed on my arm and severed my hand off, but not cleanly. They tried to reattach it—a twenty-hour surgery, but it didn't take."

"So they threw it away."

"I wish. My parents had it frozen, so it isn't really lost after all."

"Ohhhh," Jane says. "Ohhhh."

"My parents think medical techniques will change."

"Ah," Jane says.

"Too bad it wasn't just my thumb. My parents heard a story about someone cutting off their toe and having it attached to replace a thumb." Seed said. "One doctor wanted to attach my hand to my groin for a while to keep the blood supply going until they could do more vascular repair, some procedure he'd read about from Paris—can you imagine? Did you know they sometimes retrieve arms out of alligators and crocodiles and reattach them? No end to the absurd dismemberment tales I can tell you." Seed rubs his compromised wrist where the prosthesis joins it. "My parents have introduced me to a host of crippled people and dogs. You are the first one with extra material, though. That makes you incredibly unique."

"No doubt."

They eat oysters and crackers, sip water, and then Jane brings out a flask of brandy from her barn jacket pocket.

"What does your mother think of that?" Seed asks her.

"Oh, she doesn't know—I don't do it all that often anyway, but this seemed an occasion for it. And you're of age, aren't you?"

They drink out of the flask and watch the flames in the fire Jane had made. Seed doesn't know what to make of Jane. He drinks several shots, then tells her how his girlfriend likes him to take off the prosthesis and touch her with the stump, prefers it to the touch of his normal hand. They laugh.

"How did you get pregnant?" Seed asks her now. Her stomach, like her finger, seemed unabashedly part of her body and yet somehow irrelevant, even temporary, and strangely hadn't been his first impression of her.

"Guess," she says.

"I mean who is the father."

"I was raped," she answers. Seeing the question on his face, she says, "I could have, I suppose. I wouldn't blame someone else if she did, and I believe in her right to decide that, too."

"On the first hand—in my case the only hand—you shouldn't be drinking," he says.

"And on the 'second'?"

"You shouldn't be riding. You're eight months pregnant."

"I wasn't really drinking, next to nothing. You didn't notice. And I'm a VERY good rider—I could see you needed a belt, though." She smiles.

They walk around the lake, see the orange reflection of the autumn trees in the water, then decide to race back. The horses shuffle, uneasy, as they run up to them. "You're not all that fat," he says, and she grins.

They sit around the fire, again, for ten long minutes in silence.

"Who was it?" he asks.

"Someone I knew . . . a friend's father, offered to drive me home one night. He told me I'd regret it if I told anyone. He was right. I did regret it."

"You told the friend?"

"She was my best friend in the whole world. She knew everything about me, but it was more than that. It wasn't just what we knew about each other. We recognized one another. I'll miss her."

Seed is puzzled by the term "recognize" but lets it go.

Jane begins to break down the fire. Seed sees her shiver slightly and she flips her jacket collar up around the back of her sandy hair, hair that folds up on itself and sticks out the top of the jacket collar like shafts of winter wheat. He wonders what his parents wanted him to gain by meeting Jane. It was always obvious before what they wanted him to see—people overcoming great odds to accept their lot in life and still rise above it, which always made him feel invalidated, like he had no right to be pissed off for a while, like they understood and knew what was better for him. Waiting for him to realize he was lucky. Lucky to be alive and lucky that life handed him some adversity and not just a walk in the park. And what pisses him off most is that he knows they are right; he is lucky. He'll tell his children someday how lucky he is, he knows that, but he's pissed at their presumption. Even their attempt to overly pad his world would be less offensive right now. And above all, Seed realizes it is them who can't accept it, rise above it, or feel lucky. And until they do, Seed can't.

"I can't stand thinking about that fucking thing in that freezer," Seed says. "They have no idea what that's like."

Jane stands and looks at him. "Where is it?" she asks.

"The hospital wouldn't even keep it. My parents talked the medical center in Newberry into keeping it—I presume so my parents wouldn't throw it out by mistake themselves, defrosting their own freezer, or so I wouldn't see it every time I got an ice cube."

"Won't it get freezer-burned?"

"Logic doesn't enter into this equation for my parents. I'm sure if Newberry wasn't such a small-town place, they never would have agreed to it—even if they could have reconnected the arteries and veins. Once the nerves are reattached, the chance of ongoing pain is high. They seem to disregard that as well."

She smiles at him.

"It's Tuesday," she says. "It's two hours to Newberry on horseback."

"Tuesday," Seed says. "Let's go.

They water the horses in the lake and set off. They make fairly good time, but it's dark when they arrive, something they are both grateful for. Someday Seed will remember the darkness as comforting, protective.

●◆●

Jane doesn't encourage Seed to take this course of action because she's seen the past. And she certainly doesn't encourage him because she's seen the future and that the future she sees isn't pretty—or because she's seen an alternate migration in which Seed still never recovers his hand. It's none of those reasons. Actually, what she has seen is an alternate reality where he *had* recovered his hand, but seeing this reality didn't influence how she responded to his pain now. Jane knows alternate migrations don't matter to this one; she learned that a long time ago. They don't fix a particular reality, or change it; all they do is broaden perspective, enlarge experience. The fact that Jane sees time as a whole, as a type of fabric she can perceive as a long seamless runner— the past, present, and future all part of an endless sewing pattern—doesn't matter, either. It is true that Jane sees Seed's possibilities and his lack of them. She sees where he's come from and where he might go, and again, it doesn't matter to any particular course of action. Jane knows the only reality that matters is the one people believe in: now, here in the present. No matter what Jane might tell Seed about his past or future, it wouldn't change the fact that for him the world had stopped—and would stay stopped—as long as that hand remained in the boy's present reality.

Jane knows Seed feels warm toward her, and she knows the reason he does, the reason most people did, if they spent much time around her: on some deep, elemental level, they recognized Jane. She was familiar because she'd glimpsed bits of their pasts and she'd glimpsed bits of their futures as well—hovered over the continuum of their existences like a figure in a Chagall painting, and when they looked at her, she saw in their faces that sentient expression, that feeling of Déjà vu that told them they'd seen her somewhere before, or lived through this moment with her at some time before, or they were just about to, that Jane was part of their destiny. She'd watch them shake it off, but Jane knew, they had, in fact, lived that moment before, or more accurately the moment still existed like some wispy, faint memory wall. Jane was like a face they'd seen on a passing train or a bus, or someone they were sure had seated them once at the theater, or guided them on a tour of some kind; someone who had once pointed their way, or, again, was about to.

They knew her.

But they couldn't see.

Unless they were dying, of course.

Then they saw the same glimpses Jane saw.

Earlier today, Jane had seen Seed's childhood—when he was not quite two—his father Daniel holding each of his hands as Seed took a first tentative step, fingertips lacing loving fingertips. Daniel's face beamed and Seed seemed more interested in looking up for his father's approval, or to reassure himself that Daniel was holding on tight, than looking outward at his blossoming world. Jane watched as Seed let go of his father's hands, the release painful for them both, like an extracted tooth, and Seed took two steps toward a leather couch under his own steam. Certainly, Jane thought, we "feel" with our whole bodies, and yet if one closes one's eyes, it's those hands, those tentative fingers that instinctively reach out in front of us, those fingers that feel our way.

Jane also saw the women in Seed's life, the one before the accident, and the one afterward, struck by the differences in their personalities. The first one pretty and outgoing and somewhat self-absorbed; the second one quieter, with a rounder, more open countenance and an interest in Seed's new approach to life. She was less drawn to his deformity than she was interested in how it changed a person, or how it might change her, and Jane was pleased with the young woman.

Though Jane seemed to stretch across a person's time-span, she could never make anything of its entirety, or either end of it. She wasn't sure if a person's lives and realities went on in either direction or if they stopped, and she seemed to have no control over which parts of someone's existence she floated over. At times, she had the feeling the person was cognizant of her sententiousness; at other times, she was aware of her own time span intruding upon her and maybe even her own consciousness, yet never in such clear scenes as she saw others. She didn't know what to make of her gift, and was surprised when she realized other people didn't have it—or most other people. It was not that she was "time travelling"—she wasn't—but instead it was as if every part of a person's existence, and her own, were occurring simultaneously, ad infinitum; she was simply aware of it while others weren't. And most terrifying of all, and she was not sure when she was first aware of it, she began seeing lives, migrations, moving off at perpendicular trajectories, also simultaneously, not just parts of the same existence, but shadows of alternate ones. Seed would be shocked to know there were worlds in which he never went on an ATV with his father, and never lost his hand, and even worlds in which Seed didn't exist at all.

Jane never was, and never will be, a mathematical or scientific person; what she knows about time and time spans is simply intuitive. She is not surprised, though, to find that Einstein and other great minds of physics had been grappling with theories of relativity and quantum mechanics, theories that would back up her intuition with phrases like "fabric of the universe," "alternate universes," "spooky entanglements."

Jane appreciates the darkness but not in the way Seed does; the darkness is blessedly uneventful and still, something she longs for. She sits and waits as Seed searches for his hand, her hand stroking the neck of the dappled mare. She thinks about things missing and things extra, things not asked for or deserved.

•◆•

Seed breaks the back window. There wouldn't be any question who did this, but he thinks it's unlikely anyone will press charges. At any rate, he doesn't care. He climbs in the window while Jane waits with the horses. He walks across plastic vinyl floors, down hallways of hospital green, and wanders around until he finds a locked room he's certain is a medical supply room and, through the door's window, he can make out a freezer within. He wanders around a while longer until he locates a cleaning supply closet and in it a pipe wrench which he uses to break the window in the medication room door. No alarms, none that he can hear anyway. There is a moment when Seed is afraid the freezer might be locked like the medication cabinets are, but no, thank God, it's open. It's a normal upright freezer with four shelves. Seed notices one shelf is full of Popsicles (probably for the rare tonsillectomy patient or to be used as a bribe for a recalcitrant youngster), a few Fudgsicles, and what looks like some frozen lunch meals for the staff; on the rest of the shelves are medical supplies, some kind of vials, prescription bottles of some sort or other, some kind of film. He locates his hand: Seed Fairchild, it says, right hand, severed June 5, 1998, frozen June 7, 1998.

"Look," he says after he climbs back out the window, "there's no expiration date. Probably majorly freezer-burned."

"Here," she says, "give it to me. I'll put it in the saddle bag." He hands her what looks like white freezer paper inside of a plastic ziplock bag that has been vacuum-packed.

They make good time back to the campfire site they had made next to Duck Lake. It is a quiet ride, but Seed feels satisfied; Jane rides with her right hand on her lower back like an old woman who had been cleaning floors all day. The coals of the fire they'd left are still warm, and, with a bit of fanning, they are able to get the kindling to catch fire, and then Seed adds a couple big logs to it. Seed watches Jane huddle up to it and he puts his good arm around her for a minute. She doesn't look like someone you could put an arm around like that and her look of surprise confirms it for him, but he doesn't move it right away, and she rests into it after a moment, like he's a bale of easy straw.

Seed removes his arm, takes a deep breath, and starts to unwrap the hand. Jane hands him her Swiss Army knife, and he is able to make faster headway with both the plastic and the freezer paper. He looks at her again and sets the hand on a stump next to the fire.

"Appropriate, don't you think?" he asks her. "Hey, what exactly is dressage?"

"Well, most people think it's 'tricks' you teach a horse, much like you'd teach a dog to jump through a hoop. And I suppose there's something to that. But it's really not that. Dressage is the intimacy that develops between rider and horse so that the rider's slightest movement of a foot or the slightest pressure of a rein can influence the way the horse places his own foot or moves his head, changes a gait, positions his body. It's riding techniques focused into a feeling—actually it's a language. But it can never happen unless there is absolute trust between horse and rider. And in order to get the horse to understand these subtle, subtle cues, every movement of the rider needs to be hyper-focused. It takes intense concentration on the part of the rider since any confused movements will confuse the horse. It's why a rider training his horse for dressage would never, even for a moment, consider putting another rider on him. People think of the Lipizzaner stallions when they think of dressage, all those incredible feats a horse can perform, but dressage is as simple as a horse moving his body sideways with a crook of the rider's foot, an unnatural movement for a horse."

"Having an extra finger increases your sensitivity? Just think what an extra toe might do," he jokes.

"Well, no, but having an extra finger makes me more aware of everything, I'd say. I'd say it tuned me in. I think you'd be good at it. Dressage. There is nothing like the synchronicity and the feeling that develops between a horse and rider, how they become one. Nothing like the raw power of a horse running underneath you at full speed. With a car, you're always separate from the power, but with a horse, you're inside each other, you are moving stride for stride with him. And he's as aware of the connection as you are. It's a rush."

Seed thinks of himself moving through the world and wonders if he'll ever be in sync with anything in this way.

The hand has begun to thaw slightly.

Seed is expecting green, but it's remarkably white-ish pink except for what looks like a bit of freezer burn along the fleshy ragged dismemberment. He looks at the third finger, the one he used to wear his middle school class ring on and imagines slipping it over the swollen, slightly bent knuckle. Thing, he thinks, from *The Addams Family*. Bruce Dern's hand in that Bette Davis movie, *Hush . . . Hush Sweet Charlotte*. He has imagined it crawling through the years like some deranged appendage from a multitude of horror movies, but now he can see it's his hand, really his. The nails look whitish-blue and remarkably clean, though the index finger appears to have a slight hang nail. Not monstrous, suddenly, but familiar. He imagines it fondling Nancy's breasts and feels a moment of intense sadness, but then thinks of his stump against her back, pulling her to him, how she says it feels more solid, more real, than a hand. Somehow more supportive. And he realizes that that's how the hand has come to feel to him—unreal, a fantasy, an impossible dream. He thinks about power like Jane talks about, feeling the horse under her, and wonders how it would feel three-legged.

The hand has been in the freezer four years nearly. It appears slightly smaller and less calloused than the hand that had grown and worked and stretched with him these last several years; it is remarkably unchanged otherwise. The skin on the fleshy palm of the hand is jagged just as Seed remembers it the day his father picked it up, the day he'd seen that horrible, terrified look of guilt on his father's face, that look that never fucking leaves, frozen there like this frozen hand.

"Not too late to change your mind," Jane says to him.

He picks up the hand, which feels cold and slightly rubbery, and drops it into the flames.

"God, you could have just dropped it in the lake," Jane says. She leans back against the stump, stretches her legs out in front of her, and rubs her enormous stomach. "It's stretching again and has the damned hiccups, too."

He responds to her remarks in order.

"I could have buried it, too, but I don't want to think of it as having shape . . . hiccups. Never thought about a baby having that inside you. Doesn't it need air to have those?"

"You'd have to have a very hot, long fire to get rid of the bones," she says. "It's harder than you think."

"I can live with bones," he says.

The hand shrivels at first as it thaws, and they can see tiny hairs on the knuckles which sizzle and smell rancid. It's sitting on a piece of pine firewood and Seed wonders if Jane can see the pain, then relief he feels at being done with this hand forever. She hands him the flask.

"Here," she says. "Maybe I can give you a hand." She smiles at him. "We should celebrate, don't you think? I'll have a tiny sip, too."

"To things unnecessary," she says.

"And to things not not necessary."

"Your parents are going to be really pissed at me," she says.

"Yes, won't they be."

The skin on the hand is now becoming crispy, filling with air, swelling, making it look like a browned, hideous balloon. The rancid smell has disappeared and the smell of roasting flesh is not all that unpleasant. The fingernails drop first, then the skin melts. Seed expects to feel phantom pain as the hand shrivels, but he doesn't. That would be his father's role—to feel physical pain—and he wonders if he can feel it from wherever he is, hopes that at last he'll let it go.

"Do you think it would taste like chicken?" Jane asks.

"Nah, alligator."

"I'm gonna buy Stony," he tells her. She nods.

●◆●

Jane sees a glimpse of what looks like a hand superimposed upon a bright blue sky, hovering, its palm lightly cupped the way you see old renderings of God's hand, reaching down to lift his children toward heaven. She sees a glimpse of Seed's life, or one migration, at least, sees him progressing on, more stutters than stops and even periods of smooth sailing. She feels—like she does with all the people in her glimpsed lives—as if she's entwined, and knows she will be all her life—part of life's continuum.

They add up, like layers.

But then her attention becomes riveted on a shadowy form at the edge of Duck Lake, and she's certain it's a coyote, though it looks the familiar human form it always does when she sees it—like a very old woman hunched over a warming fire—and she knows it's a rare bit of her own destiny intruding.

Time expands and Jane expands with it.

Seed finishes the flask while Jane dozes next to the fire. An hour later, he pulls the hand out with the Swiss army knife, now just bones and a small amount of blackened flesh. Jane wakes and walks over with him to the lake where he quietly dumps the bones.

AISSA

JUNE BUGS
AND PRAYERS

"I don't pick up hitchhikers," I'd said.

"You ain't pickin' up anybody, lady." He'd laughed back.

What are the odds? I'd asked myself when the car had started to sputter.

I'd looked down and seen the gas gauge dive below empty, the little gas pump picture winking at me from the dashboard of the '88 Lincoln. It had coughed a few more times then quit as I hit the top of the next hill, so I threw it into neutral and coasted off the Bloomington exit. I should have stopped an exit earlier, at Normal, Illinois, but I just couldn't—goddamn it—make myself go to *Normal*.

So it had been Bloomington and I was out of gas. No way I'd make the inclining grade of the ramp, and I saw him walking the shoulder, backpack slung over his own shoulder like a cowboy toting a bronc-busting saddle, a part-shepherd-looking black mongrel between him and the road.

Running out of steam—maybe we both were—I saw him glance over his shoulder as I came abreast of him, and since they were on the shoulder, he and the dog, and I couldn't pull off without hitting them; I didn't. Pull off, that is. Just kept rolling down the tarmac.

Ten o'clock at night, June 10, in the year of our Lord 2005.

I waited the full minute it took for the car to stop on its own, him walking alongside, only slower and slower, waited until the car came to a complete and total stop because this time, no matter what else happened, it would not be me who put a foot on the brake.

No way, not this time.

Not until I felt the car settle backwards did I, with great reluctance, reach a toe toward the brake, and then only to keep from sliding back the way I came.

Only one rule now: *no going back the way I came.*

As the Lincoln sighed back and caught, the cowboy coasted to a final step as well, a step like a final tick of a wind-up alarm clock, or the last beat of a heart, and all I could think is how we've ended together, the car, the cowboy, and me. On this spot at this particular time in history. It was silent except for the far-away whoosh whoosh of the passing cars.

He was wiry like the quick end of a day, and I couldn't lose the cowboy image. He turned his head and looked me right in the eye and then he nodded slightly. The dog growled. I had the windows rolled down and didn't for a minute think of rolling them up and locking the doors (though that would normally have been my inclination), because all I could think of, all I kept asking myself is: what are the odds?

"Where you headed?" he'd asked, of course.

When I said Tulsa, he said he hadn't been able to get another ride for the last five miles and was headed in for something to eat, but he'd buy me a can of gas, plus fill my tank if I'd haul him along as far as 65 South, the turn off to

Eureka Springs. I didn't think twice—"okay," I said, "but grab me some jerky and maybe a Danish while you're gettin' the gas? Then it's a deal." And he nodded.

"Hey, and a cream soda," I yelled at his retreating back, "orange."

I watched him drop the pack and walk toward the Shell station, his boots kicking up dusty gray clouds in front of him. When he disappeared, I closed my eyes, humming the lyrics from "Rawhide," ("rollin, rollin, rollin") asking myself what exactly the odds might be of running into the love of your life in a situation like this.

Or maybe getting introduced to your murderer this way.

Too young to be the love of your life, I told myself, old enough and strong enough to be my murderer for sure.

The real tragedy, I knew, is that more than likely he was neither. That running out of steam together most likely meant nothing, nothing at all.

But I kept thinking it anyway: *What are the odds? What are the fuckin' odds?*

That was yesterday.

I watch him watch me.

He's stopped eating entirely, his mouth hanging slightly open, head tipped sideways so his center-parted blondish straight hair—hair long enough to tuck behind an ear—swings to the right corner of his mouth, gets tangled inside with a forkful of hash browns; he slides knobby yet somehow attenuated fingers down the strands like you'd squeeze toothpaste from a tube, retucks it but without closing his mouth.

"What?" I say then. Open my own mouth wide so he can see it's stuffed full of blueberry pancakes—something I'd never done in my life and can't believe I'm doing now. But I don't speculate why I, Aissa Alspaugh, player of all (most) things safe, would do something like this.

"I read once that dreaming about your teeth crumbling or falling out means you're losing your potency," I say. I think of my ex-husband, Ben, and it seems pertinent.

He smiles a little but doesn't answer so I pour more olive oil (which I've had to ask for special) over the top of what's left of the pancakes, and follow that with half the pitcher of maple syrup. I miscalculate and the mixture pours off the edge of the plate, a plate the neon color of pond algae, and oozes onto the faux-wood table top. A small tow-headed girl leans over the booth behind us, her face hanging over my companion's right shoulder. She bounces a little, puts her mouth on the filthy wood that lines the seat back and blinks at me. The waitress is still hovering at the table where she's just handed me another pitcher of syrup, but now she's backing away in horrified slow motion as if I'm holding a bomb and she can't tear her eyes away from me.

I keep shoveling.

"Look," the cowboy says then. "I hardly know you and I suppose you got a right to do whatever the hell you please, but that's really disgusting. You're ruining my damn breakfast. Are you in some kind of crisis or something?"

A ten-second pause. Then he goes on.

"I was just wonderin', ya know, 'cause we been on this road for exactly a day and a half and if my calculations are right, you've gained about eight pounds from when you picked me up off the damn road."

More like eleven, I think. I've gained eleven pounds easy figuring in the water weight. I've had to unbutton the top of my jeans early this morning and I can feel my bra cutting into the sides of my lats forming that sausage roll I don't have to touch to know is there. Unseasonably warm, the humidity has plastered the jeans to my thighs with sweat. "Four ax-handles wide," my father used to tease, referring to my ass. This should be a record, though: weight gain in a pounds-per-day ratio up until this point has been ten pounds/four days—maybe half in water weight?—who knows? But that had been when I was trying not to eat. Just one of many chronic symptoms: the result of a lifetime of holding back.

This is a different prospect all together.

I don't explain my eating habits. And I don't feel guilty for behaving so repulsively.

"Surely blessing I will bless thee, and multiplying I will multiply thee," I say. "Hebrews 6:14 . . . God is definitely blessing me, wouldn't you say?"

"You're religious, I take it."

"I've certainly been anal-retentive enough for it, but 'religious' is a slippery word, you should be careful with it."

"What's in Tulsa?" he asks.

"Red dirt," I say which is what an old boss had said to me fifteen years ago when I first said I was headed there. "That's all they got in Oklahoma, red dirt," he'd said. Yep, they had red dirt and they had religion. No doubt about it. And floods, tornados, gales that swept things way to hell and back. I loved how the boys stood at the bottom of the steps of Mabee Center awaiting the blast, the draft that when the girls forgot would wrap their skirts around their necks. I remember hoping one of them would be mine.

Jani Mortensen (who I will find out is Finnish) nods as if an answer of "red dirt" makes perfect sense to him. He looks like an artist or a bull rider, I will think, over the days to come. The way he totes that backpack, he looks like someone who could stay on if he had to. I'm not interested. At least not much. The piped-in music is playing an instrumental song I can't quite place, though the line "try to make it by Friday" pops into my mind. Then I think Oklahoma. Oklahoma in June.

I flag down the waitress. "Hey, bring me a couple of those apple fritters, will you? When you bring the check?"

Jani has stopped eating. He raises a crumpled napkin to his mouth covering the cleft in his chin, holds it there, frozen. I keep shoveling pancakes and watch the expression on his face as I dive back in.

"Don't worry," I say, "you will not be required to sleep with me."

"Good," he says. "Where'd you get the car?"

"My grandmother died and left it to me."

"Where'd you get the gun?" he asks.

"Came with the car," I say.

• ◆ •

"Christ," Jani Mortensen says when I tell him I went to Oral Roberts University. "Did they make you go there?"

1985. I'd had to write an essay to get in.

I'd refused to lie, assume holiness, or profess to "spiritual gifts" I didn't possess. My best friend had gone off to school there while I was at Michigan State. She came from a family of charismatic gospel singers, holy rollin' Bible thumpers, my parents called them. Despite different backgrounds and despite the fact that my boyfriend had cheated on me with her, we had recognized in one another a generosity of spirit we had never, either of us, found elsewhere (she forgave me— right then and in perpetuity—for being a sinner, and I forgave her—right then and in perpetuity—for being somewhat crazy) and a year out of high school I had missed her. So I wrote the letter explaining to the admissions board that God indeed spoke to me (which was complicated, but I felt true), but always in private. That my relationship with him was as private and personal as I could only imagine a relationship would be with a lover. My friend said they'd never let me in writing stuff like that, that it sounded perverted in fact. I didn't think they would let me in either, but it turned out they did.

"How's the Big O," my father would say when he called me at school, and I'd tell him, imitating the evangelist the way we all did, "I made it, with God's help, through the tuberrrr-ka-lo-sis and through the many other TRIals and TRIBulations of my life and I did it by looking to God as my source, by not limiting Him, and by applying the principles of seeeeeed-faith, which if you open your Bibles with me nowwwww you will find in Mathew 17:20: If ye have faith as a grain of mustard seed," I'd go on, "ye shall say unto this mountain, remove hence to yonder place; and it shall reMOVE!" I'd imitate his southern drawl, and shake my right hand when I spoke, imitating what Oral called his "shakey hand," the one God endowed with His healing power.

The hand motion was like Al Jolson doing an old tap number.

"Nope," I tell Jani now. "I chose to go there of my own free will."

When Jani tells me he's off looking for the younger sister his rich mother has written off as nothing more than a junkie and a whore, and when he tells me he wants nothing to do with his family's environmentally-polluting-fuck-ass mining operation that encompasses much of the Yellow Dog River basin west of Marquette, Michigan, or his family in general (which is why he doesn't have a car or a job at the moment), I tell him sisters and family are one thing, but we might be pushing things talking about both politics and religion on just one measly trip.

"Yeah," he agrees. "We might be at that."

"My mother lives near Tahquamenon Falls," I tell him. Which, coincidentally, is also in the Upper Peninsula. "She's dead now."

Back in the car we're quiet a while. And I think back about the school.

About the dresses, women always had to wear dresses . . . High-tech reflective glass on space age buildings that reflected back to me a pudgy body, one teacher who felt sorry for me—maybe too sorry? Celebrities who whipped through the university in frenzied barrages. Elvis, Merv Griffin, rock bands of all kinds. Kathie Lee Gifford was a fellow student then, only her name was really Kathie Epstein. Later she'd sing on *Name That Tune* as Kathie Lee, then marry, divorce, and finally end up a once-again-divorced Kathie Lee Gifford.

The celebrities are a faded blur, but Kathryn Kuhlman will never be; a faith healer with the gift of being able to "slay people in the spirit." Her voice had vibrated and rolled like thunder. I had watched, horrified, as masses of people went down in frenzied spiritual waves beneath her outstretched hand.

I'm suspicious of that kind of mass emotion and I had resisted the pressure of the place. Pressure to talk like them, emote like them. I just watched the competitions for possessor of the most spiritual gifts: gifts of discernment, of wisdom, of speaking in tongues. Of prophecy. They had pressured me to take down "secular idols" like my *Jesus Christ*

Superstar poster. Fuck 'em, I thought, while they prayed for my soul. Praise the Lord, I'd say, as they backed out of my room shaking their heads.

I learned early and from then on to tolerate religion in people who kept it to themselves. As soon as they started "talkin' the talk" I prepared to be violated.

One guy from the Middle East, Nabhil, a converted Christian, explained to me things I had forgotten about the English, those imperialist busybodies who stole from the Palestinians the promised land and started it all. And how we'd made it all worse by siding with the Jews. I felt sorry for him, this person from Iraq. He wanted to drive my car, so I'd let him, yet I could feel the coldness, the disdain: I was a mere woman, after all, and worth nothing.

I remember thinking back then, what a perfect place for someone to drop a bomb: Oral Roberts University. The flame that never went out at the Prayer Tower. Someone praying at the top of it for the world, 24/7, or so they claimed. Yet it seemed they preferred economic symbols to religious ones.

It's all fascinating stuff, but it is not what sticks in my mind most: it was the june bugs. Thousands of them littering the ground like scattered acorns. How even though I wanted to miss them, I couldn't. How with every step I'd hear their hard bodies crush under the leather soles of my dress shoes.

It's the june bugs I can't forget.

"Why you going to Tulsa?" Jani asks me again after much time passes. I don't answer him because it's none of his business. I don't care what he thinks about me or my plans; I know I'll do what I came to do and he won't stop me. Though it doesn't seem he'd try. You can't talk someone into or out of something they don't already incline toward in the first place. That seems to be something he knows about people. I can see it in his face. He doesn't ask me anything else personal and I don't tell him anything. Certainly not about the gun, which did come with the car. I had told him the truth about that (my grandmother knew how to shoot and thought the possibility of needing to not all that remote).

Instead we talk about rivers and mountains and how it feels to beat nature. We agree you don't really beat her; it's just that she hasn't gotten you yet. We talk about how you start loving her like a hostage starts loving a kidnapper. And then we don't talk at all for two more hours.

Jani drives the Springfield stretch and I flip in CDs: Bonnie Raitt, Alison Krauss, B. B. King. We'd had to wait from eight a.m. this morning until two p.m. this afternoon in Litchfield while they sent out for a part to repair a broken alternator. It's late and hot and I think the air conditioner could use a good charge. I roll down the window and as Jani drives historic Route 66, I watch the freight trucks with names like Old Dominion, J. B. Hunt, Peterbilt, Kenworth, Midway. We drive past happy places: Happy Trails RV, Happy Time Tavern, Happy Truck Stop. During the trip we will (or have already) crossed the Des Moines River, the Des Plaines River, the Mississippi River, and the Arkansas River, to name the biggies. In Illinois mostly black faces wave to us from the Illinois State Corrections bus.

I ask myself if I were to pick up someone on purpose, would I have picked Jani.

I watch his face for what I always look for in everyone's face: those misguided signs of faith I am so disdainful of. Religion is only the smallest part of faith, a symptom of it, and I'm curious, like I am with everybody, if he has the capacity for it, and the reason I am is because I never really did. "Keep the faith," people would say, but I know faith isn't something you hold onto like a miser.

I think I can see it, that propensity of Jani's to give it, evidenced by his casual grip on the wheel, the relaxed bend of his leg which is not on the gas pedal due to the cruise control, the lazy lopsided set to his jaw.

Not sure exactly where we are when I decide what I have to do has no real time frame, and since Jani is paying for gas I might as well drop him at his sister's friend's house in Eureka Springs, two hours out of the way. He's grateful, though it turns out when we find the house, a small weathered gray bungalow perched on the side of a mountain that she isn't there after all. She'd left two weeks ago amidst rumors she was headed to Oklahoma City.

We drive past a glass cathedral. Glass churches designed by famous architects you can see right through (the churches, not the architects). Can you talk to God better through glass I wonder? We stop to eat and pay twenty-one dollars for a chicken and shrimp linguini in Alfredo sauce I know is Stouffer's frozen food.

"How can they justify this slop?" I ask Jani.

"I can't sleep in this car again," Jani says when we get back to it. I had originally thought when I left that I would live in this car permanently, never again own or latch on to a patch of stagnant earth. But I had lain awake in the back seat most of last night myself, listening to the dog rustle around in the front seat and Jani snoring lightly. I thought about the dog. Why is there always a dog, I wondered, and I thought of my mother's ratty strays, one dog I had to shoot after her death. There always seemed to be one at every critical juncture in my life, though this one seemed entirely indifferent to me.

Its presence seemed, nevertheless, like a vibration under the skin, a nervous tick.

Eighty-five during the day, it had nevertheless dropped cold. There were no clouds and the air had been still and I had felt the emptiness of my own heart. I smelled my sweat, dried and salty on my skin, but what I could smell oozing from Jani's pores was not salty, or even sweet like honey, but creamy and white like an emollient. I felt parched in comparison.

"I hear you," I say, thinking about another night like last night. "We'll get a room."

"Arkansas is known mostly for chickens and tourism," the lady at the Angel Inn tells us.

Despite the beauty of the Ozark Mountains, Eureka Springs is a funny plastic sort of place full of old people and honeymooners and bad food. Rubber chicken I think, remembering dinner. The inn is new made to look old Victorian, fake topiaries and silk flowers everywhere, pictures of Christ, and framed sayings like the marriage blessing:

> A Blessing the Heart Divine
> On Cana's marriage Fell
> The Blushing water Turned to Wine,
> It's faith in Christ to Tell
>
> And May a Three Fold Blessing
> Upon You Both Descend
> Of Love and Happiness Sublime
> And Peace That has No End

I wonder what kind of people get married in a place like this, so like Las Vegas despite its plastic morality and sugary platitudes.

"Married?" he asks me when we get to the room.

"Divorced two years ago," I say, "he's a dentist." He nods. I throw my leather valise on the bed. "My daughter is with him now, but she'll be living with me in September." I tell myself this is true, she will be.

"Where?"

"I don't know yet. Maybe at my mother's in the U.P. She's dead."

"No one else since?" He means the lovers not the dead people.

"Yes, but things are iffy." I think about Sam. Another Sam like my mother's Indian Sam. I'd collided with him, literally, in a canoe at the confluence of the Two Hearted River (what were the fuckin' odds?) He was bearded, slightly round, red-haired Irish, and prone to fishing metaphors. Keep that rod tip up, it's how you catch the big ones, he'd say, and when I told him catching the big ones is more trouble than I cared for, he'd told me living in fear was no way to live. He hadn't ended things between us despite my aloofness, but the last few months I'd felt him pulling away, a cue things probably wouldn't last between us: the men I ended up with kept on coming . . . and of course, I always held back.

Jani touches the silver necklace at my tanned throat, a fine Native American necklace with tiny birds every half inch around. It falls right at my collar bone.

"I used to like gold when I was young," I say. "Now I like silver. And I have an idea that if I live long enough, I'll enter the bronze or stone age." I am not sure why this is.

Jani's eyes move from the necklace up to my mouth and finally to my eyes. "I think I'll get married," Jani says. "Though I don't suppose I have to."

No, people with faith never have to, I think. I know he isn't talking about marrying me.

I get undressed in front of him, head naked to the shower. He isn't embarrassed and I realize he isn't embarrassed because I'm not embarrassed. And I think that it's the first time—ever—I haven't been. When I come out of the shower, he seems to be studying my body with curiosity. Despite my age, the weight doesn't hang on me, but seems to press outward, something that pleases me.

"Why do you eat like that?" he asks me.

"Because I want to," I say.

"When will you stop?"

"When I want to." I'm surprised I know the answer. At first there had been this idea with the eating that I'd just get it over with, this gradual wasting, the irony of a slow torturous decline providing a satisfaction I didn't want to give Him. He, I believed, had to be a sadistic bastard, and must be getting a good laugh over watching creatures as vain and superficial as we humans are, slowly decomposing before His very eyes.

Later, I will realize the eating may have been my first real act of faith.

The air conditioning causes goose bumps to rise on my skin and when his hands touch my breasts I reach for him instead of resisting slightly, the thing I'd learned kept them coming. Then he is on his knees, hands cupped around my backside, face upturned and between my thighs. When he looks up, I see a rapt expression on his face. I'd never thought of sex as an act of prayer.

"I would wish that ye all spake with tongues," I said, "Paul, First Corinthians—if you're praying, the only answer you're gonna get is a 'yes' from me."

"Praying ain't like a conversation."

"Nope," I agree with him. "It sure ain't."

Still on his knees, he unbuttons his shirt, while I never think, never wonder what I'm about, what this is all about. And the truth is that if I'd recognized it for what it was—my second true act of faith—I might have left things at that.

Gone on home without doing what I came for.

Later, I lie awake, watching the blinding road sign through the drapes, and thinking. Once at Oral Roberts, I had had a casual friend who found out her boyfriend back home had died in a car accident. She had come to my room, expectant. I'd rather have died than pray aloud, but I prayed anyway. My best friend looked on as I filled the room with empty words. I felt a fake and my best friend knew it. My friend's face held the look of a betrayed lover—the least I could have done was faked it for her, something I refused to do, and I had felt despicable and small inside. Then we both looked at the girl who in spite of the prayer, in spite of the cheat, looked remarkably and irrelevantly at peace.

Jani puts the windows down on the Lincoln and the hot dry air whips our hair in clouds in front of our faces. The night before is ours to keep as each we see fit, and for me the memory of it swirls, too. Not dry, though. But not warm and life affirming, either. Jani is driving and I see he's sweating and I know if I lean a hair's breadth to the left and hike up a little I'll see the mole on the left side of his hairless chest, a small mauve colored spot the size of a partially used eraser on the end of an old pencil. I can smell his shaving cream and the tarry smell of cold coffee left in his cup, the near-empty Styrofoam lodged between his thighs. When he tires of the wind noise, he rolls up the windows and turns on the air which blows stale, barely cool air at us, like somebody's soggy breath. There are several flies left inside the car and I swat at them with a small red fly swatter.

"Bad karma," Jani says.

"Environmentalist bunny hugger," I say back.

"Actually, I'm a conservationist hunter/fisher person," he says. "Killing is part of life."

"It's part of death, too," I say. "In case you haven't noticed."

"Have you done it?"

"Sure, you just saw me do it."

"Something that bleeds," he says, "a grouse, a rabbit, a big fish?"

I smile. My mother had once shot an intruder in her place on the Little Two Hearted River. She'd heard him cut the screen in the kitchen window and when he rounded the corner of the bedroom, she'd been standing there stark naked with a twelve gauge staring him in the face. " He'd said, "you ain't got the nerve." He'd taken a step toward her and she'd taken off most of his right thigh.

A fly lands on Jani's right arm just above the elbow. "Go ahead," he says, nodding toward the fly. "Give it your best shot."

I swing at the fly and the red plastic makes contact, but the fly buzzes off, circles my head twice, then lands on the left side-rear window where, the shepherd/mongrel (Horace is his unlikely name), smashes his nose against the window, traps the fly, and promptly eats it.

"You held back at the last second," Jani says. "You were influenced by the idea that you'd be hitting me."

"I was not," I say. "Your arm simply didn't provide the proper resistance to support the swatter—it's a scientific principal."

"Nope, you were influenced. Something inside at some elemental level prohibited you inflicting pain on another fellow human being."

I shrug. "Think what you want." I eat two king-sized Snickers bars one right after the other as if to prove how wrong he is. But Jani is at least partially right. Up until this trip, I had never been like my mother. I had possessed the infinite fear of the faithless.

I hadn't held back this time.

And if that fly still lived, it wasn't because I hadn't given it my all.

"Do you believe the death of one person is ever justified?" I ask him then. "Like one person having to die so that fifty people can keep on living? Do you believe in that kind of sacrifice?"

"If it's the person's choice to be doing his own sacrificing, I do."

"And what if it's not?"

"Well, who's doing the deciding, then?"

"Suppose it were you deciding."

"Then it would depend, of course."

"On what? Suppose the person deserved it," I say.

"Then I'd be less inclined to decide on that person dying since that would entail judgment on my part. I wouldn't want to have to second-guess my motivation."

"You would never judge," I say. "You'd let fifty people die because you might have to make a judgment about one sinner."

He picks up the cup between his legs and throws it on the floorboards at my feet. "Look, I don't like thinking about shit like this. I didn't sleep good last night and I don't like being fucked with. What is it you want to know precisely?"

Silence.

"Okay, goddamn it, so I do make judgments," he says. "I've lived in the U.P. all my life and I know exactly what order I'd have bugs eliminated."

"Oh?"

"Flies. The first to go would be the mosquitoes because they buzz so loud inside and outside you think they're gonna lift the damn house and make off with it. Then the small house-fly ankle-biter types that bite hard enough to bring tears to your eyes, worse even than the black flies, but they're next. They don't hurt as much, the black flies, they got some kind of anesthetic that numbs you, lulls you into complacency, and then they get you right by the hat band line on your forehead and on the back of your neck and you swell up for a week. While you're busy slapping them away from your face in clouds, they're biting the shit out of the back of your neck—cows have been known to die from the lack of blood. Then the deer flies. Then the no-see-ums. If they asked me, that's the order the sons o' bitches would go."

"What about spiders and bees and ants and stuff?"

"Nope, they don't make the list. You got a list like that for people?" he asks.

"Maybe."

We drive through the Ozarks, along the Trail of Tears. Yesterday we'd driven through Branson, Missouri, through Mark Twain National Forest, on into Arkansas, past the Cosmic Caverns and the Onyx Cave, through the land of Jesse James, on to Eureka Springs. Today we drive Highway 7 through Hobbs State Management Area and on down to Fort Smith. We pass one of those Calvary hills on the edge of a farm; the three crosses jut skyward on the small hill, the cornfield stretches green behind it, and every hundred feet or so an oil well pounds methodically up and down. "I have planted, Apollos watered; but God gave the increase. First Corinthians 3:6. Funny, the Bible making reference to a pagan god," I say. "Must have been something the Catholics forgot to pull out of the Bible."

I think about Oral. He was at least part Cherokee and I imagine his ancestors on the "trail where they cried" and I think maybe that's enough—justification enough for who he was. After all, he's just getting back part of what we'd denied him as a "People." And I think maybe I should leave it at that, but of course you know I didn't leave it at that.

"My uncle is a Buddhist," Jani says.

"Ah," I say. "My mother had a shaman, an Indian medicine man name Sam. American Indians and Buddhists make some sense to me. At least they aren't exclusionary religions."

"What was he like? Oral Roberts?" Jani asks.

"Charismatic, as they say. The ultimate medicine show. He had a modest house in Tulsa, but they say he had a million dollar house in Palm Springs, a two-million-dollar house in Beverly Hills, a Fan Jet Falcon. They say when his daughter and son-in-law were killed in the '80s, they left a ten-million-dollar estate. But people believe in him, despite the fact half a dozen people have actually died attending his 'healing' campaigns. The icing on the cake for me was years later when I'd use my lunch hour to retrieve certified letters he'd sent begging for the eight mil he needed to build his City of Faith—a medical center he was building in order to cure cancer. If he didn't get it, he said 'the Lord would call him home.'"

"My uncle has never been so at peace," Jani says, somewhat irrelevantly, I think, but I know he's talking about the Buddhist stuff.

"No doubt because he has learned to 'be' instead of 'do.' Never made sense to me, though, why you can't 'be' in the very act of 'doing'"—I've since found you can—"Or how they can deny goals of any kind, even spiritual ones. Nirvana is the state of not wanting, but isn't nirvana a goal for Christ's sake?"

"You got to have passion for something or someone," Jani says. "My father told me that."

"You do?" I say. "Who do you have a passion for?" Smile at him when I say it. I'm surprised when he tells me Sarah Jennings. He has a passion for Sarah Jennings.

"Really?" I say. "Why aren't you with Sarah Jennings?"

"She doesn't have a passion for me—don't matter, though."

"Don't it?" But I can see it "don't." I can see in his face that flat-out-run-on emotion, a free-fall maybe, something I know nothing about.

It's quiet for a while.

Then we tell stories. He tells me a ludicrous one about a woman in the U.P. who apparently had stopped at a completely unnecessary stoplight on a remote bridge under construction in the middle of the night, where apparently she'd then been raped and left for dead alongside of the road, her car still parked at the stoplight. And then I tell him a story about how on one of my trips to Tulsa on our way to school, my friend and I had seen a little woman driving along next to us, going the wrong way down the highway. It had been almost dusk, obviously no traffic on her side of Route 44. She had a little orange scarf tied over her head and could barely see over the steering wheel. We honked and flashed lights and did everything we could to get her attention to no avail. Finally we sped ahead a couple exits in hope of heading her off. But it seems Roberta Sands (we were to find out later—an eighty-year-old widow), had run head-on into Burton Landsdown (an eighty-seven-year-old widower), each driving no more than thirty-five mph, between the exits of Buckhorn and Waynesville, Missouri; they had both been killed instantly.

A match, I couldn't help thinking, made in heaven.

It got quiet again and I thought about my matches made in heaven. And how I'd held back. Not everything, just the things I knew instinctively put me at risk. And what I held back was different with each one. The first one I held back sex—why buy the cow and all that. Later I held back money with one who leeched off me, time from one who was always late, affection from one who clung. Ben, the dentist husband, wanted me to be a screamer during sex, but I refused to even moan; later I held back orgasms altogether, or perhaps they held back from me. I held back approval, one way or another, from all of them. I realize that, like me, they had all been faithless which is not the same thing as being unfaithful. Inevitably they would be that, too. It didn't end with lovers. I held back things from myself. Joy and pain and demonstrable grief. Laughter.

It all boiled down to faith, really.

It's noon when we pull into Tulsa, third day on the road. I ask Jani if he wants to get on his way, if he wants to be dropped by the exit at Highway 44 but he wants to know how long it will take, what I have to do at the university.

"Not long," I say. "Won't take me long."

"I'll wait for you here in the car, take a nap, and then you can drop me before you head back."

"No," I say, "now that I think of it I might be a while."

"Do you know anyone here anymore? Teachers?"

"I doubt it," I say.

He watches me closely. "Drop me at the closest motel to the school," he says. "You can come there afterward and either stay the night or get cleaned up before you head back out."

"Okay," I say and drop him at the Motel Six, a mile from campus. Before I leave, I call my daughter Jane. It's Monday and it's now four in the afternoon. I get no answer at her father's, so I call him at work. He tells me Jane is at a nearby stables cleaning stalls for five dollars an hour.

"You can call her there," he says.

"Just tell her that I called please," I answer.

When I come out, Jani hands me the leftover donuts he'd paid for early this morning. "How's the food at the school there?" he asks me with a smile. "I'm sure you'll need a snack soon." He lifts his backpack out and slings it across one shoulder. Saddle-style again. Dogs are okay, so I don't have to wait and help him sneak Horace into the room.

"It used to be great," I tell him, referring to the food. But I have no intention of eating there. "I'll see you after a bit."

He looks at me like he doesn't believe he'll see me at all and says, "Nothing's inevitable."

"Keep the faith," I say.

As I'm pulling out he calls after me, "Hey, what's your name?"

"Aissa," I yell back.

As I drive, the road seems to radiate heat. I remember this tire I saw once rolling down the shoulder of the highway. Just rolling and the whole time I drove next to it, it kept on rolling. No idea how it got there. I drove next to it a half a mile or so, but it rolled past my exit, and I got off without seeing where or how it stopped.

The Prayer Tower is a ridiculous blue and silver reflective space-aged-looking spire with a round observation deck two-thirds up it, exactly like the house that George Jetson lived in, and as I walk around the side I see my reflection in the side of the building, like I used to see in all the buildings here those many years ago. Back then I looked round; now I look square.

The june bugs are still here. I'd never seen anything like this. No way to miss them and as I walk, I hear their bodies crunch under my feet.

I walk into the lobby, wiping the bugs off my feet on the mat, and a beaming college student asks me if she can help me. She has that "nirvana" sort of look on her face, that penetrating invasive frankness, and I brace myself for the onslaught. She tells me where the bookstore and gift shop are located, and I tell her I want to go up to the observation deck. She nods and points toward the elevator. My purse is slung over my shoulder and I tuck it under one arm as I push the button.

"Is this your first visit with us here at ORU?" the girl asks me.

"Oh no," I say. "I went to school here myself many moons ago."

"Praise the Lord," she says then. "It must be great to be here again."

"Yes," I say.

"But you don't look happy," she says. "Can I pray for you?"

"Oh, I'll take care of that upstairs," I say. "But thank you."

A fat lady comes in just then and asks the girl where she can find the bookstore, and she points in the opposite direction. As the elevator door closes, I see the girl at the desk is wearing a bracelet with one charm, a cross, dangling from it.

As I get off the elevator, I decide there's no rush and I look at the view. From one side of the tower I can see most of the campus which doesn't look that different than it did all those years ago. From the other side, I can see the "City of Faith," the medical center that almost was; I wonder how Oral justifies crawling around the planet since the Lord didn't "take him home."

Then I close my eyes and try to feel the holiness. I imagine all those prayers, whipping past my head, try not to think of them, but I see them anyway, swirling heavenward like phantom whispers, sometimes in foreign tongues. I'm tempted to offer one myself, but I stifle the feeling. I stand there a full five minutes until I start to sway slightly, then I open my eyes and look at the inside walls. I see the plaque that notifies people there is always someone praying in this prayer tower. Praying for the old, the infirm, the meek, the unhappy everywhere. Praying for the world. Twenty-four hours a day, seven days a week since the day it was built.

Guardians, I think. Like the knights guarding the Holy Grail.

The walls are flat, laminated, and the rooms have no door handles on the outside, just slots for keys. So I can't tell which room is the prayer room or if it in fact really exists. So I start pounding on the walls and yelling that I am in urgent need of prayer. Nothing happens immediately, except that the fat lady who has come up in the last several minutes, looks apprehensive and pushes the elevator button to go back down. I keep pounding and my fists make a muffled thumping sound on the wall. I'm hoping that means they can't hear anything down in the lobby and I keep at it. Finally, one of the doors opens and a slight lady in her midseventies opens the door timidly. She's small, and not very official looking. I realize it's not a prayer room, but a bathroom she's come out of.

"I'm Alice, can I help you?" she asks.

I've been keeping my hand inside my purse and now that the door is opened, I pull the gun from it and point it at her.

"Are you the one praying?" I ask her.

She nods.

Are you up here alone?" I ask her.

"Yes," she says. She looks at the gun, then back at me and the one thing I think as I look into her face is that she doesn't look particularly frightened.

"You might as well come in," she says and points to a small room next door.

"So it's just you up here praying for the whole world, eh?"

"I'm afraid so," she says. There is a small desk in the room and no windows. There is a picture of Jesus at the last supper on one wall and a large silver cross on another. On the desk are several versions of the Bible and some other books. There is a pitcher of water and several glasses, as well. Along the wall there is a small kneeling bench. "Do you want to see me pray?" she asks.

I stand with my back to the door, the gun bobbling out in front of my hand. "How long have you been up here?" I ask her. I have the absurd idea she is going to say "Twelve hundred years," but she says, "Three hours."

"How long do you stay up here?"

"Oh," she says, "it depends. Sometimes four hours, sometimes six. I don't leave until someone comes to relieve me. There is always someone praying here, dear. Didn't you believe it?"

"I'm not sure if I believed it or not."

"Maybe you need a drink of water," she says. "Are you in very great need?"

"I'll ask the questions," I say. But she continues to ask them. She asks if I've ever been here before, if I watched the television program, how far I'd come, if I was married and had children, and I answered her. I told her I was a reporter for a small newspaper, but that I wasn't writing what I wanted to. She asked me if I was in good health and I told her I was as far as I knew. She talked about herself, her husband, and her sons who were both grown up, of course.

One lived in Brazil, she said. And one in Broken Arrow, Oklahoma.

"Are you going to shoot me, dear?" she asks.

I ignore her.

"I'm going to get a drink of water now," she says. "Can I get you one? I have a couple cookies here in my purse."

"Who do you think you're talking to up here?" I ask her.

"God, of course, dear, that should be fairly obvious, I would think."

"Ah," I say. "The great Unmoved Mover."

"Aristotle," she says.

"Only He could be 'unmoved' after an eternity of this."

"Unmoved," she says. "I always took that in a physical sense, not an emotional one. He's stationary, largely, though He moves everything else? Like an axis maybe?"

"The axis tilts," I say. "That's not 'unmoved.'"

"Yes, you're right, dear, the earth's axis tilts, anyway, just enough so the sun can illuminate things, warm things up periodically."

"And you think He hears you? Does He talk back and all that?"

She pours water into two glasses and I see that she has a plain platinum wedding band on her left hand.

"Prayer isn't like having a conversation, you know, dear." Jani's words.

"Really, then what's it like?" Oral claimed it was like a conversation, that's for sure. "Who was here the morning of September eleventh?" I ask her.

"Actually, I was," she says. And I doubt that somehow. The odds seem so incredible, and the thought occurs to me that she is saying that so no one else becomes involved. I will never know if this is true.

"Really, and what exactly were you praying for?" I ask her.

She smiles. "Well peace on earth of course. I had a few individual needs to include, I usually have a list, you see, but basically that's what we pray for. That God's will be done and for peace. At least that's what I pray for."

World peace, like the Miss America pageant.

"And you don't feel somewhat derelict in your duty? Perhaps there's a better lobbyist out there."

She laughs. "Well, I don't feel responsible if that's what you're alluding to, dear. Why blame just me? Or just us? Surely, there were people of other faiths praying that morning as well?"

This was something that had crossed my mind earlier. But I didn't care whether the Jews were at fault or the Catholics or the Baptists or the Mormons or the Buddhists or the Hindus or the American Indians. It wasn't a matter of responsibility anyway. I knew she wasn't responsible before I drove the 1,243.6 miles out here (not including the detour to Eureka Springs). It only mattered what she thought. It was what she thought that frustrated the hell out of me.

"How did you get here, dear, did you come alone?"

"Started to, but I picked up some hitchhiker, a guy looking for his sister. His trip, his thing, though, is some kind of protest against his family's mining operation which is killing all the fish in the Yellowdog River in Michigan's Upper Peninsula. I think that's it, anyway."

"What kind of fish, dear? I like salmon."

"Trout primarily, I think. Do you know what my mother would have said to him? She'd have said it didn't matter whether the fish died or not. She'd say it doesn't matter what happens really, it's only our reaction to it that matters."

"I'd say your mother is right, can we call her, do you think?"

"Be a long distance call. She's dead. So to all you people with faith, those people that died on 9/11 or in Oklahoma City or during hurricane Katrina or in the last tsunami don't matter, either, right? It's just our reaction to it." I'm waiting for her to invade my space. Offer to pray for me personally or at the very least lean over and touch me, spout off platitudes about "God's mysterious ways she doesn't need to understand to believe," but she doesn't. Just takes a sip of water and sits primly on the edge of her seat.

"Did you know the Catholic church took a vote way back when and declared Jesus a deity, the son of God?" I ask. Sort of like making him president of the club in absentia.

"Did they?" she asks.

"What about the big O," I ask her when she doesn't seem inclined to go down that road. "Does he pray here, too, or does he just delegate that duty?"

"They say he does."

"But you have no personal knowledge."

She doesn't answer. We continue talking like this for over a half hour, she asking me about my divorce (my fault; he couldn't be expected to know me when I didn't know myself), the length of my drive (the twelve-hundred-some miles) and places of origin (I was born in Pontiac, Michigan. She, it turns out, was seventy-two years old, originally from Saskatchewan, married to a man who sat on the board here at the school, she had once taught poetry when she was very young, had a corky terrier aged two, and a pork roast in the oven as we spoke, seasoned she said with rosemary and orange juice.)

"Is that true, what you said?" I ask her. "Was it you here that morning?"

"Yes," she says, "it was."

"Well, maybe you were in the bathroom that morning, too, huh, like today?"

"I pray in there, too, dear.

"Well, how can you keep your mind on your prayers? Maybe it's like meditation. For instance, maybe your mind wandered and you started thinking about how bitchy your sister May was the day before on the phone, or what to pack for an upcoming vacation to Hawaii? Having the den recarpeted? Or your legs waxed? Who knows? And maybe that's when the shit hit the fan."

"I know I prayed the best I could," Alice tells me as I point the gun at her chest. "Truly, I did. If there was something I could have done differently, I would have."

"Of course," I say.

Alice tries to decide if I believe her, and when it seems I do, she looks puzzled for the first time. "Then what do you want, dear?" she asks me.

That was the question of the week. What did I want? I think about that for a good five minutes. I run that through my mind. I start with what I don't want, or at least what I didn't expect. I know I haven't come for healing—either spiritual or physical. Or maybe I have, but not in the straightforward sense people normally think it. And it isn't epiphanic in nature; I don't expect the whole world to suddenly become my oyster. I don't expect to come away understanding all the relationships in my life, or with a sure purpose or clear direction on my future pathway or with a light for the world. I don't expect "world peace" or even the temporary illusion of harmony—within myself or without. I don't expect the secret to life, eternal or otherwise.

I do want fried chicken, suddenly, biscuits and butter. Or maybe grits smothered in redeye gravy, topped with a couple runny eggs. Or maybe a couple dozen oysters—now that I'd thought of them—raw on the half shell with lots of lemon. I am tempted to tell her so, but instead I close my eyes for a few minutes. When I open them I say, "I want you to come with me. Just come downstairs."

So we go.

Alice pushes the button on the elevator that indicates the lobby, and we descend, leaving the prayer room empty for the first time, presumably, since the building had been dedicated (except for when someone was in the adjacent bathroom of course). Seeing the question in my eyes, Alice assures me, "I haven't stopped praying, you know, dear." And I say, "but you aren't in the tower are you? You aren't even in the bathroom."

The girl at the desk in the lobby looks terrified. Her hands are over her mouth and the cross dangles in front of her Adam's apple.

"I called the police," she says. "Ten minutes ago."

(Later when the police arrive, the lady whose name is Alice will tell them she isn't personally going to press charges because it is obvious to her that I am not truly dangerous. And Jani will later tell me that I obviously didn't intend to kill anyone since my gun wasn't even loaded. When I tell him I had had every intention of loading it and that I thought it was loaded already, he will shake his head and say it was just like me and the fly swatter, that on some deep elemental level, I didn't want to hurt anyone at all. And that is what my defense attorney will argue when ORU does press charges, a strategy that convinces the courts to settle for three months of community service. They will ask me if I believe in God and when I say yes, on some days I do, they say good, that my community service will be at the university there. And the service up to them. Every time Alice has her shift, I am to" pray" with her, or go wherever it is I go inside my head, do whatever I do instead of pray. But what I end up doing is watching her face as she prays. I look to see if her mind wanders. If I can see evidence that she is thinking about what she is going to make for dinner, or if she is thinking about that ill-fitting pair of pants she intended to take back to the department store. I will watch to see how many times she goes to the bathroom (once most days), and I will wonder about the nature of her prayers. Not conversation, definitely. Meditation? Affirmation? I will look for moments, even fleeting, when it seemed she might waiver, lose her faith altogether.

Later it will be Alice who testifies for me in the custody hearing since obtaining joint custody of my daughter under the circumstances will not be a slam dunk, Prayer Tower incident notwithstanding.

Jani had left the dog that day and decided to head to the university since I'd made him feel so apprehensive, and this is why I notice him in the crowd. He'll come to the jail, and I will hug him and hand him the keys to the Lincoln so he can go off to Oklahoma City in search of his sister. He will have no luck, something he will later say "don't matter," of course, and a week later, he will drop the keys back off to my hotel room, before hitchhiking home to Michigan. "Keep the faith," he will say to me. And I'll tell him maybe I will keep it. I'll think maybe I had no right blaming Oral Roberts or his ministry for pulling the wool over people's eyes. Maybe they got their money's worth and more, who was I to say. But even that had nothing to do with what I wanted. I wanted to know what kept that tire rolling, what kept Alice praying, what, for God's sake, did it feel like to hit that floor beneath an outstretched hand of a faith healer?

So I will call Sam with my first-allowed phone call.

I'd like to tell you that I had the faith to tell him how much I loved him and how right we were for each other and how I could hardly wait to get back to Michigan and start my life with him. I'd like to say that—and maybe you're hoping that I did. But for now I am still in that Prayer Tower where there's something I want more than any of these other things. Maybe more, even, than I want Sam.)

"Come, Alice," I say, and she follows me into the elevator and downstairs to the front door of the tower. I hold it open for her.

She looks back at me questioningly.

I can see the june bugs littered all over the sidewalk, thousands of them, their hard shells gleaming in the approaching evening light, like thousands of chestnuts dropped out of some enormous bug-tree.

I know Alice sees them, too.

Then I imagine the obscene crunch, the feel of their bodies collapsing between the soles of her shoes and the concrete, the brown gelatinous smear.

Like so many sacrifices—no no, like so many prayers.

I think of her pork roast in the oven with the orange juice and the rosemary. I picture those oysters again, braised rabbit compote, roasted racks of lamb, brook trout over my mother Norna's wood fire, sautéed sweetbreads mixed with wild mushrooms and sage, wild blueberries in cognac and cream, grilled racks of venison and roast grouse with plank roasted grapes in sherry wine.

I point with the gun.

"Take a step, Alice," I say.

She looks at me for what seems eternity.

"Just take one step," I say.

And then she does.

NORNA

NOTHING HE CAN
PUT A FINGER ON

1. STICKS AND STONES

Until two weeks ago, Davis couldn't have told you the last time he'd looked inside the '55 Willys Wagon. But now he looks every day. His stiff fingers grip the door frame as he lowers rack-like shoulders into the car, eases his aching body onto the ragged leather seats that burn the backs of his thighs. He's careful of that trick left knee, not a Korean War wound as most people assume, but the result of a childhood fall out of a tree. He stretches the leg straight once he's seated. And then he takes stock.

The first thing he'd noticed wasn't a thing at all. Not the smell of someone, not physical evidence of someone. Nothing he can put a finger on. More significant than the sense of trespass: an altered perception. As if he no longer sees the inside of the old automobile through his own eyes.

The Jeep had been twenty years old in 1975 when he restored it to better-than-mint condition: vinyl seats for leather, vertical front grill and headlights replaced, the engine overhauled. But now nearly thirty years have passed. Sell it, his wife Norna had said once, many years ago. No, better yet, sell the Jaguar. Shit, no, he'd told her, he'd be damned if he'd sell either one. He'd imagined himself hunting or fishing, using the Jeep in that capacity, but instead it carries Irish whiskey and Bombay gin from the Canadian Soo. Not to say that he wouldn't hunt or fish someday. You got to have those *possibles*, he tells himself. He keeps the wagon parked across the road in a metal pole barn with the left-over wood scraps and garden tools.

It's hard to say how many days have passed without it registering inside his head, but now it does: the McNally *Road Atlas*, curled and soiled at the edges, has been moved from the dashboard onto the backseat. And when exactly did he become aware that it's served, rather poorly, as a headrest, a pillow of sorts? Whoever sat inside his car probably assumed no one would notice something so inconsequential, but Davis is a man who notices much—drops of glue: on the edges of repaired plastic or along the edges of window casings; asymmetry: on faces or buildings; weakness: of joints, mechanical or human, of cloud cover, of emotion.

An article in the *Drummond Island Digest* sticking out from under the atlas catches his eye. About a pecan nut fundraiser, the proceeds to be used to fund a university reading room at Saginaw Valley. That's what I need, he thinks. A nut fundraiser.

He checks the glove compartment: a flashlight with batteries long burned out, a pair of binoculars he'd lost track of, an odd assortment of loose screws, a faded yellow car registration from 1974 but no current one. Shit, he thinks. Where has that gotten to? There's a pair of dime-store reading glasses, folded but caseless, with scratches and smudges in a vertical pattern down the lenses. His? He isn't sure. He exchanges the glasses for the ones on his face, and is aware of only the slightest improvement in the newspaper's fine print.

He looks carefully at the odometer. It's turned over at least once, that he knows. It registers 12,623 miles now. Isn't that a hundred miles more then he remembers? A few loose wires dangle from below the dashboard and swing slightly from the impact of his knees. Has it been hotwired? He is convinced not only that someone has been squatting in his car, but that the wagon has been covering ground without him.

He feels his stomach lurch. Nerves? Or is it those damned runny eggs he'd fixed himself for breakfast. Norna had once fixed him glorious breakfasts when she hadn't been up all night working on one of those bleak sculptures of hers. Another jutting, post-modern rendering in stone to be placed against the cracked concrete walls she had poured in place all those years ago. Concrete walls and floor, post and beam open-framed construction. Her ideas of simplicity. A reduction, she would say, of the psychic distance between people and things.

Davis wants to build her a new house—a new start—but so far she is unwavering.

Today, in this ninety-degree heat, concrete is a blessing.

Though Davis notices much, remembering is another story. Did the eggs upset his stomach or did he even eat eggs? He isn't sure.

Hundreds of stray details lurk inside his head, not linked in any contiguous order, forming for him a jumbled and disordered present. He'd watched Norna sleep back then, watched her slight chest rise and fall. Counting breaths as if each would be her last. Not because she was in ill health, but because, like always, despite his notion about the possibles, he simply couldn't imagine a future for himself; consequently, he couldn't imagine one for her, either. Sometimes she opened a tentative eye in a face like white alabaster.

"Are we there yet?" she'd ask, her running joke with him.

"No," he always answered her. "We're not there yet."

"Thank God," she'd say. Then, perhaps, he'd rest a hand on one of her breasts and she'd close her eyes again. She never once moved his hand.

He climbs out of the wagon, searches for fresh tire tracks, but last night's rain has washed away any sign of them, or any sign of a footprint. He sticks his head back inside the wagon. It's nearly imperceptible, but Davis is more certain each day that he can divine the essence of an odor where he hadn't been aware of one initially. He's pretty sure what the odor is: tobacco. Not cigarette smoke, but tobacco. And there's something more.

But he's having trouble *putting his finger on it.*

Something makes a rodent-like rustle in the corner of the pole barn. He strains to lift his head, but isn't fast enough to catch a glimpse. It's so fucking hot, he thinks. Even for me, a person whose blood is barely pumping. He figures it's maybe noon, and he knows he needs a drink of water, but instead he walks down to the end of the long drive, in search of what he's not sure. A sign of anything out of the ordinary. Before he knows it, he is at the edges of the Maxton Plains.

The Plains look like sheets of crumbled concrete, shimmering white in the choking heat, neglected weeds erupting between the cracks. Something like chalk dust hovers a few feet from the ground. He looks east and then west across the treeless expanse, expecting to see nothing less than divine judgment written across the horizon. But there's nothing in any direction but pitiless blue sky. He looks down and sees the cairn fields in front of him, and has a dim recollection of Norna all those years ago, pregnant, forcing him to gather rocks with her by the hundreds. Or did he dream it? How she'd laid them around a house they'd owned back then, one by one, each rock touching the next in a linear progression that connected one to another, yet leading nowhere.

He's never believed in rocks, and despite the fact he knows it's against environmental regulations, he picks up as many now as he can carry, and as he walks through the dried alvar grasses, a blast of musty-sweet air hits him in the face. Butterflies float around his head and into each other, and as he walks back into the line of trees, he puts up a ruffed grouse. It whirrs away sounding like a small engine in need of repair. Why would a ruffed grouse be here? He makes thirteen trips carrying the rocks, sweat dripping down his face, along the sides of his stooped back, sand chafing raw cracks on his hot, gloveless hands. It occurs to him, finally, to use the wheelbarrow and then he makes another twenty trips. A song from a forgotten childhood runs through his head. I've been working on the railroad.

It's twenty degrees hotter inside the pole barn than it is outside, the late morning air silty and hideously orange due to the translucent red metal roof overhead. He transfers every load into the back of the wagon, throwing each rock with as much fury as his shoulders can muster.

He hasn't seen the woman in years. Can he picture Sally Crow closing her eyes, resting her head against the seat bottom, long black hair streaming onto the floor? Sort of. He can picture her *sort of*. He continues to carry rocks of all shapes and sizes, and as he heaves them into the cargo body of the Willys, he tries to picture that black head, not just as it might appear now, but how it might possibly look ten years from now, and fails. He finds there is no future to be imagined for her, either.

He's been counting, and as he drops load thirty-three into the back end, as the rocks knock one into another like a pile of discarded days, he dismisses the future and tries for the past. It exists, but in random flashes, like black and white film negatives of someone else's life. But then, as one old tire blows (that will fucking show her), and then two others, one memory crowds his mind like phantom pain from a missing limb. He remembers clearly what he'd said to her.

"Get the hell out of my car."

2. GRAVEL

"Get the hell out of my car."

It's September 1980, and he has just walked out of the Northwoods Bar, and found her in the front seat of his '55 Willys Wagon. It's still light out. Maybe six p.m., and the car is parked right in front of Sune's Grocery. Will Jansen has just stumbled out of the bar as well. Davis knows sure as hell that Will, pompous bastard that he is, won't believe he doesn't know the woman from Adam. She's asleep, but she moves her head, and her long black hair sweeps across the driver's seat, a maple leaf stuck in the silky strands. He smells something sweet and moldy, like old beer as he leans over and shakes her by a meaty shoulder. She props herself up in the passenger seat in a kind of daze.

"I just want a ride home," she keeps saying.

"You're an Indian, aren't you?"

She smiles at him, and he sees what looks like a tiny piece of lettuce or some kind of herb stuck between gleaming, healthy-looking teeth. She's wearing blue-jean cutoffs and a red-and-white striped peasant top gathered at the neckline. She's maybe midtwenties, average sized, breasty, and there's an open hole under the string tie that reveals a dewy cleavage. She seems to read his mind about the lettuce and her tongue searches her front teeth and when she smiles the next time, it's gone.

"Look, I'm hungry," he says, "and I need to get some dinner. I'm not driving you home."

But then Davis thinks what dinner will be if he goes home to Norna. Since they moved to Drummond two years ago, she's taken up power cooking. Soups, shoulder ham, capons, salmon, quail, confit of duck, assorted breads and pies, even a cold timbale of woodcock, all cooked in one day on either the wood stove or over a fire pit, refrigerated or sometimes frozen. A week's worth of food that she might or might not sit down with him to eat. The meals taste remarkably good warmed up, but it's the lack of ceremony, the lack of celebration of a day well spent, that he misses. He imagines that in some way having a week's food prepared ahead of time anchors her to survival—of at least that many days. Or does it free her from him instead? He isn't sure. But cooking day is the only day they sit down to dinner formally, when she cooks lamb or thick steaks on the wood fire. They'd sit across from one another; beef tongue and jars of mincemeat would fight them for elbow room. The mountain of food filled his mind with gluttonous thoughts of excess which tended to make him lose his appetite. But cooking days hold out the only hope for him, with just the table between them. So he'd sit there swilling gin, watching her fork hearty portions of red meat into her mouth, while he wished for pastry or confections. Of any kind.

"I'll wait while you eat, then you can drive me home," Sally Crow says now. "I'll pay for it."

Take what you want, Davis's father always said (purportedly quoting God), but pay for it. Davis believes in that. It's the creed he lives by. Some people would say he doesn't know the meaning of the words, but that isn't true; he knows what it means to pay for things.

"Goddamn it, get out of the Goddamned car."

But he's afraid someone else will see him sitting with this woman and since he can't feature dragging her out by the hair, he drives to Chuck's Place for dinner. They don't talk on the way. The Andrews Sisters sing "Boogie Woogie Bugle Boy" on the Jeep radio, part of Stage Door Canteen.

Norna loves to dance, but prefers quiet when they drive in the car.

Sally Crow moves a crossed foot in time to the music. It's dusk now and Davis drives carefully, watching for deer alongside the road. Wind gusts blow Sally's hair around inside the car like a black funnel cloud, and he leans slightly left to keep it from obstructing his vision. A strand catches in the crease of his neck and he leaves it there. Though he doesn't ask, Sally Crow tells him she lives with her uncle on the south side of the island, in a house with no plumbing and no electricity. Ever since her parents died of food poisoning, that is, and they had buried them in the back yard, which, yes, she realizes, is against the law.

"What do you want?" he asks her, indicating Chuck's Place as he pulls into the parking lot. She looks hungry but says, "Nothing."

After grabbing a burger to go, Davis stops across the street at Johnson's and gets a six pack. Then he drives out Johnswood Road to the southeast side of the island. Wordlessly, he hands her a beer. Then he passes her the burger and she takes a big bite, her tongue sliding out to catch the grease which nevertheless runs down her chin. As she hands it back, a slice of onion falls between her legs. He watches Sally Crow wipe mustard from the inside of each bare thigh and considers. He listens to the wheels slip against the gravel, each stone slightly diminished from the friction of his tires. He can hear the stones becoming less.

"My people believe there are spirits in everything, even stones," Sally Crow says.

She must be watching the stones, too. Then, he thinks: *stones that blanch powdery-white under his headlights, moments before his tires roll over them.*

He sleeps with Sally Crow in the end, not because she owes him anything, and not because he has a burning desire to, but because it makes no difference to anything. He tries to imagine the price, the implications of a future that will tie this night to the next, but try as he might, he can't picture a day when he'll be loading the Willy' full of rocks, hauling his ass across the Maxton Plains. He can't project to the rock heaps he'll gather in the future. Neither can he summon the past, a past far enough in the past, to jog a familiar chord of youthful optimism.

And if he could, it still wouldn't matter.

Sally Crow will fade away, at least in a physical sense, and he will never discuss her with Norna, though he might, God knows, tell her anything. Even that wouldn't matter one way or another.

Sally Crow smells like tobacco, and he sees she has unrolled a pouch of it along with some herbs. "Are you a medicine woman?" he asks her.

"Holes," she says. "I heal holes."

"You better be careful then," he tells her. "That could ruin not only your sex life, but your records won't play very well." She laughs and her voice reminds him of blues harmonica, the way it seems to travel in pitch and emotion, sliding around, not staying put.

"That's what you wanted to hear, though, wasn't it? That I heal people?"

"I don't know."

She takes his hand and moves it to her left breast. He keeps it there, moving a tentative finger for a long minute, then lets it drop. They don't say anything for a while and then she starts talking again.

"There was a neighbor lady once who got me into Girl Scouts," she says. "I used to believe in brownies, fairies who come and do all your work while you sleep. For cookies and a bowl of milk. Then I found out it was me who was supposed to be the Brownie."

He sees a stack of magazines in her lap he hasn't noticed before. "Isn't that a catalogue for Superior State you've got there?"

"Maybe."

He drives on and the stones spurt out behind the car, leaving rolls of dust hanging in his rear view mirror. As he drives, he tries to imagine a future with this woman, their bodies joined, the taste of her smoky lips ripened with age to them, and he fails to form any tangible picture of it. Nor can he picture her feet gracing a college campus, or see her enrolling in the inevitable accounting classes. Or maybe he's wrong about her altogether and it would be premed classes? What would she look like working at one of the casinos? Or summoning Great Spirits to heal holes in lonely white men in her uncle's rundown shack on the southern part of the island? He peers through the dusty windshield, as though it's a window through time, hoping to see how it all might happen. How Sally Crow would, in fact, do all of the above and more. But it's impossible. He's not sure he can visualize even the next half hour, in spite of how hard he's grown watching her. So he tries again for the past. He'd like to remember being a child, the feelings of being a child, but once again that past eludes him.

He pulls off the road onto an overgrown two-track. A mixture of pine and hardwood branches reach into the open windows, familiar figures with almost-recognizable features that tap them each on a shoulder. They hunker in closer, and pretty soon the two-track ends at an enormous granite boulder. Another road block. As the grill of the wagon comes to rest against it, as Davis sees Sally Crow pull off the red-and-white peasant top, he struggles to picture even the next thirty seconds in which surely his hand will touch that olive skin. But he can't. Can't imagine even that, and the Maxton Plains flash inside his head instead, those two thousand acres of grasslands and cairn fields. And he remembers just what he'd said his first trip there.

"What the hell could you possibly want with all these rocks?"

3. ROLLING STONES

"What the hell could you possibly want with all these rocks?"

1954. He looks around him. Pon-ta-gan-igy, A View of Beautiful Islands, is what the Indians called Drummond Island. Glacier revealed, it is a silent land of limestone bedrock surrounded by water, much of the island forested evergreen and hardwood. The edge of Potagannissing Bay, where Davis will one day live with his wife, Norna, is forested as well. But not the Plains, of course. The Plains consist of two thousand acres of alvar grasslands, lying atop the Niagara cuesta, a resistant landform of dolomite and shale, a landform found only here, a few places in Canada, and the Baltic Sea coasts of Scandinavia. The thin soil atop the bedrock accounts for soggy conditions in spring and early summer, searing heat and drought conditions later in the year, supporting vegetation unique in that it consists of both arctic and desert-loving plants.

Weeds, really. Davis thinks it looks like the surface of the moon—a chalky cracked desert.

"I just want them," Norna tells him, a rock in each hand.

The Plains remind him of Alaska, where he'd been stationed for the last three years during the Korean War. He watches Norna standing on top of a stacked pile of rocks, arms spread wide like a soaring eagle or hawk, in some ritualistic, sacrificial sort of posture. The soon-to-be endangered prairie smoke gathers at his knees, pink cotton candy in the approaching dusk. He wonders what the cairns mean, if they are Indian memorials, or some kind of direction markers. Years later, he'll ask that question and be told that they have no meaning at all, that it's just a "monkey-see-monkey-do" kind of phenomenon, and that will seem jarringly ironic as well.

"There's a whole beach here comprised of fossil rock, did you know that?" she asks him. "Why so many in one spot do you suppose?"

Davis has no idea, and can't imagine living on this island. What did he have in common with people like these, he wonders? The island will draw a few influential people, but for the most part the inhabitants will seem largely unremarkable. Yet frighteningly impervious. The kind who, years ago, had actually bussed their children over the frozen ice to school in DeTour. What kind of people do something like that? He will think every time he crosses on the ferry how interesting it is that they made you pay to ride over, but they let you off for free.

Yet he'll come. Soon he'll belong to the Lions Club, golf on occasion with a few of the other retirees, join the snowmobile club, though he'll never quite understand the cold metal, the whine of the engine screaming its misplaced frozen horsepower. He'll feel like some kind of mechanical cowboy one shadowy night when he and the rest of the club race around great herds of deer the sportsmen feed on the south beach in winter. It will be an absurd and ghostly roundup, the deer fanning out in random groups of panic, some forced out onto the ice, heading, seemingly, toward mainland, others breaking wildly inland, hooves clattering in a thunderous crescendo, the moon a chunk of gleaming ice overhead. "Refracted terror," is how Norna will describe the event when he tells her about it.

"Are you happy here?" Sally asks him.

"Yes," he'll answer. "It was Norna who wanted to come here, but it's me who is happy here."

And he'll walk that fossil beach one day with Norna, his feet crunching over the echoes of remaining life forms. He'll think about mistakes and wonder, when it's all said and done, if they could ever be viewed so simply. What hope would he have, after all, without the mistakes?

"Do you believe in a defining moment?" he'll ask Norna, pointing at a stone he'll hold in slippery fingers. "A moment that hardens your life into an impression like that forever?"

"Maybe," she'll answer. "But then, it would necessitate standing still, wouldn't it. For a very long time?"

But these thoughts of indentation and immutability come much later. For now, and for the next five years, they will be merely visitors, he and Norna, and each time, she'll abscond with at least thirty pieces of stone. Stone that has nothing whatever to do with the art mediums she'll later work in. No thought yet of carving and shaping it; she has not yet learned "how to walk" as the sculptors say. She knows only about dreaming so far. She appears so light and ethereal, he is sure that at any moment the wind will lift her from her perch on the rock. He has the odd notion that for Norna, the rocks serve as emotional paperweights, a grounding that even the eight months of her advancing pregnancy cannot afford her.

"I want them," she says again, because it's still 1954 and for now he's suspended in this cairn field.

"For God's sake," he answers. "Don't you think I can get you all the rocks you could possibly ever want?" And then he says, "You married me for my rocks, and now they're not good enough for you, is that it?" He's kidding and he smiles, but he sees a guilty, sideways look cross her face.

"As long as your rocks are good enough for you, I guess that's what matters," she says, and now she's smiling back at him. He holds her and lowers his face, sandwiches it between her breasts and the protrusion of her abdomen. Keeps his head there, but turns and looks out across the Plains. It's almost dark now, early June, but off in the distance he can just see the heads of sandhill cranes bobbing slightly above the grasses. In the autumn of years to come, he'll watch them fly overhead in groups like hovering pterodactyls. But tonight, in a matter of moments, they'll disappear into the depths of the alvar fields and into the night.

"Are there bears out here?" she asks.

"Well, if there are, you'd see them coming from a long way, that's for sure . . . well, at least during the daytime."

"I look like a bear," she says. He wonders if his face looks guilty now, though he's not sure why it should. They've been married only six months, but what mattered, what was important, was that he'd asked her before she became pregnant, before they'd even made love, for Christ's sake. That's what matters.

"I love you," he says. "Do you know that?"

Her face is hard to see in the evening light. He's glad he can't see into her eyes as he says these words. Not because he doesn't mean them, but because he just doesn't want to see her eyes.

"If there ever is someone, you should go for it," she says.

"What?"

"What possible point could there be in me stopping you from anything you want to do?"

He grabs her shoulders, off balance at her words, off balance like he feels most days with her now. "So you don't give a shit if I go to bed with anyone I want to? What kind of marriage is that?"

"What possible meaning could there be in a relationship between you and me, if I am standing in the way of your desires."

"Well, for Christ's sake, why did you marry me then?"

She smiles. "For your rocks, of course."

His rocks. He pulls her to him, and tries to picture himself sitting at the desk of Associated Aggregates ten years down the road, and he fails. He can't picture himself with a child, or even with a wife five years down the road, despite the fact that he has one and is about to have the other. Did he feel like this during the war? He doesn't think so, but he isn't sure. Was he capable of imagining the future back then?

What about the past? He remembers it, of course; he isn't fucking crazy. But it seems to belong to someone else, like a story he'd read once.

But the fact is, he will inherit that desk in Oxford, Michigan, once his father dies of that coronary embolism that has loomed over him for years. His mother has been dead since Davis was five, a rare form of bone cancer, so that will leave only Davis. He'll sit there after his father is gone, at the great mahogany desk covered with glass, and wonder why the desk makes him so uncomfortable. Norna will tell him one day, it's the psychic distance of the glass between himself and the texture of the wood that is separating him from his father and even from himself, and she's right in a way, but what he hates most is that he can see his own reflection in it.

Despite this, he'll never remove the glass.

He'll take it as long as he can, approximately five years, and then he'll hand the reins over to his vice president, Leonard Kranston, the man who runs nearly everything anyway, and move to Drummond Island, where Norna thought she wanted to be. But before he does, for those five years, he'll sign purchase orders and pay checks and memoranda until noon each day, the glass desk top hard and cold beneath his hands. And at least once a week during that time, he'll drive down the road to a small gravel pit owned by a friend of his, Jerry Shaw.

Jerry is older than Davis, and had once worked for Davis's father. The first time Davis saw him, he was seated on a boulder, eating a pastrami sandwich, the crack in his rear end showing above soil-covered jeans. Davis would complain about his father to Jerry, and Jerry would shrug, and say, "He's fuckin' aces to me, man."

Jerry's bad eye had kept him out of the war, so he'd purchased his forty acres with a small inheritance, and taken to mining it all by himself. He had no employees and delivered his loads of gravel in a rusty old Peterbilt dump truck. Jerry had an excavator, a loader, and a backhoe, and Davis would sit and watch him load yards of oversize into the Austin-Western jaw-crusher. Or some days he'd just run the roll crusher on the smaller material and rely on the Grizzly to separate out the slightly bigger rocks. There was a shaker, a harp screen, and the sand classifier #1, like a giant strainer lifted from a child's sandbox: one-inch stone and smaller is used for basements; 10-A pea stone is used for septic stone in drain fields; potato stone (the size of potatoes or bigger), is bought by landscapers. Piles of ready-mix concrete sand and yards of mason sand, like small Egyptian pyramids, surround the pit.

On rainy days, Jerry makes road gravel since that is the only thing he can do on wet days; winter he does mechanical work on the trucks and designs new equipment. Business is carried out from Jerry's home, a mile down the road. Jerry travels only the distance from the yard to his house, sends his wife on necessary errands. For years, he'll run the yellow excavator in the pit, displacing the dirt, the layers of clay, much of which is simply discarded, eventually uncovering valuable veins of sandstone and granite.

Now and then, Davis will watch him do his pit run with the big excavator. He'll sit at the top and listen to the crusher grinding and scraping, listen to the engine stutter. And then when Jerry is done, he'll offer him a beer, or sometimes a shot of whiskey. Jerry will wipe the grime off his face, and smile. Talk about how there are all kinds of dirt in this world, and he prefers the kind he can see.

"I've been working the front twenty for the last eighteen years," he'll say to Davis one summer day. "In another two

I'll move to the west ten, then ten years after that, if one of these Goddamn walls doesn't come down on me, I'll do the south ten."

"How can you fucking do this?" Davis will ask him, though something about it fascinates him, "And then what?"

Jerry smiles. "Then, I'll dig myself my own Goddamn grave."

At this point, Jerry's years are all in front of him in designated slices of earth. He'll raise his children in the front twenty, bury his wife in the next twelve. Jerry had been able to afford only limited test-core drilling on the site, so before he can finish the last eight, the vein, like his life, will disappear on him. Layers of ground are called horizons and Jerry's "sky" just dissolves one day into useless overburden. Eventually he'll sell the pit to prospective golf club developers. He'll lose his leg to diabetes and die in a leather chair there in his front room. A chair he bought used the same day he bought the pit. "Ya takes your chances," Jerry will say to him.

And it will turn out that Davis's rocks are indeed not good enough for Norna. At least not exclusively. After she takes up sculpting, she will occasionally buy a chunk of dolomite from the limestone quarry on Drummond Island, but more often, she buys exotic material that must be imported. Sandstone from Spain, travertine or alabaster from Italy. All-white or cream-colored stone. Davis will watch Norna create figures out of clay, watch her use a da Vinci-like pointing machine later to copy the figure into stone. Norna's days will take on the same planned-out quality as Jerry's. Her future is full of mallets and chisels and drill sanders and rasps. Years of vessels followed by approximately the same number of years in wall sculpture. Another few talisman-type years; a couple years of headless human torsos. The thing Norna will work on last, just before she leaves him, looks to Davis like a big chunk of rock. A rock turned into another rock, which, amazingly, only looks larger. And this is the part that will always get him, something he will never understand or be comfortable with, in sculpture or otherwise: the requisite process of removing mass, things becoming less to create something more.

But for now, only one thing has gone missing. They are standing in this cairn field in 1958, and Davis's face is enveloped in the contours of Norna's body. Davis is aware only that he's pushed her into a future she has not envisioned for herself, and that something small yet significant has been lost, something he can't quite put his finger on. The rest eludes him. And will continue to: he will fail to recognize how Norna will simply envision for herself a new future.

But now, Davis pushes away from her body and lights a cigarette. He sits on one of the rocks and tries to imagine it, the rock, sitting in front of the house they would someday build here on the island. Moves it in his mind to different locations. Next to the light pole, out by the edge of the drive, off by the west corner in a flower bed sitting next to a tree. But the rock seems out of place everywhere, or rather, can't be two places at once. It's under his ass, after all.

4. GATHERS NO MOSS

It's under his ass.

1953. His body glistens wet from the dip in his father's quarry pit. He's reclining on a huge boulder that has retained the day's heat, his body cooler against the warm rock. He's looking at the stars and the moon, thinking how there was no such thing as a summer "night" in Alaska. He'd spent the last three years at Shemya Air Force Base at the western tip of the Aleutian Islands. "The Black Pearl," or "the Rock" as they called it, an ideal refueling stop on the Great Circle Route during the Korean War. Most of them who fueled there were "Pole-vaulters," the name they gave for the Reconnaissance Squadron stationed at Eielson, south of Fairbanks, a squadron who flew frequent missions over the north pole. The pilots told him tales of earthquakes through the mainland, and Davis had sworn he could feel the tremors all the way out at Shemya, feel the land tip sideways, threaten to dump him into the sea. For three years, airplane landing lights descended upon him like falling stars in what is certainly an endless night, then lifted off again like great birds running for air speed, the island little more than a momentary touchdown. All of it leaving him rootless, groundless, like the island itself. Three years of keeping fuel logs, occasional trips to Fairbanks or Juneau, endless nights passing into endless days.

He rolls over, pulls Norna's wet body toward his and remembers the first time he saw her. Norna's adopted father worked for the Road Commission and had been murdered by a disgruntled employee, and Davis's father had insisted they all attend the funeral. Norna's mother, stood next to the grave at the interment, wearing a straw bonnet, looking graceful and wilted and flower-like. Norna had stood back, slightly, behind a massive stone memorial, like some unwelcome illegitimate daughter surreptitiously watching her father laid to rest. She had been staring off when their eyes had connected over the stone, and he'd felt that rush of reciprocated lust between them, a feeling like sticking his head out a car window, a car traveling at great speed.

Now, his engagement ring sparkles on Norna's left hand, the rock glimmering in the dark like those landing lights he was used to in Alaska. He pulls her, feels her resistance.

"I want to wait," she tells him.

"Wait for what?" he answers. "What difference will it make, a few more weeks mean nothing. All we really have is this moment, you know. That's all that really belongs to us. If we let it go, it'll be gone. You aren't a virgin anyway."

She smiles at him. She isn't sure about what belongs to her, she tells him, whether a moment lost is lost or simply preserved. She does know her love for him has nothing to do with time one way or another. Her smile is tender, and she puts her mouth against his, her breasts showing full against the soaking T-shirt. "I like the future and the past because they make the present stay put, right where it belongs."

Her reluctance, he will find, has nothing to do with the past, the present, or the future. Or with whether or not she loves him. In fact, there is nothing extenuating or complicated about it. Nothing that fills her mind with dire repercussions. He will understand soon that she simply prefers to wait, like she likes the color red over the color green, or apricots over oranges.

He pulls her wet shorts and panties off, his hand between her clenched thighs.

"I just want to wait," she says again, giving him one more chance at it.

"You're everything I could ever want," he tells her. And then he doesn't talk anymore. He doesn't have to because he feels her body relax under his hands. This will puzzle him for the rest of his life. Norna got her way when she wanted it. He'll never understand why she relented.

He starts to pull her off the rock onto the soft ground, but she says no, it has to be here, and he puts his hands under her hips in an effort to shield her body from the hardness of the rock, the knuckles on his hands and his knees scraping raw with the motion of his body. She moves his hands from beneath her thighs and he tries again to move her into the sand, but she holds to the sides of the rock, clings to it, her back arched. Their bodies fit together despite the rock, her body compliant somehow, not rigid as he expects. He has the odd thought that she's protecting him from the rock, but only partially. He thinks he hears her whisper that she loves him and when he comes, it seems nothing compared to the exquisite pain of the rock shredding the tissue of his bloody knees. And then he stops moving, Norna as still as death beneath the weight of his body. And for some inexplicable reason he thinks of the future, gets a glimpse of it for a moment, an image like old movies flipping through a projector. He sees flashes of limestone bedrocks, and cairn fields and sculptures and fossils. And then it's gone, his future, as if he had never had one. As if this is the last moment of his life. And so he does the next thing, a thing he will become used to doing through the years. He searches for the past. What was it Norna had said to him a few moments before? There was something.

He struggles, overturning rocks in his mind but under each is an empty hole. He looks up into the moonlight, expecting to see Norna's face turned from him, but it isn't. Instead the moon shines full across her countenance. What is it he sees there? Disappointment, resignation, validation, love, pity?

Something he can't put a finger on.

And his mind races on in a blur. He knows there is something of significance that has just happened to him, some chance he might have taken, some suggestion he might have heeded, some impression of himself he'd had that is already missing. Who had he been ten minutes ago? He looks again into Norna's eyes, which reflect bits of stony light and he feels his body flush. There is a stirring of recollection, a hint of familiar ground he'd once covered, an echo of the past, some memory of a past when he still possessed a future.

Isn't there?

There must be something there, he's sure. But for the life of him, he can't put his finger on it.

AISSA

GENITALS

Genitals: The organs of reproduction in animals, especially the external sex organs.
—*American Heritage Science Dictionary*

Third week after conception marks the beginning of the embryonic period. This is when the baby's brain, spinal cord, heart, and other organs begin to form. The embryo is now made of three layers. The top layer—the ectoderm—will give rise to the baby's outermost layer of skin, central and peripheral nervous systems, eyes, inner ear, and many connective tissues. Baby's heart and a primitive circulatory system will form in the middle layer of cells—the mesoderm. This layer of cells will also serve as the foundation for baby's bones, muscles, kidneys, and much of the reproductive system. The inner layer of cells—the endoderm—will become a simple tube lined with mucous membranes. Baby's lungs, intestines, and bladder will develop here. By the end of this week, baby is likely about the size of the tip of a pen.

1981

The bathroom stall at work, Aissa remembers, was green with several long diagonal scratches down one side. She has propped herself, hands on each side of it, bent over the toilet in endless heaves that mostly produced phlegm then reduce to the dry heaves. She hears someone else enter the bathroom and she covers her mouth to stifle the noise, unwilling to answer questions, but they come anyway: You okay? You've been in here a while. Doris, executive assistant to the owner, while she, Aissa, is his executive secretary.

Sure, something I ate, Aissa responds. The nausea should have been related to the fact she isn't yet writing and is instead fetching coffee for an egotistical, tyrannical construction contractor.

But it isn't.

Over the last month, she had become so exhausted she went home each evening at five p.m., pressed her clothes for the next day, then whisked eggs she picked at before going immediately to bed, only to repeat the day again, over and over, endlessly. Weekends she slept away.

Take a leave of absence, her shrink tells her, until you can make sense of things, a couple weeks at least. She'd never seen a shrink before in her twenty-six short years, and can't believe the guy says nothing as she outlines her predicament. She'd explain the situation. How do you feel about that, he'd respond as if she had years ahead of her to waste on cognitive therapy. As if somehow this circumstance could be tied to an abusive childhood or poor nutrition and once the cause was determined, it would disappear as if it all never happened. Shrinks, she will come to discover, are parasitic, useless people, having gone into their professions because they themselves struggled with abusive childhoods, eating disorders, bi-polar disorder and the like. Which may make them more qualified, not less, and even deserving of her compassion, but Aissa doesn't care. They are trained to say nothing and/or to play devil's advocate, and she spends the little time she has to decide the future course of her life, analyzing *him*. She'd just told him, yet again, the circumstances that had led to her present predicament and he had just, again, said: What do you think about that? Without providing a bit of useful information, giving her things to think about. Nothing.

She leans over his brown leather chair and pukes violently on his faux Persian rug.

Fetal development four weeks after conception:

Growth is rapid this week. Just four weeks after conception, the neural tube along baby's back is closing and baby's heart is pumping blood. Basic facial features will begin to appear, including passageways that will make up the inner ear and arches that will contribute to the jaw. Baby's body begins to take on a C-shaped curvature. Small buds will soon become arms and legs.

Aissa is caretaking her best friend from high school.

They are both sixty-two now and there is no one else, so Aissa has brought Eva to the Little Two Hearted to care for her.

Aissa has spent a lot of the time the past few days hauling and splitting wood to leave Eva alone with her thoughts. Eva tries not to let her eyes rest on her chest as Aissa aids her in changing her bandage. Aissa tries to ignore the ravages of radical mastectomy which they rarely perform anymore, but upon which Eva had insisted, a look like someone had scraped a pebble off her chest with a machete. It is a description Aissa had once told Eva about her own mother's chest, the damage extending into her armpit and slightly down her left side, red and angry and so final.

Funny things, breasts.

They'd once felt like they were full of knots or pebbles or jaw-breakers, large and alien to her in some ways.

It doesn't hurt, Eva assures Aissa. And they turn up the radio—the Tigers game Eva loves—while Aissa makes her cups of tea and late lunches of oven-browned shredded wheat covered with butter and half and half, something Eva would eat, followed by the inevitable cigarette smoked in an elegant manner, her legs crossed, as if she was an old-time movie-star like Marlene Dietrich or Gloria Swanson.

Norna's voice floats back to Aissa through the years: I don't care what they say, she had announced to Aissa. It's a collection of cells, nothing more.

> *Seven weeks into your pregnancy, or five weeks after conception, baby's brain and face are rapidly developing. Tiny nostrils become visible, and the eye lenses begin to form. The arm buds that sprouted last week now take on the shape of paddles. By the end of this week, baby might be a little bigger than the top of a pencil eraser.*

Eva tells Aissa that when was thirty-five years old and childless, her husband George had said to her, You know, it's the same as being seventy years old, you know that. If you're seventy years old, you think you don't have much time left, but the truth is you might have thirty years left, while the five-year-old child sitting beside you might be dead tomorrow. It's exactly like that, you know. Nobody knows.

Aissa is aware that George is right, but reality has never mattered as much to her as potential, possibilities.

My daughter, Jane, says time doesn't matter, Aissa tells her. George is right.

> *Eight weeks into pregnancy, or six weeks after conception, baby's arms and legs are growing longer, and fingers have begun to form. The shell-shaped parts of baby's ears also are forming, and baby's eyes are visible. The upper lip and nose have formed. The trunk of baby's body is beginning to straighten.*

> *By the end of this week, baby might be about a half inch (thirteen millimeters) long.*

Last days of elementary school, Drummond Island, where Aissa's parents had lived for four years. She is eight and it is the day of the school carnival where she'd played ring toss and pin the tail on the donkey and a toss-form of tick-tack-toe. Balloons made by a clown into the shape of a donkey and a wiener-dog bobble and squeak as she cringes. She stumbles upon a tee-pee-looking tent setup in the gym: a gypsy fortune-teller. When it is her turn to enter, and after she awards the woman the two tickets it takes to see her, she notices the scarf around the woman's head, the big hoop earrings, rings on all her fingers, the long red and orange and blue skirt, but most of all she notices the breasts, ponderous, mountainous, intrusive breasts with colorful beads dripping off them, the shelf of them forcing the beads to drop and hang suspended in the air over the table which hold tarot cards. The gypsy, who says her name is Madame Zelda has a large snow globe sitting on the table covered with a clashing paisley tablecloth which makes Aissa slightly nauseous. But she's excited, too, because she wants to know what her future holds for her. She imagines, even at her young years, that this will be a fun thing to do, that the woman will tell her about her science grade coming up, about how many boyfriends she'll have in her lifetime, about where all she might live, what her future career will be.

How many children she will have one day.

But none of those things happen.

The woman shuffles the cards, then spreads them out like she's playing solitaire, not commenting as she goes, which Aissa will later learn is more the norm, and when she is finished, she simply looks at Aissa for what seems five long minutes and says nothing. Then she speaks.

I have only one thing to say to you and it is this: you are a very headstrong and stubborn and arbitrary child. I can promise you that if you do not change your ways and your attitude that the future will be a very hard one for you; it will not be a prosperous or happy one for someone like you.

She stops speaking.

Aissa feels the room spin, the colors in the fabrics run together and she is struck motionless in her seat. She doesn't vomit, though, and when it passes, she sits and stares at the woman. Who is she? Aissa is eight, but she knows this woman is no real gypsy. She studies her features and her breasts, the way they heave and seem to have a life of their own, notices a smell that wafts off her that later she'll think reminds her of mushrooms, moldering and sort of festering. She isn't a teacher, not the principal (Aissa has never once been in trouble in school and is a good student), she's not a friend of her mother's—something like this was not Norna's style. She would never have told this woman to say this.

Aissa doesn't ask if that is it, and at last rises from her folding chair and exits the tent. For the rest of her life, she'll try to imagine what kind of person curses an eight-year-old child in an elementary school carnival.

Aissa is thirteen years old and walking down Maxton Plains Road the quarter mile necessary to catch the school bus. It's six thirty a.m. on a Monday morning in mid-September, and she's wearing a new miniskirt with fishnet stockings, and even though it's hot still, she's wearing her new short wool matching jacket, knowing she'll be perspiring the entire day. She's walking the left side of the country road when a blue pickup truck approaches her and stops next to her, rolls down the passenger window. She assumes he wants directions. Later, she'll describe his body part as a wobbly sort of balloon like that circus clown would use to make a dachshund instead of a donkey, wobbly because his hand is moving so rapidly to form the body of the dog. She rolls her eyes and walks on to the bus stop. As she's waiting with the other children, she sees him drive by, staring at her.

In the ninth week of pregnancy, or seven weeks after conception, baby's arms grow, develop bones, and bend at the elbows. Toes form, and baby's eyelids and ears continue developing.

By the end of this week, baby might be about three-quarters of an inch (twenty millimeters) long.

Aissa keeps Eva's mind off things. Eva tells Aissa over coffee and English muffin bread: I asked them in the hospital what they did with my breast. They looked shocked when I told them I wanted to keep it, that the Native Americans made very nice coin purses out of them.

Aissa, who has grown somehow both wide and thin at the same time, smiles at Eva and tells her that story reminds her of something her mother Norna might have said, Norna who had gone through the same loss of body parts.

My daughter, Jane, raised horses, she reminds Eva, who nods. I was visiting once when the vet arrived to geld the yearlings, she tells Eva. And Aissa recalls to her the morning of butchering out in the south pasture, all performed with a mild general anesthesia—a procedure they claimed was fast and relatively painless recovery-wise, something Aissa tells Eva she has her doubts regarding. They would slit the sac, pull out the testicles until they looked like stretched-out, partially inflated balloons (again), and attach an electric power drill, which spun them until they thinned and detached, something that caused little blood.

Aissa recalls for Eva the red orbs of flesh lined up on the ground, which hadn't been there long before Jane's dog, Hank, had indulged in a late morning snack.

Yes, Eva, responds. The very least they could have done was thrown it to the dogs.

It's cold in the front room, and Aissa wraps Eva's shawl around her, pressing her hands to her shoulders and across her chest for a moment in a gesture they both know can only replace so much.

She was sixteen.

Aissa is blown away by his modesty and the sheer force of his energy, and that absolute quiet that could explode like compressed steam. He seems at times like someone she doesn't know, reckless, even brutal, but when he kisses her finally, his lips tremble. He kisses her every chance he gets in any place they can manage, buried in mountains of maple leaves that covered her front lawn, shoved up against cold refrigerators, under the Ping-Pong table, up against the massive box-stall door of her horse barn.

They start taking drives along back roads in his mother's green Chevy Malibu. Because other trucks or jeeps would slow down past their parked car and the drunken inhabitants would holler "Get some for me," he finds places even more remote, driving through brush-covered two-tracks until they come one day to a clearing with a large willow tree hanging over a small pond. His mother complains. The weeds in the bumper are making her suspicious, he tells her. But she knows it isn't that. It's the desire that pours out of their skins, mixed with the guilty sweat and the smell of stale smoke from the cigarette butts his mother leaves in the ashtray (and occasionally, if it is hot enough, the water from the creek bed). Aissa knows that all this moisture between them had condensed on the steaming windows and that it had run down, like fermented cider, into the slots in the doors or the seams of the long shiny vinyl seats. She knows his mother can smell it as soon as she opens the car door, if not before. That the evidence of his hands traveling slowly over her body quicker and quicker until it flowed like the wide river in front of them is apparent to her and everyone. Still, this touching was all that she allows between them. Then. It was enough; he didn't need more than that.

Of course it turned out he did.

If she wasn't keeping her man "happy," it was understood that "somebody" would.

Years pass.

Three years later, her best friend Ann calls to tell her someone had seen him with another girl in the parking lot of the Quick-Mart, sitting in her father's truck, drinking beer and smoking cigarettes. The next day, Ann phones to say rumor had it that Dawn thought she "might be pregnant" and that he was the father, which Aissa knows didn't happened all in one day. It turns out she isn't pregnant, but Aissa had silently gone her own way without once ever confronting him.

They drift away from each other for ten long years and when they come together again it is the pent-up explosive years of abstinence from one another—built up in *her* mind at least—that accounts for her lapse.

She, Aissa, had been uncharacteristically *unprepared.*

And, it turned out, he *still* had someone else—

> *By the tenth week of pregnancy, or eight weeks after conception, baby's head has become more round. The neck begins to develop, and baby's eyelids begin to close to protect his or her developing eyes.*

There is no reason for her to talk to Eva about most of this since Aissa has told her about all of it throughout the years. And they don't talk about whether the surgery and chemotherapy would be successful, nor do they talk about the emotional aspects of losing intimate body parts after being understandably attached to them. So they talk about college years, some of which they'd spent together at Oral Roberts University. They talk about Aissa's irreverence there and Eva's striking beauty, Eva's husband George, who had died several years back, and Aissa's feelings about her husband Sam and her years with him. They don't talk about Eva's childlessness. And they don't talk about the one thing Aissa has never shared with anyone and never will:

Aissa's mother had had a friend named Iris, who looked like a peony to Aissa. She wasn't elegant and slender and delicate, but squatty and plebian and abundantly plain. Aissa had been home alone when Iris had arrived and when Aissa informed her Norna would be back later, Iris, who had never liked her, said, You'll be a horrible mother, you know. And then Iris had walked out.

> At the beginning of the eleventh week of pregnancy, or the ninth week after conception, your baby's head still makes up about half of its length. However, your baby's body is about to catch up, growing rapidly in the coming weeks.

> Your baby is now officially described as a fetus. This week your baby's eyes are widely separated, the eyelids fused, and the ears low set. Red blood cells are beginning to form in your baby's liver. By the end of this week, your baby's external genitalia will start developing into a penis or clitoris and labia majora.

> By now your baby might measure about two inches (fifty millimeters) long from crown to rump and weigh almost one-third ounce (eight grams).

Aissa has a lovely patch of woods behind the camp. It's filled with white, red, and jack pine; maples; and poplar.

It's a hundred yards behind the work shed and the graves of her mother's four dogs dot the landscape. Eva and Aissa walk along the path silently. Aissa is carrying a shovel and a pouch of tobacco her mother Norna had once given her, and a portion of their lunch meal. When it seems right, Aissa stops and digs a hole three feet long, two feet wide, and two feet deep. Eva is carrying the red blanket and when Aissa is done digging she opens it for a moment and looks at everything inside. The small yellow romper and the rattle; the picture of Iris Aissa had found in her mother's trunk right after Norna had died; a picture of Norna and her father, her father looking bigger than life and grand and imposing and proud to have a lovely woman like his wife on his arm; and the picture of herself taken that summer, the rust-colored blouse covering the slight pouch that had become her abdomen; and the picture of *him*, of course. Someone had shot it of them sitting at a picnic table that summer, their heads leaning companionably together. They each had a beer in their hands.

Now Aissa wraps them all back together, lays them in the ground along with a gardenia, her mother Norna's favorite flower. Eva throws in her "pouch," having decided not to make a coin purse out of it and not to throw it to Maggie, Aissa's two-year old dog. Eva watches as Aissa covers the ground. They put the tobacco and the portion of their meals next to it and stand in silence for five long minutes before turning and walking back to the camp.

NORNA BRIEFLY

NORNA'S HOUSE

Limited by space, a frog in a well cannot
Understand what is an ocean;
Limited by time, an insect in summer cannot
Understand what is ice.
—*Chuangtzu, The Tao of Architecture*

They will wonder during the inevitable forensics, pointing fingers in their minds, if it had been the proper balance of form and function, or whether the process had broken down, each of them accusatory, each of them suspicious of the other. Or perhaps it had been Drummond Island herself—in an angry indignant tirade over their presumptive hubris, who tore the whole thing down, who ripped at not only their hearts—yes, obviously it was their hearts that had been ripped from them—but more than that, before it was said and done: even the generosity of their good (or bad) intentions would lie in the dust.

They had become, once again, insignificant particles on that fossil ledge overlooking the North Channel.

They came together the first time over the blueprints Davis asked Forrest to draft. They sat in the construction trailer, the three of them, on an unseasonably warm day in June of 1967, and watched as that unnaturally sterile bleached-white beach seemed to waver in the heat like some distant dessert oasis, despite the great water that slapped against the rocky shoreline.

There wasn't enough water to quench this alvar substrate and it seemed the woman knew it.

Norna's eleven-year old daughter, Aissa, sits in the chair next to her, and plays with a tendril of her mother's blonde hair which falls in short, haphazard golden waves, somehow sterile and untouched like the beach they can see out the windows. They would need air conditioning and a generator out here soon, at least by late June. Forrest's gaze is fixed upon the beads of perspiration gathering on Norna's boyish chest while Norna gazes out the window, her colorless eyes reflecting the green water one minute, the white sand the next. Somehow, Forrest will miss the disconnect. Norna looks up at Forrest occasionally which makes him shift in his chair like a naked child. She somehow seems fleshless, like so much electrical current, a force of energy. Did she even speak that day? It can't be said with certainty that she did, not even to her small daughter who looked so like her father and seemed as perplexed as Forrest was by the negative space surrounding her mother. That negative space, as in all design, completed her.

If she had spoken, her voice would have wavered in the air like a chord from a plucked harp.

"I believe in design," Forrest says now. "Like some people believe in Santa Claus."

Simple, hollow structures floating through white space with nothing to ground them. Certainly nothing that could possibly hope to contain them and though Davis appears skeptical about "belief" in design, he does express a confidence in structure, foundations.

"Are we on budget?" Davis asks, the next time they meet.

"Close," Forrest answers, smiling. "When has a project ever been on budget?"

Davis smiles.

"You're a builder," Forrest says. "You probably didn't need my services at all—that would have kept your costs down."

Davis has done well for himself, owning a fairly large resort on the other side of the island that had been popular with rich tourists from Detroit and Chicago.

They look at the plans, the three of them. Forrest shows them elevations, floor plans, describes orientation and aperture views. Though Forrest's work shows a familiar influence of Frank Lloyd Wright in the way in which the house will become one with the landscape, he will not be the last one to be influenced on the island; Fay-Jones will someday continue the nod and do much Wright-like work here as well.

It's as if Forrest can feel it, aligns himself with it. They all agree that in order for the house to become Wrightian, "one with the landscape," it will take enormous limestone members along with steel, and Davis says he has connections with the dolomite quarry on Drummond and will special order. His face lights up at the description of the foundation and the strength of the framing members.

"It'll stand forever," he says, but he nods for Forrest to go on, to continue his description of the dream. "Go on, go on."

Steel was one thing, limestone something else.

Forrest explains that despite the massive materials Davis insists upon, that there will be large expanses of glass through which the outside world will be invited, this to the point the steel and limestone will fade into the background, become nearly nonexistent, providing foundation for what really matters: that view of the world, of the heavens. That limitless horizon that one can gaze upon forever.

A place from which you can watch.

And it isn't long before the house begins to personify the woman herself.

"It'll be, in many ways, as if you are perched on the edge of the world," Forrest tells her. It was 1975, after all, and that meant they possessed the technology to build the house so it would hang out over the rocks, over the water, and Norna would be part of it all. The structure was there merely to support the dream, Forrest tells her: that's how structures work. She looks into Forrest's eyes, then, with nothing less than rapture. Forrest promises her it will all happen, that dreams never end, they have that capacity to go on forever, and that was a strength no amount of limestone could replace. Norna seems lit from within. Does she see it too? Does she believe it can happen? Not a single thing has been built, but she can see it all through his eyes. The dream the only reality.

The "dream" gives Davis his only chance to hold her and he needs Forrest to get it done.

Davis nods again for Forrest to continue.

So he describes her studio where she can sculpt her strange figures and objects out of white stone. Unexpectedly, the studio is located on the second floor. The north windows are unobstructed, but those on the east will have electronic shades which can be lowered in the morning, retracted at noon.

This was the best it got: a set of blueprints and all those possibilities.

"Future Home of Davis and Norna Hanson" Forrest had written on the plans.

• ◆ •

Norna refuses to be rushed. Davis accommodatingly disappears for months while Forrest and Norna tinker with the blueprints. The drawings achieve perspective: three-dimensional spatial relationships described on a two-dimensional surface. Lines that converge and recede. The challenge for the drafter: resolve the conflict between what people know of a thing, how they conceive its reality, and the appearance of it.

It is their house, Norna's and Forrest's.

They move walls together, they shift orientation, spend hours staking out rooms on the beach. They sit at the table and look out over a flat sea. She doesn't "confide" in Forrest, but she will talk about the life she might live in their house, an unspoken covenant that it is, indeed, their house.

And she listens. She dreams. Mostly of the sculptures she'll create in that house on the edge of the world. And she'll carve a new life. A different life from the one she's led. A life she can steer and control the way she molds those sculptures.

However, it's only real because it *isn't*.

"Color can blind," says Forrest, quoting Laotzu.

"That's good," says Norna. "I'm color-blind."

"Negativism in color, also according to Laotzu, means that whenever a color contains greyness, it has its intangible content of its opposite, and thus is capable of harmonizing with its opposite, at ease. He says the human organism is created to receive the negative side of nature, receives reflected light better than the light itself."

Norna absorbs the words, becomes one with the design. "To him who regards nothing as persistent, what is important is the 'becoming something,' not the opportunity of remaining as something confronting deterioration."

She swims in Laotzu.

Do they make love? Yes . . . and no. Does it matter?

•◆•

They tried.

There's no question about that. Perhaps his judgment had been poor: perhaps Davis should have hired an architect named "Brick" and not one named "Forrest." Though an architect could never be named "Brick." Forrest had been recommended, highly recommended, having worked with Frank Lloyd Wright.

There was a flaw in the design, even the damned architect would later admit it. That was what caused it.

Davis and Norna had met at her father's funeral in Curtis. He'd gone because he'd had to be in the Upper Peninsula anyway and John Ansgar had been a war buddy of his father's. Davis had gone with his father annually to the U.P. to hunt grouse with John. They had stayed at a camp on the east branch of the Tahquamenon and Davis had found that around John his own father had become accessible; the only good memories he had of him were associated with John. Two days after the funeral, her eyes meeting his over the casket, she had asked him to go dancing. Davis didn't know how to dance, but she stood on his feet and Davis stomped her around the dance floor like a father would his little girl.

"If only you could walk me around like this forever, my feet would never touch the ground."

"I can support you," Davis had said. "No, I'm kidding," she replied. "I don't want support."

But she would later tell him she married him for his "rocks," he being in the gravel business.

Now, they have pored over the blueprints, the three of them, tinkering with the floor plan until it seemed to please her. Norna asks a few times if the design pleases Davis, but the design is out of his realm, a problem that clearly escapes him, which is what has induced him to enlist Forrest's help in the first place.

He'd lose her without him.

"Do you like it?" Davis asks her, waving the plans in her face. This after he'd watched them for weeks adjust site orientation; go over material lists; change from brick to concrete and back to limestone, the only choice for the support members on the façade. After they'd moved the kitchen from the back of the house to the front, reduced the house from five bedrooms to four, shifted Norna's studio upstairs to accommodate the northern light, added another bathroom off the master bedroom. After all that, Davis waves them, the plans, in her face—they are paper, after all, and that seems to startle her. She looks at Davis as if he'd thrown cold water on her in her sleep.

"Yes, maybe so," she says.

He could see she'd been entranced listening to Forrest's words; they dazzled even Davis like they were so many dancing spirits, the words possessing a life of their own the way his mistress Sally Crow had once told Davis they could. The Native Americans said everything breathed life, rocks, trees, water, words, and Davis can see Forrest's words have that effect on Norna. Davis knows that as long as they are talkin' "plans," as long as they are still in that no-man's land of the "possibles," as long as they remain, the three of them, hangin' out in her head, Forrest has the advantage over him. And when Davis waves that paper and the air moves over her face like a Chinese fan, she's seen them, for a moment, for what they are: plain old lines on paper, nothing more.

•◆•

Davis knows Norna and Forrest have spent the last three months gazing out the window of that construction trailer, and for hours on end they'd erected imaginary walls in the rocks and in the sand out front. They'd cooked elaborate and decadent meals of the mind consisting of exotic ingredients obtained from the far reaches of the universe, delicacies that they both knew would escape Davis, delicacies that might excite the taste buds, but could never really satisfy the appetite of the soul. They'd done the same thing with her studio, and finally, inevitably, with her bedroom.

Forrest was an idea, he knew—Norna was a thought.

Davis keeps waving those plans, and they walk the beach, too, that fossil beach, the stones crunching under their shoes, and she'd become aware of Davis, suddenly, as if, again, she'd awakened from a deep sleep.

"I'm sorry, you know," Davis says to her, and she nods.

He grabs her hands in both of his and rubs them together like you would do when someone suffers from hypothermia, and that seems to bring her even more to herself. There is strength in those hands. Norna looks delicate, but it is she who responds to this inhospitable landscape, she who had dragged Davis here those years ago, not against his will; he'd known it was his only hope of holding her. And she is worth it; she is still worth it.

Davis has time.

Eventually, they'd break ground.

The day they poured the foundation footings, she stood on the beach and saw how those footings anchored her in place as if each of her running shoes were filled with concrete. They watch, Davis and Forrest, to see if she'd struggle, try to wrench free, but she doesn't move. She watches each footing as it is poured, as if she is grateful they prevent her from sailing off into the heavens, and Davis smiles. Next, they pour the concrete flooring she had preferred over wood and as the steel support columns go up, and the limestone façade is lifted into place, they watch her face which looks as enraptured as it had the day Forrest first told her about the dream.

Forrest knows he is in trouble.

Davis puts in the plumbing pipes from which the water pours, electricity which lights her way. Davis builds her a real kitchen in which she can cook food you can smell, food you can smear all over your face, or roll around in on the rock floor if you're of a mind to, and Davis builds four bedrooms, two bathrooms with bronze fixtures from the Sears catalogue, and her studio, which yes, has those windows, but also has walls and a floor, and the day they carry in the sink and her first pieces of alabaster quartz—along with a chunk of her limestone, it is she who smiles. The bedroom is not made of heavenly clouds, but the headboard is fashioned from copper, copper mined out of the ground from the Keweenaw Peninsula, real men scraping ore from the earth, at times crawling on their bellies like humanoid snakes, that's how brightly that copper shines from their labor. They clawed through those mines like Norna and Davis clawed at one another, scraping through layers of flesh until they'd grown hard and lined from the scraping.

The bed has steel side frames manufactured from the sweat of more real men, and the mattress is firm and real under their backsides, like the rock they'd first made love on. The day they move the bed in, even though they are a long way from moving in permanently, she reaches for Davis, even pulls him on top of her, and they move in time to the wind blowing through the eaves.

Finally, they finish Norna's daughter's room. Soon they will move in Aissa's furniture and her clothes and her phonograph and her radio and her ice skates and her books and her writing journals and her tennis rackets and her tap dancing shoes and her report cards and her track medals.

They'd soon move it all in.

• ◆ •

The woman is not unlike the island herself, especially the North Channel, the Maxton Plains and the Fossil Ledges. Drummond Island supports a fragile ecosystem, has a delicate skin upon which little will thrive, yet she is brutally rugged underneath that skin. She isn't lush and full and attractive to tourists, yet she possesses a sort of dangerous beauty that holds a fatal charm for some. The starkness of her is surrounded by Lake Huron to the south and east, the Sturgeon and Potagannissing Bays to the West and the North Channel to the north.

There is a kinship between Drummond and the channel and a kinship with the woman, and this escapes the two men that first day as they three sat hunched over that set of blueprints. The woman spent most of the time looking out the window at the ledges and the channel, not even speaking to the young child beside her, but there was no question that the "plan" pleased her. Despite her expectations, it pleased her. She responded to its air-like quality, its noninvasiveness, its benignity. She liked the wispy lines on the drawing, the way they floated and seduced her in her mind. The architect had a way of communicating that design that pulled her out of that trailer and up into the air.

His words had power.

They seemed charming and innocuous.

She could be safe within those lines, float there forever, and nothing could hurt her again. She'd nearly been complete within them.

She had never before seen a design so perfect, but it was hearing him describe it in words that gave it a life of its own. Without the words, the lines would fade slightly, and seeing this, the architect would talk faster, and not just faster but more eloquently until the lines and the words lifted her out of the trailer and she seemed to be hovering there—though the lines, wispy as they were, kept her from sailing.

She has hovered for months.

But this day is different. It's the first day she realizes the plan needs adjustment—the kitchen is in the wrong place, the orientation of the house slightly wrong, her studio not quite where she wanted it.

"Dreams are just that," she says.

"We'll tweak it," the architect says to the woman. The lines seem heavier somehow, more permanent, and she seems to lose her ability to float.

"Do you like it?" the woman asks her husband. He seems to respond to the architect's words as well.

"It'll stand forever," he says, waving the blueprints in her face as if to cool her off.

"I'm sorry, you know," he says when she doesn't respond.

They break ground. Her husband knows how to build this house, even does some of the work himself, and at first the plan loses none of its beauty for the woman. The limestone and steel members that form the face, that hold in all that precious glass and her vision on the world, seem right somehow.

She catches his eye.

But then they start the finishes: window trim, cabinets, fixtures, sinks and toilets, and with each addition, the woman grows slightly tired. The architect talks faster, the builder builds more furiously, but the woman gets tireder and tireder. It seems the house will suck every bit of life from her. Drummond, the North Channel and the fossil ledges, the Alvar Plains all begin to churn somehow and become one with the wind, and the churning fills the woman with its own energy.

Incredibly, the woman notices a design flaw the architect has missed, a steel girder that seems to span slightly too far for stability, and she notices, too, a slight but substantial crack in the foundation; she says nothing.

The talking and building goes on and she allows it because there is no stopping it now. *She cannot deny the house because it has become her—alive with every flaw.*

It can't exist in her head and it can't exist on the ground.

And so she waits for the storm.

She watches as the movers move in all her possessions. Her furniture, her clothes, her sculpture and art materials, her pots and pans, and she watches as they move in her daughter's belongings and her husband's. She sits on the couch and watches all things of her life pass by her as if they are someone else's. It's July and the windows are open, those that do open or slide, and there is a thick humidity in the air, a pulsing quiet that fills her to the top of her head, and down the lengths of her hair so that she feels like a picture a child might draw of the sun. The horizon is orange, has taken on a warm tone, no longer the cool white and blue/green it has been almost constantly since they started this project.

As the movers work away the afternoon, the storm brews; the channel now a frothy gray, the wind whipping papers off her husband's desk, swirling them around the room. He closes a window or two, but she insists the rest remain open. She walks the beach for a while, feeling the intensity build, looks back toward the house and sees for a moment, for half a second, inside the shell that is her.

An essence that could never support an edifice like this. Whatever made her think she could belong here?

She looks away. The fossils crunch under her feet, centuries of bodies holding her to earth, but the sky swirls overhead, threatening to lift her off her feet, and she feels stretched like an elastic band, like she's now hundreds of feet tall and yet made of nothing.

She returns to the house when it starts to rain in earnest.

The movers are nearly done. Her husband hands them a check. The architect is here for their big day. He and her husband walk out front despite the rain, to look back together. She wonders if they can see her through the glass. The woman watches them and thinks of Laotzu.

"To him who regards nothing as persistent, what is important is the 'becoming something,' not the opportunity of remaining as something confronting deterioration."

Things are only process, she thinks.

The wind howls and she feels that first shift of the great foundation, starting, she knows, at that crack—that cleft in the limestone that had been there from the day they started building the house, a crack she had known in her heart was there all along.

Had it been laid into the concrete? Or was it inherent all along?

She feels the steel sway from that design flaw, that steel joist too weak to span the distance.

Had it been drawn into the plans?

Drummond Island heaves and tears, but she knows the chasm is coming from inside.

The woman becomes one with the house, the island, and her life.

She watches the horrified looks on their faces through the glass, that glass through which she was to dream. She doesn't move as it all comes down, disintegrates around her into a heap of limestone and glass.

•—◆—•

The woman lies in a coma.

While she has been gone, the architect has drawn beautiful lines accompanied by more and more words. The builder builds on, too, perhaps a bit more competently, but without enthusiasm. They both come to see her for a while, but when she doesn't wake up, they finally lose interest, or hope, or both.

She waits until they give up.

When the woman wakes up, she sees a picture on the wall—a chalky desert of wild lavender and choke weeds that remind her of the Alvar Plains.

JANE

DEATH NOTES

We physicists believe the separation between past,
present, and future is only an illusion, although a
convincing one.
—*Albert Einstein*

Today is a good day to die.
—*Crazy Horse*

George Giltner pushes my body against the wall of his double-wide, hand at my throat. I can see the black hair in his nostrils, which are flared like my mare Hannah's in a high wind.

"What are you doing here?" he asks. "Who asked you?"

"I did," his wife, Shirley, answers from the couch. "George," she says softly. George glances toward her with an expression like ground glass, then it softens to a milky sad glaze as he watches her. He moves away from me for a moment and adjusts the blankets around his wife's legs, checks to see her water glass is filled.

"You think because she's old, it doesn't matter." The man sits down on a chair, the seat partially missing, and I can see his overalls bulge through the hole in the seat of the chair. I know I will think forever about how sad that bulge is.

He puts his head in his hands.

"Get out," the man says. "I see you near this house again, I'll kill you."

"Jane," Shirley Giltner said, "he doesn't mean that."

He means it, I can see that. This isn't the idle threat of a person stressed. George is soon to be a man adrift, and he isn't equipped to grapple with the incomprehensible. He runs a small nursery in Newberry; perhaps if he'd been a full-scale animal farmer instead he might have been able to accept the way things were. Or perhaps the lack of acceptance has nothing to do with life experience; George seems off somehow and I catch a glimpse of him as a child: a stern, silent boy twisting his red hair, the bald space at his crown creeping ever larger, his mother standing off to the side with a worried look on her face.

"Get out," George says again.

◆

Forty-nine-day rituals. Not many Jews observe the Counting of the Omer, a forty-nine-day period of self-reflection and spiritual renewal anymore, but Tibetan Buddhists have burying rituals that last forty-nine days. I'll spend forty-nine days contemplating the end of my marriage someday; I'm soon to get a glimpse, but for now the idea is intriguing.

◆

Helen had a younger sister named Della who was eight, and I knew immediately that Della was ill. I would find out later that Della had leukemia and had been to many doctors until the money ran out.

Della's sister Helen is my new friend from school. We were twelve at the time.

I visited Helen and Della often that summer, picked them both up to visit Jane's horse she boarded in Newberry. I would lift Della up on Hannah's broad buckskin back, waving off Helen's concern about Della riding bare-back.

"She's gentle as a fawn, Helen," I would tell her. "Let her feel the warmth of the animal under her legs."

Helen nodded and we lead the girl slowly down the path and into the woods where we'd walk for hours, Helen and I walking ahead quietly, so that all you could hear was the squawking of a crow or a sandhill crane in the distance, the gentle click and thud of the grasshoppers as they landed on our thighs or into the tall grass, scattering like parting wheat as we walked, and of course, the crunch of the gravel under Hannah's feet, the swish of her tail. Della wrapped Hannah's mane in her hands, and sometimes she'd lay her cheek against the mare's long neck to feel the rhythm of her steps, her eyes closing in pleasure.

"My parents would have heart failure," Helen said once. And I nodded. "What if Della tells them we didn't get ice cream."

"Don't they notice she stinks of horse to high heaven?" I asked.

"No, I throw her in the tub the second I get back," Helen responded.

It had seemed a long summer, Helen and I becoming fast friends without really noticing. But we did notice the child growing weaker until Helen's mother would no longer allow the girls to go off leading Della in the red wagon they used to transport her to the stable—a mile out of town. Not seeing

Hannah seemed to take the life out of Della more than the illness, I thought. But Helen reported that Della would perk up the second Jane arrived.

"How did it happen?" Della asked her once.

"What?" I asked.

"How did you know about the horses, Jane?"

"I rode one once downstate with my dad," I replied. "I knew they took to me, so I saved my money."

The girl nodded and asked a hundred questions about how to care for a horse, the parts of the saddle, the conformation of a horse, what they ate, how long they lived, if horses went to heaven, and over the next week her health declined rapidly with each question. Helen's mother Ann declined as well, the life in her disappearing along with the child's energy.

One day, I walked in as the doctor was leaving and when I saw Della, I knew this would be the day. Ann hovered around the edges of Della's room, tidying things up, dusting, freshening her water glass, while Helen sat by the window and watched the leaves which were starting to fall, listening as a sudden gust blew sand against the siding. Della was sleeping when I arrived, so I sat in the chair by her bed and waited. Finally, the child opened her eyes, and we saw—Della and me—sunflowers, a sea of them, Della kicking a soccer ball before it blurred into a whole fabric of experience the child understood perfectly.

Ann stepped toward me. The woman looked startled and I thought perhaps even Ann had gotten a glimpse, but then it was gone, replaced by terror and grief, and some kind of suspicion that I was somehow responsible for what was about to transpire.

But there was no terror or grief on Della's face, just gratitude.

"Thank you," the small child said.

I think sometimes they see me Kevorkian-like and expect my home to be chock full of equipment like Dr. Death's Thanatron ("death machine," from the Greek thanatos meaning "death"), or the carbon monoxide gas mask he called the Mercitron ("mercy machine"). Kevorkian was strange, but not as strange as they want you to think and there were much more interesting things about him than his assisted suicides; mostly he was funny. His *The Kevorkian Suite: A Very Still Life* was a 1997 limited-release CD of five thousand copies from the *Lucid Subjazz* label that featured Kevorkian on the flute and organ playing his own works with the Morpheus Quintet. *Entertainment Weekly* called him "weird" but "good natured." He was also an oil painter. He sometimes painted with his own blood and he painted one picture of a child eating the flesh off a corpse; I'm guessing he made some money from those.

●◆●

A man had had a bad car accident and I gathered next to the car along with a large group of townspeople, the movie theater having just let out. Car accidents were uncommon in Newberry, but this one would later be blamed on brake failure and driver error as Tom Jensen had begun down the hill much too fast. They pulled Tom from the car which had crashed into a telephone pole (Tom trying to avoid hitting a young girl who had started across the street) because they were concerned the engine was going to blow. The steering wheel seemed to have crushed the man's lungs and there was blood in the corner of his mouth, but he appeared fully conscious. He seemed unaware of the people who had summoned help and who were trying to make him more comfortable, until I squatted next to him.

"What is it?" he asked me as he looked into my eyes. "What am I seeing?"

"I don't know," I whispered. "I think of it as kind of a glimpse, I guess."

The people standing around asked each other if they had any idea what we two were talking about. They looked uneasy and said that Tom must have been hallucinating, though they watched me warily.

Since time was not linear in the glimpses, not sequential, and since there were so many possibilities to it, I never bothered looking either direction much.

"It's nice," he said to me. He seemed to be turning his head slightly each direction as he looked into my eyes. The crowd watched him search my eyes. "It's a gift," he said. And while I hadn't been sure of that at first, I had, in fact, come to think of it as a gift, or as an aberrant kind of accomplishment, like standing on the seat of your bicycle or juggling gourds.

"Don't leave," he said, and I assured him I wouldn't.

The crowd shook their heads, and after Tom died, they asked me if I had been humoring him.

"Of course not," I'd answered, and walked away.

This was the second time I'd been present when someone died.

They talked about me after that.

Paradoxically, some asked for me and though I didn't want to, I always went.

● ◆ ●

Time is irrelevant.

I didn't know what the glimpses were back then, would never really understand them in a way they could be articulated, but they stopped surprising me. They didn't necessarily reveal the truth about the human condition, nor did they disprove anything about spirituality. It was simply part of the way things were, a reality I was somehow aware of, that others couldn't see without me. It was a glimpse of the fabric and each glimpser made of it what they would. Sometimes they were alternate possibilities that paradoxically seemed part of a whole.

I'd see someone's past, maybe a birth, parts of a childhood superimposed on the present, but I also saw the future, almost as if someone had taken a huge brush and smeared them all together so they ran into a continuous whole. If a person was dying, they, too, would see. I would turn my head one way and see a blurry past, the other way and see the future. More confusing yet, there seemed to be different migrations, other worlds. I knew the dying could see them, too.

They usually smiled.

Sometimes I can't see the glimpse myself, but the dying person always can. And though I can see that these glimpses take away the fear from the dying, and though I know with certainty that death, as a state of being, or as a point in time, has been diminished by this reality, it still hasn't, somehow, removed all fear for me. I'm not sure if it is still death I fear or the glimpses themselves or the reaction I get from others, but something still makes me uneasy.

Perhaps it is simply because they expect me to have all the answers, those who survive, and I don't have answers.

I see George leave for the nursery a few weeks after our encounter, so I stop in to see Shirley. She looks the white-gray color of unprinted newspaper somehow, a thought that arrives to me partly because her skin seems nearly like paper, maybe tissue or crepe paper, as if it might shred away at the slightest touch of a hand, but her eyes blaze with life still—and gratitude for the fact that I'd consider again stepping foot inside her home after George had threatened me.

"It's perfect timing," she says. "The visiting nurse won't arrive for forty-five minutes yet." She motions to the stove. "George left me some tea simmering. Get us each a cup. Cupboard above the stove."

I take down two green paisley cups and pour what appears to be green tea into them. I hand her a cup and notice she has beautiful hands still, her nails remarkably pink, though ridged and pitted. She takes a couple sips and watches my face as I sip mine. I'd known Shirley a long time. She'd come, sometimes, to chat with Norna and she'd seem interested in me, asking about my horses or what I liked in school.

"George's special tonic—green tea and some concoction of other herbs he refuses to disclose," she says now. I nod.

"You know," she says, "I saw you, your mother and your grandmother once at the vet with a very black dog. The dog had pinned the vet and his staff in the back room, I think."

"Yes," I tell her. "Norna made the mistake of leaving us with the dog for a few minutes while she ran across the street for hotcakes."

"What I thought as I watched the three of you was how alike you all were."

I shake my head. "My mother was dark headed and thought she had nothing at all in common with Norna and me—wild creatures she thought we were."

"Oh, no," Shirley says. "No. You were so alike."

I look around the room. There is a picture of a young girl in her teens on the coffee table with straight center-parted brown hair and eyes that look eternal somehow, and when I enquire if she's a grandchild, Shirley shakes her head.

"Miriam," she says. "Our daughter."

"She does look like you," I say. "I never met her?"

Shirley smiles. "Your grandmother did. Miriam went downstate to Kalamazoo to go to college. Her freshman year she was murdered next to a small stream in a remote area several miles from campus." Shirley seems content with my calm acceptance of this news and my careful nod, so she continues. "Apparently, she had become secretly pregnant, and George always suspected the child's father, though they couldn't ever find evidence or be sure if she'd been sexually assaulted even. She'd gone missing for almost a month when they found her. She'd decomposed and had what they called a 'coffin birth' where the mother expels the child—probably from the body's own gases and breakdown of tissues—but essentially, Miriam's corpse gave birth to her dead child. The birth had either recently transpired or the animals had respected the child's body. It about drove George out of his mind. I know this sounds strange, dear, but I always felt it was symbolic, some kind of message from Miriam, somehow hopeful, that even death could not stop rebirth. And that wherever they were, they were together and starting over."

"What do you know about all this?" she asks me, and I know she means death.

"Not as much as they all say."

I don't tell her about other people's glimpses because they are private, and she seems content when I tell her I see things, but I can't really make sense of them.

"You will be able to understand, though," I tell her. "That's one thing I'm fairly sure of."

We talk about the hard winter and how welcome this spring has been, even to her, here at the end, because, she says, the new growth always helps George. "I dreamed of being a physicist," she says, "and I could still dream, I guess. Physicist or not. On the day George proposed, we sat in a corn field. He said it was a sure thing that plants would sprout again year after year, he could count on it. And he'd be there for me always, too. I'd studied enough physics to know there was random chaos, uncertainty, underneath it all—at infinitesimal particle levels—things George would never understand or believe in and I suddenly wanted to protect him from that, but, of course, I couldn't."

I nod again.

"Do you know there are processes now, other than cremation, that can return you to the earth as water? Or freeze-dry you and turn you to compost? Neither require the need for a casket or embalming, nor do they require the energy of cremation. I'd like that, but George would never hear of it. You'd think he would."

We talk a while longer about how Shirley had loved to cook; and how she had a brother now estranged from her, she being peripheral to some altercation with their parents; and how she liked game shows.

It's May. "It snowed in Paradise last night," I say.

"I'll see you soon," she says.

● ◆ ●

George isn't there when I arrive. Shirley had had the health care worker call us both, but made her wait twenty minutes before calling him.

"Don't worry," Shirley says to me.

I wasn't precisely "worried." It's hard to explain how I get about dangerous events in my own life. I'm aware of them, I'm apprehensive, perhaps anticipatory. At times I've been briefly fearful, but I'm never worried nor do I project to worst-case scenarios because I know there are so many scenarios—both bad and good—it would be futile.

Shirley doesn't have long, a half hour if that, and I stand in the corner while the health care worker opens the shutters. Shirley, too weak to talk, waves her away, and the nurse gathers her purse and goes quietly for the door.

When George's lumpish figure fills the doorway, he doesn't see me immediately, but when he does, he wastes not a moment. He rushes to the kitchen drawer and pulls out a .38 revolver and levels it at me, but Shirley holds her hand out to me and despite George's fury he allows me to take it for the briefest of moments, and when I do I see Shirley playing piano with her brother, a duet. I'm not certain if this is in the past in this migration or another one, but Shirley smiles, and when it's all done, her face holds an expression not of rapture, but of amused contentment, then peace. Time swirls together as if it were a kaleidoscope, or a prism. I normally watch the glimpses with the dying person, but I'm intent on George, who grabs me by the arm and hurls me across the room and against the window, which shatters over my head and rains over me like an ice shower.

"Don't waste it," Shirley says to him. He moves to her side, takes her hand.

"I love you," she says, and before he can reply, I know she is gone.

He turns to me, pulls me from the floor where I've been sitting under the window, and shoves me again against the wall, the gun shaking in a hand that is dirty, nails black with planting soil or maybe mulch and I think of Shirley's burial wishes. I see the thought cross George's mind to pull the trigger and send a bullet through my chest, and his finger moves imperceptibly. I expect to see glimpses of my own life, and I do. Some of what I see is shocking, but the glimpses are interrupted by those of George's own life. I see a time when he is trying to read in a classroom with a teacher who isn't yet familiar with dyslexia; a gift of a blue wind-up alarm clock he'd given to his mother for a particular mother's day; a ring he meant to put on Shirley's lovely hand. Miriam. They blur together, the past, present, and future into a purple/blue/green/yellow smear of time—experience and alternate lives. I have a moment of confusion when I see George's expression of hate turn to peace and gratitude.

He smiles at me.

He puts the .38 against his temple and pulls the trigger.

• ◆ •

In Mexican tradition, Death is teased and made to dance and merrily cavort in "Calaveras," sugar death masks. The Grim Reaper is unmasked and revealed to be a jolly fellow underneath his macabre exterior. Death is thus seen for what it is, a temporary point between what has been and what will be, and not as the black hole of oblivion.

When the gun had been pointed at me, sometimes at my head, sometimes at my chest, wobbling in George Giltner's hand, I'd seen a lot of things I'd never seen to date. They'd been interrupted when I realized I was seeing glimpses of George's own life, but they had all run together—Shirley's life, George's life, and my own in a way that had never happened before. Shirley's glimpses continued on long after they would normally have stopped and they ran together with George's glimpses, something I didn't expect to see at all, and then I'd seen why. I'd seen all the possibilities and so did George, and I'd seen his gratitude.

But George and I had seen things simultaneously. I saw a migration in which George pulled that trigger, sent that bullet into my chest, and ones in which he hadn't. Migrations in which he'd turned the gun on himself as he was about to do, and possibilities where Shirley had never been exposed to the chemicals that had given her liver cancer; and even migrations where Miriam had given them grandchildren— live ones. Migrations where none of us —Shirley, George, or I—existed at all. And that was when he had smiled at me. The moment he'd seen the earth populated only by graceful fauna and sprouts of virgin green—streams that ran clear and cold through pristine forests.

But I had seen possibilities of my own. Migrations that ran into one huge fabric so fast I couldn't separate them in my mind. But then I'd seen a couple stand out. One in which I'd one day hold Alex's exotic dinner party of braised rabbit and slaughter; and one in which I would never return home to him after some enormous fire but would move past those forty-nine days of self-reflection and on to day fifty. Scenes in which I'd gone off with John and we'd lived a challenging but rewarding life together.

And, of course, there were migrations with none of the above.

NORNA

FREEDOM

It was nothing more than a flutter, she would think later. A sound like a piece of plastic rustling in no more than a wisp of a breeze.

But Norna recognizes it.

The cabin is log, and it has settled some, jacking the window apertures, making it more difficult to remove the screens each year. Since they are old like the cabin, they are framed in wood, too, and they have warped along with the settling house. Norna doesn't remove them except to clean them, so she puts them back in exactly the way they come out.

Still, they catch some.

It's three a.m. and winter, but Norna believes in fresh air and always leaves a front window cracked. She imagines she is about to hear that window rise ever so slowly, and she imagines what it will sound like: a slow, gentle whisper. Sssssshhhhh, she hears, a sound like she'd once whispered to her daughter, Aissa, during a funeral in church, holding her finger over her lips, a tolerant smile on her face. Stop fidgeting, she tells herself now, holding that finger there now as if to steady her heartbeat.

She doesn't lift her head.

The structure is three rooms: a bedroom, a main living area, and a corner she has recently partitioned off for her future bathroom which so far contains only a claw-foot tub and a drain; she still uses an outhouse. It's one story, and she contemplates for a moment escape through the bedroom window, but knows she doesn't have time. She is certain he is climbing through the window now, though incredibly she hears nothing more. The loaded twelve gauge is leaning behind the set of bureau drawers shielded from sight if he should set foot through that door which she knows he's about to do. She's lying on her left side and she can see the gun, the bureau, but the doorway is partially obstructed due to the chest. The moon is close to full but approaching snow clouds race past the window, plunging the room into darkness. She's grateful it's not completely pitch dark like so many nights in the north country.

The door is open so the heat from the wood stove can travel through the structure—though it's become cold—time to stoke that fire, which may have been what had made her restless in the first place. She'd left the door to the stove open a smidge, and she can see the glow of the dying flames shimmering at the doorway casting flickering shadows onto the bedroom floor. She sees his shadow now, but still hears nothing. With a single motion she stands, grabbing the twelve gauge with her left hand, and as he gains the doorway she swings the gun to her shoulder and levels it at him, the sheet still wrapped around her legs.

He doesn't say anything and she's not sure if he can see her as clearly as she sees him, but finally he says, *you don't have the nerve.* She releases the safety as he makes a lunge for her. He leaps into the air, something she didn't expect, and the shot she had aimed at his heart strikes him, she thinks, in the upper left thigh. His trajectory carries him forward and he grabs the gun from her.

She regrets not shooting him the moment he stepped through the doorway.

The odds of this being someone she knows are next to none, but she had to be sure. Oddly, she hasn't heard anything from him other than a small "uh" sound when the bullet entered his thigh.

Get some lights on, he says now.

I need the matches, she says, gesturing to the bureau. He nods and she lights the lantern on the chest of drawers, and when she does, he says, more. Light more. As she passes him to go into the front room, she notices a smell that reminds her of rotting fruit. The jumpsuit he's wearing is orange making it hard to see how much blood he's losing, though a good sized puddle is forming at his feet.

Get me a belt, he says. Or a piece of rope.

Do you want lights or a belt, she asks, and when he impatiently says belt, he gets up and drags himself and her back to the dresser where she grabs a fairly thin one from the top drawer. As he pulls it tight around his thigh—groin level—he gestures again. Get the lights, all of them.

She has three gas lights mounted on the walls—two in the kitchen and one in her living space—

And she lights them while he watches her.

You missed the artery, he says. Actually, you mostly missed my leg or I'm sure it would be gone.

I was using a slug, she says. I was aiming for your heart. If you hadn't jumped, I'd have hit it.

She turns and faces him. The shotgun is double-barreled and there's only one shell left in it.

I want the rest of the ammo, something to eat, and that rope I asked for before, he says.

I'm going to tell you right now, you better go ahead and kill me, Norna says. You will not get me tied up without doing it. It'll be a lot for you in your condition, trust me.

Well, he says, you got no phone. I checked. And it's snowing to beat hell out there. Give me your car keys.

Artery or not, there is a substantial pool of blood under the chair he's been leaning against, and Norna can see he looks drained.

Get 'em, he says. She hands him the keys hanging on the peg by the door. She doesn't tell him the car has been temperamental at best or that she knows better than to head out in this storm. Few people are year-rounders and the closest one to her is eight miles; there is a memorial near Pine Stump Junction to a couple who tried, once, to walk two miles in a storm like this.

Now the ammo, and get cookin'. No, first, you better get me some bandages and something to clean this wound.

She doesn't have bandages big enough to deal with a shotgun wound to the thigh, so she tells him she'll tear up a sheet, and gets a clean one from the chest at the foot of her bed. He strips out of the jumpsuit which is wet from the snow and blood and she notices he is big but fit, the fine blonde hairs of his thigh matted already in congealing blood. He had had what looked like an old furniture blanket around him which had dropped to the floor of her bedroom as he leaped into the air. So she hands him a red flannel blanket she has lying against the back of her pine rocker.

She notices the bullet seems to have gone through the thigh, missing the artery and bone, but still it's an enormous gaping wound. She knows he needs antibiotics, but she cleans the wound and his thigh with soapy water then pours peroxide on each end of it, wrapping the leg finally and tying it with the clean sheets, which turn pink almost immediately. She somehow manages not to touch his flesh with her fingers.

Where's the dog? I expected a man or a dog, but saw no sign of one outside.

Just lost my last stray, Norna says. Died of liver cancer. I am about to find me another one. Timing is everything, she says.

He sits on the floor, back against the small leather couch, wraps the blanket around his body and closes his eyes, his hand ready with the shotgun that sits on the floor to his right. He cracks an eye, gestures with the gun toward the kitchen, and she picks up the peroxide and soapy water and makes her way there. She has fourteen dozen eggs in the propane refrigerator (enough for a couple months at least), smoked ham, a pound of bacon, eight pounds of assorted cheeses, five pounds of butter. She makes her own bread twice a week. Tins of sardines and oysters and tuna fill one of the open shelves. Canned tomatoes and pickles and green beans line another shelf above a row of flour and sugar and salt and pepper; dried rosemary, thyme, tarragon, and oregano hang from the rafters. Outside is a locked corrugated metal shed full of ice blocks, ten pounds of frozen bacon, a dozen chickens, twenty pounds of whitefish, a rack of lamb and one of venison (given to her by her Anishinaabe friend Sam) for special treats, and frozen vegetables from her garden.

She has a propane oven and cooktop and she starts frying slab bacon, seeing he's watching her through half-closed eyes. She assumes he wants eggs over pancakes to get back his strength, and she gets a dozen from the fridge along with a loaf of bread she then slices and grills over the open flame of one burner.

The bacon will take a bit.

I've got to use the outhouse, Norna says.

Fine, he answers, don't take a coat.

It's still dark, and the moon is covered now by heavy snow clouds, so she feels her way to the toilet, listening as the wind and snow howl past her head, sure nevertheless she hears a coyote in fairly close. She wastes no time in only her flannel pajamas, and when she returns, she notices his eyes are still open but his mouth is hanging open some as well, and she knows it's from the pain.

Got any whiskey or brandy, he asks, and she grabs a bottle of each off the shelf where they stand next to bottles of dry red and white wine. Tylenol? That won't make me bleed.

Just aspirin, she says. I'm out of Tylenol.

He gestures toward the Calvados brandy and she knows he's cold, so she pours that and grabs the blanket from the rocking chair. After he's eaten, which he does haltingly—still sitting on the floor as if he might be sick any moment and any movement might precipitate it—he seems to gain strength and gestures for her to help him to the couch, and when he's comfortable, he says, sit here, motioning to the floor next to him. She sits and he grabs her wrist with his left hand, the shotgun still in his hand next to the couch back.

I'm a light sleeper, he says, and as he closes his eyes, and before she closes hers, she notices that he looks like John F. Kennedy.

Norna dozes a while. She isn't concerned about being sexually attacked immediately. Partly because of his injury and partly because she doesn't think this is what this about. Though she hasn't ruled out the fact that he might need her dead for one reason or another.

She knows she's useful to him for now.

A clear head requires sleep, she knows that. So she forces herself to rest, her wrist becoming sweaty under his grip. The stove could use stoking again and she shivers from the cold of a bare floor.

She figures it would be a fluke if Sam happened to stop by. Sam, her Anishinaabe lifetime friend and long-ago lover. She'd once thought he was a twin and that they were tricking her—both sleeping with her at different times, so she had set a trap for him. Hog-tied him for a couple days to see who came looking for him or missed him at work—and if not that would say something, too. She'd been twenty years old at the time and spent the winter with him in his trapping shed.

The whole town had talked about her.

She'd helped skin the animals and learned something about traps along the way.

She remembers what Sam had said about traps, that there was an inherently volitional aspect to being trapped and a psychological aspect to it as well. What if I choose to view being trapped as a vacation, he had said to her back then, and she sees positives to his line of thought now with the big criminal's hand tight around her wrist. At any rate, she's no longer sure if there is one Sam or two; she's long since stopped caring. What she cares about now is if he might check on her in this snow and she can't make up her mind if that's something she hopes for or against. Her daughter and granddaughter would never come here in January, she knows that, and she's grateful. And even grateful she's between dogs since she's certain her last stray wouldn't have survived long around this man. She'd read the presence of a dog can sometimes send a criminal to the next house in the first place; but in her case, that would have been eight miles.

Situations like this, Norna knows, call for a particular mind-set. A person like Norna—who had been left in a dump by her biological mother—knows about mind-sets and about her place in the grand scheme of things. She does not subscribe to circumstance in the way some people might. That circumstances matter as much as people think. And this circumstance is just that—a circumstance.

She wonders what in the world has sent this man her direction instead of a geographically desirable southern route. She wonders what prison he's escaped from. Marquette and Munising are closest, but she somehow envisions him coming from Jackson or Detroit or Lapeer or Adrian despite the days it would take him to travel, pictures him sleeping in people's sheds and outbuildings.

He's snoring lightly now, a putt-putt motorboat sound with an occasional clicking in his throat. It appears his left eye is open a slit and the grip on her hand hasn't lessened at all. She has dozed enough to remember jumbled incoherent thoughts—always her clue she's getting some rest even when she thinks she's awake. She watches him sleep and thinks now that maybe he's a cross between John F. Kennedy and Robert Redford and smiles to herself about how some women might want to handcuff him to their bedposts or offer themselves up as hostage. She makes him to be mid- to late thirties. His speech mannerisms haven't told her much yet. He seems more accomplished than the average criminal, yet somehow not, she figures, for white collar crime.

His good looks make the whole thing seem oddly disconnected, at odds with the orange jumpsuit on the floor and a bullet in the thigh.

He's perspiring lightly despite the cold and light blanket and she can tell by his hand he's running a fever. It must be around ten a.m., Norna thinks, though in the gloom from this snow storm it's hard to tell. She shifts and pulls on his arm and when he opens his eyes, she gestures toward the kitchen and he nods, releasing her arm.

I'm using the outhouse first, no coat, she says. When she returns, she starts the coffee and begins slicing ham for sandwiches. She opens a jar of pickles. She watches him heave himself to his feet, struggle past her to the back door. He leans against the house while he relieves himself, then staggers back to the pine harvest table and slumps into a chair.

Why didn't you just break into an empty cottage up here, Norna asks him.

I needed heat and food, he answers. I've been doing that all the way up here.

From?

Jackson, he answers.

Why are you out here alone, he asks.

Norna isn't one to answer questions, but she knows her survival depends on any rapport she can establish with this man.

Been married, she says. I think clearer on my own.

That's important, I suppose?

Yes.

She looks at him questioningly and he says, I haven't killed anyone. Not yet. But I don't got an aversion to it. Need some water, he says, so she fills a glass. I'm part of the Posse Comitatus group downstate. We sent letters to state officials protesting the tax policies directed toward a guy named George Kindred. Two years later, a guy in Wisconsin named

Thomas Stockheimer and several followers lured an IRS agent to a farm and assaulted him. He was part of our group; we all paid. The group is becoming anti-government, and subverting the government is not something you want to do.

Something had to be done, he says. There were local abuses and that doesn't take into count the federal abuses. The sixteenth amendment is unconstitutional.

What does it mean, Comitatus? she asks.

Feudal term in England and Germany compelling rulers to rule in consultation with their subjects and warriors. Ironically, the government is now using the idea so they can turn the military into a civil militia in order to use deadly force against people like me. You aren't one of these people who believes breaking the law is always wrong?

Of course not, my mother's family is German—no German believes you should always obey the government.

Norna has always been suspicious of groups: governments, organized religions, even some charity organizations claiming to help others. Sometimes they did good, but ultimately, it was about controlling other people and often in ways they shouldn't be or for their own benefit. She tells him as much and he nods his head. Still, she says, a group like the Posse Comitatus is also a "group." It's true that the thoughts of a whole room full of people can potentially accomplish things not possible for even the smartest man in the group, but groups making decisions together rarely do the right things. At its worst, they can be persuaded to do acts of horror they would never do individually.

He nods. That may be so. Guy named Gordon Kahl getting involved in it these days, I hear, who is a religious nut and kind of a Ku Klux Klan kind of guy, something I'm not into. I'm not going back there.

He'd asked her again about her marriage and she'd reluctantly filled him in that she was separated. She didn't tell him her marriage had been something she was not sure she wanted—ever—with anyone, but Davis had been persistent and Norna had agreed. Early enough, they'd found themselves at cross-purposes over the simplest communication, unable to read one another's signals and incapable of the faith it took to wait it out. Norna was desperately lonely sometimes these days living alone and she didn't tell her captor that, either. And it *was* lonely. But Norna didn't disappear here the way she had in her marriage. Some people found her lifestyle courageous, but it was marriage that took courage. It took a kind of courage she sometimes thought she lacked, and when Davis began befriending other women on top of it, the communication stopped altogether.

Norna lost faith for a while even in herself.

Their daughter Aissa had been a casualty, of course, though they'd both done admirably raising her together. And Norna thinks again about how it came down to faith. About how Davis and she had become simpatico in their failure, in the shared failure of their marriage, a commonality that had never occurred when they were together. It was a mutual sadness that seemed to personify itself in Aissa and somehow the sadness had drawn them closer and closer these last two years. It wouldn't surprise Norna in the least if right now someone leaned over and whispered to her that someday Davis would leave Drummond Island, the inn he ran there, the great water so like his large personality and move in here with her, on her simple river, the last year of his life. And it wouldn't have surprised her to know that it would be right in a way it had never been in their youth. It would not surprise her to realize that even though their marriage had failed, their relationship had not and would not, that no relationship she had ever embarked upon had failed, that they never ultimately lost the faith they needed to endure—none more so than the one between she and Davis.

But for now, it was about freedom.

He's awake.

She sees a feverish light in his blue eyes she hasn't noticed so far, and decides to keep quiet. She builds a sandwich for him with a couple pickles and puts them on a plate, pours him some coffee. She wonders what this man did for a living before getting involved in this cause, and she wonders where he could be headed, but she doesn't ask anything more as he eats. When he's through, he tells her he wants the packing and bandage changed again, says he wants her to stitch up the wound. She tells him that might not be a good idea without antibiotics, that he needs medical attention in Newberry, but he shakes his head.

My buddy will have antibiotics for his livestock. I just need to get there.

And when she asks where "there" is, he tells her his buddy Janson has a place near Crisp Point about a half mile from Lake Superior.

That survivalist place, she says. I've seen it. Those roads are passable this time of year only by snow machine.

Somethin' I wager you got out in that shed, he says.

I need to get the road cleared out to 414, she says. Or we won't get out of here even on a snow machine.

Maybe we'll wait until it stops tomorrow.

She smiles. It snows every day up here, maybe not with this intensity, but snow.

Do it without your coat, he says, something that meant she'd have to come inside every twenty minutes—or sooner—to warm up, and it would take hours with the snow blower. But he wouldn't budge.

He permits her a sweater and about halfway through it, she sees Sam's green truck headed her way down 414. She has half the drive plowed, and he pulls up that far and turns off the motor.

Are you crazy? he asks her, and she knows he's referring to the fact that she has no coat on. There is a host of reasons she doesn't want to tell Sam the truth, but the biggest one is she doesn't know if the prisoner (whose name is Anthony) has the gun leveled on them both right now. There is a clear shot where they are standing from the kitchen window and Sam makes the bigger target. She's afraid if Sam steps closer to the house, or she takes a step toward the truck, he'll shoot one or both of them.

No, she says.

Then what the hell are you doing?

Sam is a big man but he looks small, too, in a situation like this.

I have a rash, she says. So painful I can't put a coat on. Maybe it's shingles.

Sam looks doubtful, but says, okay, go to the house. I'll finish this.

I'm fine, she says. Just be on your way. Are you headed to town?

For a couple things, but mostly just checking on you. Go in the house.

She decides that makes the most sense and she stays between Sam and the kitchen window as she walks. When she opens the door, she sees Anthony leaning over the counter with the gun propped on the window ledge.

He grabs her by the arm. I was just considering breaking out this window and screen, he says.

Just get in the bedroom, she replies.

Can I expect him to go off and return with reinforcements?

I didn't tell him, she answers. Sam is not the kind of guy to drive off and leave me here with you. Get in the bedroom.

Norna does dishes and watches Sam out the window as he finishes blowing the driveway. It is still snowing but it's eased a bit. When Sam finishes, he steps inside to get warm.

I don't get it, he says. The coat thing. If you're too sick to wear a coat, you are too sick to snow blow.

No, she says. I'm fine.

Is that jeep running? Let me take you into Newberry to the doctor.

It's running and I plan to go later today. Thanks for your help, but be on your way.

I don't even get a cup of coffee for my efforts? Sam has been part of Norna's life since she was a girl. He's grown round about the girth but straight still.

I suppose, but not if you're going to lecture me. She pulls a coffee cup from the shelf and pours him a cup of coffee, adds sugar. They talk about his job at the asylum in Newberry, and about his limited trap line, what he plans to cook for dinner. Norna is anxious and says she needs to clean up before going to town. Sam leaves at last but not before saying something seems wrong, yet again. Later, he would ask her what would possess her to do what she was about to do, and she would tell him that right and wrong were not so easy to tally up.

But what you did was illegal, Sam would say. And this group sounds like trouble to me.

They might be trouble, she acknowledges, but still a person has to actually do something wrong before the government has a right to incarcerate you. He might have abandoned the group before that happened, perhaps nothing would have happened at all. You don't round people up by association like we did the Japanese during World War II.

It's not quite the same, Sam will tell her, and she knows that's true, too. Andrew wasn't rounded up for his nationality or race but because of his membership in a small group, part of whom had behaved violently, but she still hadn't been convinced of its rightness.

She tells Anthony it's too late to take him to Crisp Point by snow mobile today and she can see he's shivering with fever anyway. He takes the snow mobile keys and then sleeps on the couch while she reads Heidegger. She prepares a roast chicken for dinner with stewed tomatoes and dried basil and roasted rosemary potatoes, and after relieving himself he slumps again in the chair.

What did the "threatening" letter say? she asks.

Just that we will not soon be tolerating government tyranny of this sort and were taking measures to end it. When the Wisconsin assault occurred, they lumped us all in together. Gave us twenty years. She watches him eat which again seems intermittent as if he's going to be sick. After dinner, she changes his dressing and tells him again he needs medical attention that she cannot give him here. But she can see he has no intention of getting medical help.

He tells her he was married once before his politics became too much for her, and they had a small son named

Ronald. She sends me pictures of him, he tells her, and he looks like my father.

What did you do for a living besides protest, she asks.

I sold typewriters to schools for IBM, he says, and when she looks shocked he just smiles. When he falls asleep, she makes her way to her own bedroom. He stirs, opens his eyes for a moment, but does nothing to stop her.

The storm rages on two more days, and Norna and Anthony wait it out. She blows the drive which he allows her to do with a coat and at night they play cribbage and she cooks dinners of pot roast and white bean chili. He shakes his head at her and smiles. They make love once and when she changes his bandage yet again for the night, his hand brushes lightly against hers in a way that expresses gratitude.

The next day, she starts the snowmobile. It takes an hour and a half to get him to Crisp Point, to his buddy's survivalist camp. When they arrive, she helps him to the camp and once inside the door—which isn't locked, he shoos her away before "John" makes his way from the back room. She nods toward her twelve gauge he is still carrying, and says, that was my father's gun. He hands it to her and as she drives away, she sees him raise one hand from the window.

AISSA

THE LOVE-CHARR

She doesn't know, even now, if she believes in Big Fish.

Just when they were sure to land it, it'd jumped six feet in the air, scissored an enormous air-borne convulsion ripping the heart from her, and vanished into the tea-colored river.

Some fantastic pooka of the sea.

An *omble de fontaine;* a glaciated, monster coaster; a speckled adfluvial sea trout. Like Daniel Webster's Devil Fish, it was a hump-backed love-charr of mythic proportions.

"Dreams and fishes are no more than wishes," Sam had said.

"Hey, I'm no fisherman," Aissa had answered back.

Maybe they'd dreamed it, after all. Big Fish had slipped through their fingers leaving emptiness, but also a pounding anticipation in the knowledge that it existed in these waters at all. It had loomed large, like their passion for each other.

Once you see something like that, you want it.

Or you want to want it.

Normally she'd go to Timber Charlie's, since it was closer to camp. But she's had to make a run to St. Ignace for a load of siding so she decides on the Bear Pitt in Eckerman for a quick dinner. It's a tavern she hasn't been to since April when she'd last been in with Sam. Nevertheless, it's on her way back if she goes through Paradise.

"Hey, when you been to Paradise with me, baby, where else is there to go, eh?" Sam used to say.

A joke of Yooper proportion.

Michigan's Upper Peninsula is a place of high good humor and mythical happenstance where folks might orchestrate their own "Labor Day Bridge Walk" which happens not on the Mackinac Bridge or the Golden Gate, but on the "Million Dollar Bridge." A dozen guys in hip boots carrying rods and flashlights—at midnight—an annual stomp of eighteen steps across the four railroad planks spanning Plumbago Crick. Where on New Year's Eve in Marquette, you can see "da Yooper ball" drop, a sphere made of chicken wire draped with Christmas lights: last year the guy lowering it with a hand pulley paused, and the year started a minute and twelve seconds late. Best of all is St. Urho's Day(s), the two-day bender March 16 and 17 in celebration of St. Urho who, unlike St. Patrick and his snakes, was said to chase the grasshoppers (or vas it dose frogs?) out of Finland.

The U.P. population consists primarily of Finns, Swedes, Norwegians, and French-Canadians; a few pockets of Italians. Livelihoods since the early nineteenth century: mostly copper mining, prison workers. Limited lumbering, farming, fishing. Tourism.

You don't get rich here.

The Bear Pitt is the only public establishment for eighteen miles. It's late September and the place is full of hunters, mostly after bear and grouse. Yooper heaven: the two weeks a year you can fish and hunt at the same time.

She slips into a booth.

"Beer, right?" the bartender, Henry, asks. "Guinness was it?"

"Not tonight," Aissa says. "Let me have a Two Hearted Ale." A tourist beer up here, but since she's in the mood for a mojito, she'll settle for the ale. She takes off her hat and wipes her forehead with a napkin, then replaces it, tucks her hair behind her ears. Henry sets the beer down along with a chilled glass and as she pours, the condensation drips down the glass like the sweat between her breasts.

"I'll take a twist of lime for this, if ya got one," she tells him. And as Henry heads off for it, she listens to the conversations at the bar. There's one local bear hunter she doesn't recognize and two hunters from downstate who'd been hunting state land south of Crisp Point.

"Been usin' chocolate for bait," the local offers grudgingly. "Got a four-hundred-pound male out there in the pickup, ya wanta see 'm?"

"Is it a bear or your twin brother?"

They all laugh and the downstaters say they sure do want to see, and they head for the door.

"Hey, we made a pact, you know." Sam slides into the booth across from her. She smells mint, the river, and the musky smell of him which always contains elements of water—as if he himself is part of the earth's watershed, a force, and she shifts in her seat. Sam is nothing like her mother Norna's Indian Sam—after all he's fair with red hair—and yet there's something so like Indian Sam. That calmness, perhaps.

"It was your call," she says.

"But it was not me who reneged. The deal was it started on the river and we agreed it would end there."

And that was true. It had started there. But it had flooded over the river banks into the semblance of their lives; he'd trespassed, truth be told, like he'd done that first day on her river.

"I can see me insisting on that, but what do you care?"

"We'll discuss that on the river. When did you get back? Where's Jane? I see they took the tether off you." Grin on his face.

Aissa's daughter Jane, almost twelve, is staying with her father who has a dental practice in Lansing and a new girlfriend (since the divorce—or really before it) in the neighboring town of Williamston. Jane has stayed with him since Aissa's trip to Tulsa.

"Who was in the tower?" he asks.

He's referring to the Prayer Tower at Oral Roberts University where Aissa had attended college for a year, and where she had, in a deranged early-life crisis, dragged a little old lady out of a prayer room at gun point, demanding to know who'd been praying on 9/11 or on the Oklahoma bombing day or on the day of the last tsunami. "Pick your disaster," she'd said.

"A little old lady. The gun wasn't loaded, you know."

"So you said."

Sam, history teacher turned river guide, is apolitical now, claiming he's tired of watching history repeat itself. Not that Aissa is political per se, despite the Oklahoma-crazy.

"Jane is still downstate with Ben." Luckily sole custody had not been something Ben ever desired.

"What you workin' on now?" Sam asks her.

"Same as when I left, the Yellowdog mining fiasco," she answers.

She doesn't have it sold yet. She's a freelancer these days having quit her job at the *Lansing State Journal* when her mother died; the Yellowdog is a trout stream and the silting the proposed mining will cause has been publicly and hotly protested, due to the endangerment of the coaster brook trout.

"Your hip boots in the truck?"

"Yep," she answers. Hip boots are basic equipment in da Yoop, but she's evasive. "Maybe I don't want to get back in that river, did ya ever think of that?"

Sam doesn't answer.

For more than ten months before her trip to Tulsa, they'd passed time, she and Sam. They'd played cribbage. They hunted for and cooked grouse—or sometimes venison—over open wood fires. They painted his storage shed. He sang her through empty Sundays; she shortened his window curtains. They planted cucumbers and tomatoes. He made her a cistern—out of a discarded gutter, an oil barrel and spigot—for rain water to wash her hair. Snowed in, he taught her to tie flies using grouse hackle, turkey quills and bunny strips. Once he'd made her laugh until she'd left a puddle on the floor; and they fought once to the point of violence over property rights—or maybe it was the unseen ramifications of technology. Still they lived casually without dissecting life much, without violation.

They made love. Not often, but mindfully.

And they didn't dissect that, either.

They fished some—

Sometimes she got quiet for days on end. At the point of ripping his hair out, Sam would leave her alone for a week without a word. Then he'd return and howl at the moon, thrash in his sleep like a dervish, pass wind from his constant diet of peppers and chilies, and swear at her purple.

One day she'd left for Tulsa without a word.

"Don't come back," he'd said when she finally called.

Aissa had heard the end in his voice and she thinks she can hear it still, now, this day in the Bear Pitt, so she doesn't see the point.

"I've got an extra rod strung," he says, "just come from a guide—that'll save you stringing one." When she doesn't answer, he takes a sip of her ale, wipes a hand across his red beard. "You got forty minutes . . . I'll meet you on the water."

She'd inherited this stretch of the Little Two Hearted River. Hemingway, though likely fishing the Fox, had made the Two Hearted famous by adding "The Big" in front of it; both rivers empty into Lake Superior, about four miles north.

Her mother, Norna, had been a recluse. She'd been talked about in the village, laughed at, avoided, and finally feared, even by Aissa. Norna had lived on this wayward creek year round, relying on battery power or at times no power. Aissa had intended living here "temporarily" after the divorce, but it has been two years now, the place having taken her hostage. Norna had been dead a year when Aissa took it into her head to "know" Norna's home water, a stretch of river as strange as the mother who'd bequeathed it to her.

Aissa walked the 2200 feet of frontage in her hip boots any day weather permitted, shuffling her foot into each sandy crevice and climbing structure, as if the prowling could somehow help her to finally understand Norna. She knew each bend, every snag of alder over every undercut, each run and riffle, every hole, every rock, every beaver dam, every deadfall. She isn't sure when she realized the process had become not one of knowing her mother, but of knowing herself. Probably when she'd pronounced to her wild six-fingered daughter, Jane, how well she knew the water.

"The river bottom changes," Jane had announced in her monotone, so like Aissa's mother. "You have to change with it."

And that had shaken Aissa. Jane, who was more like her mother than Aissa could ever be, was right.

Maybe there was no such thing as home water.

She kept wading.

She'd encountered Sam, trespassing last fall at the confluence, where her river joined her tributary. Two years after her mother had died and a year after she'd started reading her heart-river. She'd grabbed the rod that morning for the first time since her mother died. Her mother, a stickler for keeping rods broken down, had nevertheless died leaving this seven-foot-three-inch Sage strung, with what Sam would later tell her was a floating four-weight line, a 6X leader and tippet, and a size-twenty blue-winged olive dry-fly.

It had been with that rod she'd almost landed Big Fish—

She gets to the creek first, pulls hip boots on over gray hiking socks, steps into the stream. She wants to gain her bearings before he arrives and as she steps in she glimpses the churning back quarters of a fast-moving coyote disappearing between the alders. It's late September, the time of year closest to her bones. It's windless, an unsettled stillness that reveals the droning sound of flies, bees, and mosquitoes. She hears the eerie baying of bear dogs coming from near the Betsy River lowlands. A sandhill crane flies over like a pterodactyl, honking; a crow caws back, both sounds echoing down the river valley, and dying into the persistent howling of the dogs. Jane's Anishinaabek friend, Henry, says crows are their dead ancestors, and she wonders what creature Norna has become.

Sam's truck door.

He steps into the creek next to her and their shoulders bump. Though he had ended it, and though she's missed him to the point of distraction, he's still a trespasser.

"You had light tackle last time, and that's part of the reason he cleaned ya out before I could get a net under him," Sam says, "but even with this rod and heavier tackle, you won't be able to horse this one."

"Give me the damned rod," she says. He hands her a rod she figures is about an eight-footer.

"What's tied on here?" she asks.

"Blue-winged olive," he answers. "Size twenty-four."

"Christ," she says.

"Yeah." He smiles. "Wouldn't it be something to land him on that? A fish like that is a flesh-eating monster. Damn fish eats mice and lemmings and any fish eight inches or under."

Sam had claimed when they'd met a year ago that her mother had allowed him to fish here, a quiet small brook trout stream, a place he liked to go when he wasn't guiding the big water, the Fox or the Two Hearted or the Tahquamenon. Aissa had no reason to doubt him.

After they'd lost Big Fish, they'd inexplicably made love on the river bank, in a wet sandy pile of discarded hip boots and fly vests, and later as she'd started up the bank, he'd grabbed her arm, looked long into her eyes, and said "Pact. No matter what this is, how long it lasts or doesn't, it started here and if it ends, it ends here as well."

"Pact," she'd answered, shaking the hand that had roamed every inch of her body moments before. It felt callused but generous; she judged a man by his hands.

She was embarrassed at her behavior then, and remembering embarrasses her now.

"The sun's good, he says." It was low enough, forming shadows across the water.

The tannin-copper water is a murky two feet deep in most places. Aissa thinks for a moment about her mother.

And about Big Fish. Marvels at the odds of Sam and she and Big Fish evolving through the centuries and ending up in this spot on this river at this time in this place.

It was no more complex than natural selection.

Evolutionary fate.

"Shall we separate or stay close?" he asks. Her eyes meet his and she wants to look down, can't. Finally she compromises and looks over his right shoulder at the steep riverbank, sees signs of the erosion.

"I can't fish this damn long rod anyway, so it doesn't matter," she says.

"Use a roll cast," he says. "It's actually easier on a longer rod." He points. "Try the undercuts and around the deadfall . . . we can always try the beaver dam."

"Yeah," she says. "Where's your rod?"

"On the bank. You fish this one. I'll hold the net."

Then it's quiet. They don't move but rest the river, read it a while. Then she roll casts, not her favorite cast, but he's right. The longer rod is better for the roll cast if a bit awkward in close. Grasshoppers fly and hop around on the bank, making that clicking sound.

St. Urho missed a few.

She drifts the fly through the undercuts, through the riffles behind rocks and down branches. She hooks and loses the fly on a fallen sweeper and as she reties, she tries to pretend Sam isn't there. She knows he wants something from her, has wanted it for a long time, something she'd been unable to give. Not a commitment, exactly.

"Never seen anything like that fish," Sam whispers now. They both know they shouldn't be talking at all.

"I didn't really get a good look at it," Aissa whispers back.

"You nearly had it in your hands, for God's sake. How can you say that?"

"It all happened so fast."

"A coaster, I'm sure."

"Steelhead, maybe?" Aissa asks.

Sam shakes his head. "They spawn mostly in spring, and it was fall when we saw it, almost this time of year. Steelhead are more silvery in color, too. I got a good look at it."

"A spirit maybe, Mitchi Manitou?"

Aissa remembers she had played the mammoth fish almost to Sam's net, but she hadn't seen much more of it than its cavernous mouth, the row of teeth at the back of its throat like a ragged zipper, and perhaps it was seeing those hidden teeth that had made her lose concentration, ease off the tension.

Sam had held the net stretched out and just as the line broke, Big Fish had teetered on the edge of the wooden net as if it were walking a balance beam. Sam, a little far from the fish, had shuffled forward, stretching as far as he could, and then with one huge swipe of its tail, Big Fish had flipped in the air, out of the net and back into the river.

"Well," Sam says now, "what do you think? Do you think it's still here?"

She says nothing.

Brook trout; the only fish who like it colder than a brook trout, is the arctic Charr. A brook trout likes glaciated, aerated water, optimal temperature thirty-five to sixty-five degrees. The Salmon Trout River in Michigan is said to be the last river to have spawning runs of coasters, but it's not impossible they could appear in other streams along Michigan's Superior coastline. Not likely, but not impossible.

But it's not about the facts.

In other words does she believe?

Fishermen are believers. They believe in Santa Claus and the Easter Bunny. They make wishes on four-leaf clovers and buy lottery tickets. They spend hours fishing, throwing back small fry, and never lose heart.

Her ex-husband was no fisherman.

Aissa's heart-river runs cold.

The Wisconsin Ice Sheet, the last continental glacier of the late Pleistocene epoch, fifty-five thousand years ago, once sat on top of the island of Manhattan, and when at last it receded, melt-water filled vast inland depressions that formed the cold-water drainage system known as the Great Lakes. Somehow Aissa, or rather her mother before her—or rather centuries of mothers before her—had, due to the coldness in their hearts, ridden the melt northward. Some thought they followed their men-folk north, but this was not true; they were naturalized north. For years, Aissa had imagined herself different from her mother and daughter, but the truth she'd had to face in the two years since Norna's death is that she belongs here. Clean, remote, northern latitudes bring her alive in a way the cloying and decay-ridden south never could. Where the clear air rips at the lungs, where the creatures run wilder: bears, coyote, wolves, moose, bobcats; where the white and red pine can survive the rugged nutrient-depleted soil conditions—and so, it seems, can she. She responds to the harshness, the desolation.

The landscape contains high places where you can see all the way to Lake Superior, and unfathomable depths where the trees obscure the sky. It contains things so beautiful there are no words to describe them: giant red and white pines, graceful trillium, wild leeks and gingerroot. Sometimes Aissa thinks she'll die of the desolation. But it had been inside her all along, this landscape.

They all belonged here—Norna, Jane, and even she herself. The fact is: her heart-river runs cold.

They fish, she and Sam.

They fish hours and hours until the light drains from the northern sky and the moon, full and incredulous, moves higher and more northerly across a black, indifferent sky, Sam tying on flies for her, throwing back eight inch-trout, twelve-inch trout, and even a wayward perch, as fast as she lands them. He's retrieved his rod now, and Sam sometimes moves upstream, but keeps proximally within view. They look down and the river flows on around their legs, at times brown and grainy like the dregs of a last cup of coffee.

They keep fishing, neither of them willing to stop, neither of them willing to call it a night, call it finished, call it anything. And they fish on. Days pass, weeks pass, months pass, and they fish on—until time doesn't matter anymore.

It's a no contest.

A stand-off.

Some years it rains and the water table floods until they can barely hold their chins above the current and some years the drought leaves them parched and fishless, even for the small ones; the river never freezes. Aissa imagines her female descendants, wonders about gradual divergence, genetic drift. She wonders about fate and the Red Queen and if, after all is said and done, she might have already passed on traits to her daughter, Jane, traits that will eventually force her descendants to migrate out of these waters, and on north, in search of colder water yet?

They fish on. She no longer cares if they step out of the river. They fish holes where they swear, where they can just feel in their guts, that some god-awful sea-monster awaits. Over their shoulders they hear slurps of gargantuan proportions that can only be the rising of Big Fish, but when they turn, they find the water flat and opaque, possessed of an ancient calm, an infernal mystery. Which leaves them to think about destiny and about coming to grips with their own failings, their own mysteries, their own fish stories. Leaving them to think about nothing more than the evolutionary task at hand, the next shuffle of a foot.

"But do you believe?" Sam shouts off and on. Her mother and daughter believe, she knows that. She feels their hearts within her own heart, and Aissa shouts back that if it exists at all, the catching of Big Fish is irrelevant, the attempt, the emotion expended the only validity.

And though Sam replies "Sure, I know that," and though the years continue to pass with them both in the river, Aissa knows the nature of coaster brook trout. Anadromous, humpbacked loners, they head upstream in the fall in search of cold spawning water—between thirty-nine and forty-nine degrees. When the male finds a female who has dug a redd, they both open their mouths and tremble, undulating bodies, as eggs and milt are released simultaneously into the nest. Then the female trout does a dance, the only trout known to do this postnuptial dance, moving gravel over the eggs without touching them. But while the female remains to guard the eggs, the male coaster moves off. And as temperatures drop, coasters move downstream in search of warmer winter water.

So far, Sam is still in her water; there are no guarantees.

As they fish, the river bottom erodes, shifts, alters its path a little every year, more every decade. Aissa shifts with it.

Every so slightly—northward.